GOBBELINO LONDON & A COMPLICATION OF UNICORNS

GOBBELINO LONDON, PI: BOOK 3

KIM M. WATT

For further information contact www.kmwatt.com

Cover design: Monika McFarland, www.ampersandbookcovers.com

Editor: Lynda Dietz, www.easyreaderediting.com

ISBN 978-1-8380447-7-0

First Edition August 2020

10 9 8 7 6 5 4 3 2 1

CONTENTS

To everyone
who has always loved unicorns:
I'm sorry.
Really.

1

A SMALL IMP-OSITION

I HAVE FACED CREATURES FROM THE VOID – WELL, A COUPLE of different voids, actually – furious sorcerers, very small dragons, dentists, cats of the Watch who give the feline kind their bad reputation, humans who do the same for their kind, and, most recently, the ravenous undead, a mad mortician, zombie-fied chickens, and a cake-wielding reaper. None of it by choice, but these sorts of situations do seem to find me, and I'd go so far as to say I'm not too shabby at handling them.

Which is just to give some context to my current decision to take cover in the bottom drawer of the filing cabinet.

"Gobs!" Callum yelled at me. "Get out here and *help* me!"

I lifted my nose just enough that I could peer over the edge of the drawer, my ears back. "You look like you've got a handle on things," I said, which seemed like a good thing to say, even if it wasn't entirely accurate.

The human half of G & C London, Private Investigators, was crouched on the desk, brandishing an old newspaper in one hand and a can of squirty cream in the other. He opened his mouth to say something that was almost certainly guaranteed to be unlikely to motivate me, and something small, fast, and a rather delightful shade of bright blue shot out from under the desk and bit the hand clutching the newspaper. Callum yelped and tried to blast the scrap of blue with the squirty cream, which was about as effective as you'd imagine. I mean, it's designed for use on custard and the occasional sardine, not for hand-to-hand combat.

"Hey," I called. "Go easy with that stuff. I want some for my tea."

Callum gave me a look that suggested I'd be lucky to get *any* tea, let alone tea with cream, and went back to trying to squirt his attacker, who was an imp of the more volatile variety. I mean, they all are, but this one seemed particularly difficult. The canister spluttered enthusiastically, spitting all over Callum's boots and the desk until he finally managed to get it close enough to the imp gnawing on his other hand. It gave a shriek of fury as aerated cream gummed its wings together and crowned it with a tasty white hat, but instead of letting go it bit Callum harder. Callum howled, and our upstairs neighbour, who seemed to only be able to connect with her inner woo when she had outer peace, pounded violently on the floor with something that sounded like a Tongan war club. A tiny but furious blue platoon of imps erupted from under the desk, all screaming as if the sky was falling, and I ducked a little deeper into the drawer. Discretion is the better part of value, or whatever.

Callum flailed desperately at his attackers with the newspaper, the imp still clinging on grimly and splattering cream and blood all over the desk as it was flung about wildly, and the other imps dodged and dived, screaming insults in their tiny, shrill voices and making hand gestures that are rude in pretty much any language. Bloody imps. Any one of them could have fit comfortably in Callum's mug, if it hadn't been smashed on the floor. They're like mosquitoes. Far more troublesome than their size would suggest.

"*Gobs!*" Callum yelled, taking a wild swing at the imps and almost falling off the desk. "Get off your furry bum and *help me!*"

"What do you want me to do?" I demanded. "Throw more dairy products at them?"

He managed to catch an imp a solid blow as it dived at his head, sending the little creature tumbling and screeching across our tiny office/living room/bedroom/everything else. It slammed into the wall hard enough to make my ears twitch, and slid to the floor head first.

"Oh, God," Callum said, looking faintly ill. Although that might have been to do with the imp still chewing on his hand. He was bleeding quite a lot now.

Then the imp that had hit the wall leaped to its feet, shook out its wings, and came tearing back to the fight, chittering so hysterically even I couldn't understand it.

"*Gobs!*" Callum was doing some sort of panicked semaphore as he tried to keep the imps at bay.

"Well, what d'you expect me to do?"

"This is just your sort of thing," he snapped, dropping

the spluttering cream can and grabbing a tatty book off the desk as the imps regrouped. "You know, attacking small flying creatures mercilessly."

"*Stereotyping,*" I said. "Plus I prefer my prey to be less bite-y."

Callum opened his mouth to say something, and the imps rushed him, screaming very tiny battle cries. One of them battened onto his ear as he laid about wildly with the book and newspaper, and he howled with pain. "*Goddammit Gobbelino if you don't help me right bloody now I swear I'll throw you in the bath!*"

"We don't have a bath," I pointed out, hooking my paws over the top of the drawer and standing up so I could see a bit better. A second imp had latched onto his other ear, giving him a matching set, the cream-covered one on his hand was still attempting to chew his thumb off, and a fourth had somehow got tangled in his overlong hair and was rolling about on top of his head screeching in alarm. The rest were dive-bombing his face furiously, and the way he was staggering about the place he was going to be lucky not to do a header out the window.

"*Gobs!*"

"Okay, okay." I jumped my hind legs up to meet my front paws, wobbled on the edge of the drawer for a moment, then dropped to the floor lightly. Immediately one of the imps pointed at me and screamed. It threw itself into a teeth-gnashing dive toward me, waving its tiny fists in an unmistakably threatening manner, and two more rushed after it with shrieks of outrage. I yelped and bolted under the desk with the imps tearing after me in a buzz of wings and pretty unsavoury imp-language. I shot out the other side, onto the back of Callum's overturned chair, and leaped for the top of the desk with my ears back and teeth bared. As I landed, something grabbed my tail and hauled me backward while I scrabbled for grip on the scarred old wood.

"You're meant to be helping," Callum shouted, batting away a couple of imps who were apparently trying to remove his eyes with tiny but exceptionally sharp-looking tridents.

"Oh, kiss my dangling dewclaws," I hissed, giving up the fight to stay on the desk. I rolled through the short fall instead, twisting back on myself to grab two of my attackers as I landed. I trapped them to the floor with one paw on each of their skinny chests, getting my teeth up close and personal with their furry blue faces.

"Hey," I hissed at them. "You want to be cat food? This is how you end up cat food."

They chittered at me, pulling at the short fur of my toes.

"Ow. Stop that. Look, we did the job. We– *ow!"* Someone had just stuck what felt an awful lot like a toothpick in my ear, and I jumped away, releasing my captives. They went straight for my nose, teeth and tridents and nasty little talons all sharp and grabby and so close I didn't even have space to knock them away.

For one moment I thought I was going to have to bite someone's head off – possibly multiple someones – which is something I'm against as a general philosophy. And it seemed particularly bad form to bite a client's head off, even if it was fair to say they started it. Then a bucket slammed down on top of all three imps, barely missing my nose and sending the critters into a frenzy of screaming and scratching on the hard plastic. I looked up at Callum. He still had an imp swinging by its teeth from each ear, like enraged earrings, and the one on his hand was more red than blue now. Other imps were screaming abuse and attacking his legs and arms, while the one in his hair seemed to have given up and was just lying there panting.

"I was on it," I said.

"Sure," he said, keeping the bucket trapped down with his imp-less hand. "Now can you please explain to them that we did the job we were hired to do?"

I sighed. Imps are about as reasonable as sugar-crazed hippos. We'd have been better off locking them all in the filing cabinet and fleeing the country, but we'd just got the money together to buy a new armchair/bed thing, and it seemed a shame to leave it. I eyed the imp in Callum's hair. As well as looking calmer than the others, it had three prongs on its tail and a full head of bumblebee tattoos. I'm no expert in imp rank, but considering all the others had only one prong and just a couple of small, regular bee tattoos, it seemed like a good start.

"Hey, imp," I said, and it pushed some of Callum's hair aside to peer down at me. "Call off the gang so we can talk."

The imp frowned at me, then screamed a high-pitched order. The other imps shouted back, waving their tiny arms and evidently arguing, but they did at least stop attacking Callum, even if the ones attached to him decided not to let go.

"Cheers," I said. "Look, the job's finished. You wanted

to know who was creeping on your rubbish bins by the pub, and we found out. That's all you hired us for."

The imp frowned, then chittered, a squeaky, rapid-fire dialect with too many vowels and a lot of exclamation marks. I squinted, trying to make a thread of sense out of the cursing. Imps are seriously foul-mouthed. They use it like punctuation.

"They say we obviously misunderstood," I told Callum. "They say what's the point of knowing pixies are stealing all the good whisky dregs if we don't do anything about it?"

Callum tried pulling the imp off his hand, winced, and gave up. "Tell them—"

"They also say your mother must've mated with a woolly giraffe."

He scowled at me, and I shrugged. "Hey, I'm just the messenger."

"I'm sure. And what the hell's a woolly giraffe, anyway? *Don't* ask them that," he added, as I opened my mouth.

The imp chittered.

"They say it's like a woolly mammoth but skinny and blotchy and with too many legs."

"Great. That's good to know. They can understand me, then?"

I listened to the imp for a second. "They say you talk more slowly than a drunk troll three weeks into hibernation with a mouthful of muddy swamp-hare, but—"

"Gobs. I don't need all the details."

"Hey, you should hear the uncensored version."

He shook his head. "Whatever. Look, please make sure our clients understand we've fulfilled our side of the deal, and this is just ..." He trailed off, looking around our devastated office. "God. Call it harassment."

The imp on his head squawked and grabbed two tiny fistfuls of hair, hauling on it wildly.

Callum winced. "And can he stop that, please?"

I listened for a moment. "They say we may have fulfilled the letter of the contract but not the spirit, so they refuse to accept the job is done. And to please use the correct pronouns when addressing them."

"Right. Sorry. Look, removing a nest of pixies is an entirely other thing. We can't just kick them out of their homes. And it's *nothing* to do—"

He was cut off by the imp on his head saying very clearly, "Uh-oh."

"Uh-oh?" Callum said. "What's uh-oh?"

"Hairballs," I said, as a shrill buzzing rose from outside.

Callum said something stronger, and the imp said some things that were illegal or impossible, or maybe both. A platoon of pixies rose into view beyond the window, motorised rotors strapped to their backs and stripes painted across their faces in dark grease. Some of them had tiny cutlasses grasped in their hands, and a few were carrying what looked a lot like harpoons, complete with exploding heads. One of the rotors coughed and stalled, and a pixie plunged out of sight with a wail, but the rest kept coming, heading for the gap where Callum had propped the window open with a can of baked beans.

"Close it!" I yelled at him, and he abandoned the bucket, lunging for the window. The imps surged out from under the bucket and headed straight for the oncoming pixies, and the imp on Callum's head stood up and shrieked, waving its trident furiously as it tried to extricate itself from Callum's hair. The imps on Callum's ears let go, as did the one on his hand, and they swarmed past him like enraged, oversized blue bees to meet the pixies. Callum snatched the can of beans away, but the sash window had stuck, jammed firmly in the frame, because of *course* it had. He tried to force it down as the pixies charged in, and one of them took aim at him with a harpoon. He yelped, jumping away from the window, and the tiny missile tore through the side of his T-shirt to embed itself in the desk, where it exploded and left a little burnt crater behind.

The imps surged forward in rough formation, shrieking dire threats. The pixies opened fire with cross-bows and harpoons as the imps dodged and dived, faster with their fine wings than the pixies were in their machines. The imps shoved pencils and pens into the pixies' rotors to send them crashing to the ground, and the pixies unstrapped themselves from the wreckage and dived into battle, except for a couple of survivors who wheeled and spun across the room, firing indiscriminately at anything even remotely blue. Furry imps and pixies in army camouflage grappled on the desk and rolled across the floor, leaving blue imp dust smudges behind them, and there was a fierce battle raging in the sink of the tiny kitchenette, where half a dozen imps had taken cover and were being dive-bombed by the remaining rotor-wearing pixies.

I looked up at Callum. "Lunch?"

He looked around the room. "What about this lot?"

"Let them fight it out among themselves," I said, as

there was a crash from the kitchenette (which was really just a sink and a wheezy old fridge in an alcove barely big enough to qualify as a cupboard).

"Dammit," Callum said, and ducked as an imp tumbled past his head. It smashed into the window and slid to the sill, then sat up and flew off again, a little unsteadily. "Why do people always have to break our stuff?"

"You're the one who insisted we had to take the imps on as clients. You said it was species-ist if we didn't."

"Well, it would've been," he said, without much conviction. A pixie and an imp had got tangled up in a T-shirt he'd left hanging over the back of a chair and were rolling across the floor with the sound of ripping cloth.

"Yeah, well, this sort of thing is why I said *not* to."

"Can't you chase them all out?" he asked. "Do a scary cat thing?"

I gave him a disdainful look. "No, I can't *do a scary cat thing*. They're imps and pixies, not shrews."

"Fat lot of good you are."

"Yes, because you're doing really well with the whole situation."

He sighed, snagged his T-shirt off the floor and held it up. Even given Callum's charity shop chic it was beyond saving. The fighters had shredded it as they fought to untangle themselves, so he just ripped a bit off and wrapped it around his mauled hand. "Well. Lunch, then."

"Finally," I said. "And we can get some more cream on the way back. I was looking forward to that."

"Obviously the most important aspect of the whole situation," he said, raising his voice to be heard over a crash of falling pans in the kitchenette. "Your stomach."

I shrugged, and followed him as he grabbed his tatty old long coat from the hook on the wall and opened the door. Then he took a step back, his face suddenly pale, his injured hand cradled against his chest as if he were afraid that someone was about to grab it. I looked from him to the man on our doorstep, his own hand raised to knock.

"Callum," the stranger said, and Callum kicked the door closed.

2

NO IMPS OR PIXIES. WEREWOLVES BY NEGOTIATION

I BLINKED AT CALLUM. "YOU KNOW, EVEN FOR A CAT, THAT was pretty rude."

Callum stared around the room as if looking for another way out, then hurried across to the window and hauled it up as far as it'd go.

"Hey, hang about," I said. "I might be able to get out that way on a good day, but you can't. Second floor, Callum."

"I *know,*" he snapped, peering outside.

"So who was that?" I asked. "Jealous boyfriend? Spurned lover? Ooh – secret love child?"

He finally looked at me. "What?"

"Well, he's obviously *someone.*"

The someone in question knocked on the door, a hesitant little double tap. "Callum?" he called.

"I'm not letting Mrs Smith give us any more of her old magazines," Callum told me. "They're obviously a bad influence on you."

"Yeah, but I'm not the one trying to climb out a second-storey window to get away from a visitor."

He muttered something, and gave the door a despairing look as the knock came again. "Gobs, tell him to go. Please."

"*Hmm.* No." I ducked as an imp struggled past me caked in sugar, wings barely moving fast enough to keep it aloft. "Although, *interesting,* asking me to talk to him. He knows about Folk, then."

Callum scowled at me. Folk – that's the magical kinds of the world, like the imps and pixies currently tearing our little apartment apart – tend to inhabit the world very differently to the way humans do. Not many humans know Folk exist, and they have no idea that many of what they'd call dumb animals are a hell of a lot brighter than they are. Humans stopped seeing Folk and hearing animals about the same time they swapped magic for illusion (not science. Science and magic aren't mutually exclusive. Magic and illusion, however, are, because magic is real and illusion is smoke and mirrors and telling people what they want to hear, rather than what is).

Humans are pretty good at not seeing anything they don't believe in, so they take care of most of their selective vision themselves. But there's also the Watch, the cat council that enforces the divide and makes sure Folk don't draw attention to themselves – and cats like me keep our mouths shut unless we're around Watch-approved humans (like cat ladies). There's not meant to be any crossover, but no system is perfect, not even one run by cats. So things seep through here and there, and some humans are less blind than others, but for the most part

Folk keep to themselves and humans keep human-ing on in blissful ignorance. Which meant that the human outside our door was most unusual.

But then, as human as he was, Callum was *very* unusual, and recently I'd been starting to get the idea that he knew more unusual people than I'd realised. And right now he was swiping his trusty cricket bat from behind the desk.

"Right!" he shouted. "Everyone *out!*"

The imps and pixies looked at each other, then formed a united front against the human daring to tell them what to do. I ducked behind the armchair, and a plaintive little voice from the door said, "Callum? Please can we talk?"

"I am *done,*" Callum said to our tiny invaders. "I don't have time for this, and not only did we do the job you asked, you've caused more damage than the fee's going to cover."

"That's not hard," I said. "They paid us in foil flowers and out of date crisps, Callum. *Foil flowers.*"

The lead imp chittered.

"They say," I started, and Callum spoke over me.

"*I don't care.* Get out!" And he waved the cricket bat at them rather threateningly, which I'm fairly sure would be in the handbook of *Things Not to Do When Meeting Enraged Imps & Homicidal Pixies.* There was an absolute explosion of shrieks and shrill shouting and a *lot* of swearing, and the imps and pixies turned their combined forces on Callum. He tried a couple of sweeps with the bat then said something that impressed even the imps and threw himself into the tiny bathroom, slamming the door behind him. The critters attacked it in a fury, scoring the thin wood with talons and blades and sharp little teeth, and I wondered if I should beat a strategic retreat out the window myself.

Then the door to the hallway opened, and the stranger put his head in. He spotted me behind the armchair. "Sorry," he said. "It's just ... well, it's sort of urgent, and—"

"Dude," I said. "You any good at moving things on?" I nodded at the bathroom door, and he blinked at the imps and pixies, who'd already started fighting each other again.

"Oh," he said. "Um. Well."

"Oh, good. That clears things up, then." I slipped out into the room, wondering if going away and coming back later was a fair game plan. I mean, it wasn't as if Callum was in any danger in the bathroom. Then a new voice piped up behind our visitor.

"Excuse me, young man, what's going on in there?"

The visitor was pulled rather firmly back into the hall, and a new face appeared, this one crowned with a flower-bedecked beehive of white hair. She gave the man a stern look, then smiled at me.

"Hello, Gobbelino, dear."

I just blinked at her. Mrs Smith, our neighbour across the hall, had ended up at the centre of a reality storm last year, and had almost been eaten alive by a book of power. As memorable as that might sound, things had been arranged so that she didn't recall any of it, which meant that a talking cat was a bit much for a Wednesday afternoon.

"I heard a commotion," she said, examining the room. "Oh, dear! What *has* been happening here?"

I followed her gaze. The seat cushion from the brand new (well, second-hand, but brand new to us) armchair was lying on the floor looking like a tiger had been using it as a plaything, and there were ancient, coverless books scattered all over the place, spilling loose pages like they'd been disembowelled. A glass had joined Callum's mug on the floor, as had our mobile phone, all the pens in the place, half a bag of bread, two crushed apples, and the washing up liquid, which had been squirted all over the walls, mixed liberally with imp dust. I sighed. Occupational hazard, sure, but foil flowers weren't going to fix it up.

Mrs Smith rounded on our visitor. "How dare you?" she asked, reaching up to shake a finger in his face. "How *dare* you! Callum's an officer of the law, you know!"

The man took a step back. "I didn't—"

"He works *terribly* hard! And you come in here and just *destroy* his place! Look at all his poor books! *Look* at them!"

The man gave a howl as she grabbed his ear and dragged him into the room. *"I didn't do it!"* he wailed. "I *didn't!* I just arrived!"

Mrs Smith twisted his ear harder, and he dropped into a crouch as he tried to relieve the pressure. "You'll clean it up," she told him. "Right now!"

I looked around, suddenly aware that the imps and pixies had vanished from the bathroom door. I spotted them at the window, differences forgotten as they helped each other over the sill and into the summer day beyond, scrambling down the wall or taking to the skies if they weren't too caked in washing up liquid and melting squirty cream. The imp leader gave Mrs Smith a fearful look then chittered at me before they swung themself over the sill and were gone. We were even.

Not even magical Folk mess with ladies of a certain age.

CALLUM EMERGED CAUTIOUSLY from the bathroom with the cricket bat, looking slightly embarrassed, but Mrs Smith didn't seem to feel it changed his hero status at all. She just set him picking up books, and stood over our unwelcome visitor with her hands on her hips, pointing out spots he'd missed as he scrubbed unhappily at blue smudges and bloodstains. To be fair, I think some of those were older than today. It's that kind of business.

"Mrs Smith, it's really very nice of you to help out like this," Callum started, and she waved him off impatiently.

"I was just going to see if you and Gobbelino had had any lunch, because I've made far too much pasta salad," she said. "Then I saw this ruffian hanging around outside your door, and heard all the commotion. It's disgusting the way people behave these days." She glared at the sorry-looking ruffian, and I wondered if having her memories of last year's events removed had also removed a few other things, considering he'd been *outside* and all the commotion had been going on *inside*.

"It wasn't his fault," Callum said. "It was a previous client. He's actually an old … acquaintance."

The acquaintance rocked back on his heels and shot Callum an injured look.

Mrs Smith looked unconvinced. "Well, there's no point him standing around when there's work to be done, either way. I'll get the pasta salad. And some tuna for you, of course, Gobbelino."

I purred.

"That's absolutely lovely of you," Callum said, "but do you think you could maybe bring it by later? I need to talk to Art."

Art. Not a name I'd heard him mention before. But then, we didn't talk about the past much. We both had plenty of it, but it didn't mean we wanted to spend time back there. The past has teeth.

More importantly right now, so did I, and Mrs Smith always bought the top shelf tuna, which was a luxury we could rarely afford. I mewled.

"Oh, someone's hungry," Mrs Smith said, and scritched my head. "It won't take me a minute to bring it over."

"It's only early," Callum said. "We'll get some later."

Mrs Smith looked doubtful, and I gave my most pitiful squeak. "Oh, Gobbelino—"

"Has plenty of biscuits," Callum said, guiding our neighbour to the door. "Thank you so much for the help. But I won't be able to relax until we've cleaned up anyway."

She smiled up at him brightly. "If you're sure. I'll pop it in the fridge for you, so just come by any time. We can't have you fading away!" She gave his lanky frame a friendly little poke that made him wince.

"No chance of that, Mrs Smith," he said, and managed to close the door on her. He turned the lock, peeled his coat off and threw it on the tattered armchair, then crossed the room in two quick strides, grabbed the front of Art's tie-dyed T-shirt and hauled him to his feet.

"Hey!" Art protested. "Callum, what're you—"

"Shut up. What're you doing here? Who told you how to find me?" Callum punctuated each question with a brisk, almost business-like shake. He wasn't much taller than Art, and he was skinnier, but Art had his hands raised in front of him as if he thought Callum was about to go all Nosferatu on his neck, and he'd pulled back as far as his shirt would let him.

"Callum, *please.* I wouldn't have come unless it was an emergency."

"Who told you?" Callum didn't raise his voice, but there was a hard, ugly edge to it that lifted the fur on my tail. I jumped to the top of the desk, slipped on a slick of washing up liquid, and shot straight back off the edge too quickly to right myself. I landed on my side with a curse, and looked up at the two men. They were both staring at me.

"What?" I snapped. "Gods-damned imps. Why in the realms you took that case, Callum – listen to me next time, alright?"

"We took a gnome case last week," he said. "We couldn't just not take an imp one."

"Yeah, and they paid us in fungus," I said. *"Fungus."* I shook a soggy paw out and licked it, then spluttered. Lemon fresh my furry tail.

"Mushrooms," Callum said, finally letting go of Art and stepping back. "I like mushrooms."

"Still fungus," I said, eyeing Art. He hadn't bothered smoothing down his stretched shirt, just stood there with his hands twisted together in front of him. His dark hair was even more overgrown than Callum's and he had a straggly sort of beard to go with it. He smelled of hippie soap and rich earth and fresh bread and fear. Lots and lots of fear, and I didn't think it was down to Callum giving him a shakedown. I had the feeling he'd expected that. It was in the apologetic lines of his shoulders.

Callum looked at Art as if seeing him for the first time, then said, "Tea?"

"Please," Art said.

I looked at my paws and sighed. Humans and their tea.

WHILE CALLUM PUT the kettle on (the plastic lid had been broken off, but it still worked) and tried to find two mostly whole mugs, Art crouched next to me on the floor and offered me a cloth. I looked at it.

"What?"

"For your paws."

I gave him a suspicious look, then tried wiping my paws on the cloth. It didn't really do much, so Art picked up one of my paws and sponged it gently. I let him, examining him curiously. He didn't smell of magic. He had the quietly lost scent Callum and those other humans that lived in the edges, between the Folk and human worlds, always carried. They were the unseen, the ones regular humans ignored deliberately or casually (or sometimes both), the ones who passed unnoticed, who fell through the cracks in the world. They were the humans who saw Folk, but not all Folk welcomed it. The cats of the Watch discouraged it, and not too many Folk will go against cats. We have certain things in common with imps and mosquitoes, and we can do more than bite.

Callum set two mugs on the desk and righted the chairs, giving them a dubious shake. "Should hold," he observed.

"I'm starting to think we shouldn't have opened the books to Folk cases," I said, jumping cautiously onto the desk. "I know we need the money, but I thought there'd be less trashing of our office involved."

"Well, we'll make it a policy not to take any more imp cases," Callum said, putting a bowl of cat biscuits on the table. I stared at it morosely and thought of my squirty cream, wasted on an imp.

"No pixies either," I said.

"Well, we've never had a pixie case," he started, and I talked over him.

"You saw what happened! Besides, everyone knows pixies are trouble."

"That's true," Art said. "They really are."

Callum sighed. "Alright. No imps or pixies."

"Or werewolves," I said.

Art frowned at me. "They can be pretty good sorts, werewolves."

"They stink," I pointed out. "Like wet dogs *and* sweaty humans. It's gross."

"So are you when you've been eating custard," Callum said, and fished a packet of off-brand chocolate digestives out of the desk drawer. He popped them on the desk, found his cigarettes and lit one, then held the pack out to Art. Art shook his head, picking up the biscuits instead. A small green snake emerged from the desk drawer and looked around warily, and for a moment there was silence, broken only by a car alarm going off in the distance and a few people shouting in that way that makes it hard to tell if they're fighting or celebrating.

"So?" Callum said finally. His injured hand was tucked under his opposite armpit, cigarette smouldering in the other hand. "How did you find me, Art? And what do you want?"

Art stared at his biscuit for a moment, then looked at Callum with his face suddenly raw and vulnerable. Despite the beard, he seemed much younger than he had before, a child in men's clothing given a life he didn't understand.

"It's my sister," he said, the words slow.

"Kara." Callum's voice was softer than it had been. "What's happened?"

Art put the biscuit down, looking suddenly revolted. "She's been … taken."

"By who?" I demanded. "And why? Where?"

Callum glanced at me. "I expect if he knew all that he wouldn't be here, Gobs."

I subsided and tried a cat biscuit. They were okay, but would've been better with cream.

"I …" Art took a deep breath. "Well, I do know, in a way. Not who or where, but maybe why."

We both stared at him. There was an unpleasant sort of realisation dawning on Callum's face, and I decided not to say anything. The past was hanging heavy and hungry on the edges of the room, making its presence felt.

"If you know that already," Callum said, those hard

tones back in his voice, "why can't you just call the police? Why do you need us?"

Art took a deep breath. "Because the unicorns are missing," he said.

I very nearly fell off the desk. Green Snake did, although that might've been the washing up liquid.

3

EXTINCT, EXTANT, AND OTHER EXES

"DUDE, HAVE YOU BEEN LICKING IMPS?" I ASKED ART, AND he gave me a puzzled, shell-shocked look. "Imp dust? You know, gets you all a bit discombobulated? Is that what's going on?"

"Gobs," Callum said, and I ignored him.

"Unicorns are extinct. Everyone knows that. I mean, never mind the whole horn trade, they were so pathologically bad-tempered they kept shanking each other over things like who had the shiniest hooves."

"Mostly right," Art said, finding his voice finally. "Apparently dozens used to drown in frozen lakes each year because they'd see their reflection in the ice and think it was mocking them. They'd stab the reflection and fall through the ice."

"Yeah, they never were that bright," I said. "Which is why they're the only kind to stab their own entire species to death."

"Not quite the entire species," Callum said.

I looked at him. "Since when did you become a unicorn expert?"

He almost smiled. "I'm not. But Art's family had the last herd in the north."

I had the strangest sense of things *shifting,* of familiar ground no longer being stable. Of the past creeping up on us.

"Still have it," Art said. "Well, did. But it's just me and Kara left now."

"What happened?" Callum asked. He had the tone of someone who already knows, but wants to be told anyway.

Art glanced at me. "The Watch. Same time as they took your family."

Callum made a small *huh* sound. "I heard something about that."

There was a long, uneasy silence, and I tried to decide if saying something was more likely to get them talking again or to shut them up. I'd never heard of Art, or Kara, or even anything about Callum's family. As I say, the past has teeth. Sometimes it's best not to poke it.

"Kara's all I've got left," Art said finally. "When you … things changed after you left. After … you know."

"I know." Callum took another cigarette from the packet. I desperately wanted to say *I don't,* but that seemed like a good way to stop the conversation, so I just stepped on my tail with one front paw and bit down on the words.

"Mum didn't want anything to do with your family anymore. She tried to cut them out of the dust trade."

Callum leaned back in his chair. "I bet that went well."

Art gave a harsh, humourless bark of laughter.

"Really well. Your family were still controlling distribution of pretty much everything, and they weren't having it. It turned into this running feud that went on forever, and just got worse and worse. I mean, your sister burned down our barn, and Dad set a couple of goblin chickens on your brother, and Kara and one of your cousins had this complete *brawl* at some kid's party – and that was just the personal stuff. Then about five years ago the Watch came in and took out pretty much everyone."

"I'm sorry," Callum said, but there was no surprise in his voice. He'd known.

"You were trading in *unicorn horn?*" I asked, unable to stay quiet any longer. "Seriously? How the hell did you go so long without the Watch coming down on you?"

"Our village was – is – a pocket," Callum said. "You know the Watch kind of turn a blind eye as long as things don't get too loud."

"You're from a *pocket?*" I was starting to think I should've asked a few more questions about his past than I had. Well, *any* questions. Pockets – little villages and corners of towns where magic runs deep and Folk outnumber humans – are everywhere, left over from the days when Folk lived openly and magic was common as dandelion tea. Most of them were swallowed as towns and cities expanded, but there are still some. Magic always persists. And they were not the sort of places I'd ever thought Callum knew of. Not till recently, anyway.

He gave me a sideways glance and a smile that was almost his normal, easy grin. "You never wondered why I was completely cool with the whole swearing cat and tentacled monster trying to drag you into the void when we met?"

"Well, fair point. Although *cool* is pushing things. You were so high I just figured you thought it was a particularly nasty trip."

His smile faded. "Yeah. Life in a pocket gave me a taste for that, too."

"You took unicorn dust?" I demanded. *"Really?"* Talk about altered planes of consciousness. More than one sorcerer had ended up literally folding themselves into different dimensions after taking a nip too much of powdered unicorn horn. And sorcerers aren't even really human. Gods know what it does to a human head.

Although that wasn't the reason the Watch would've shut down the trade. No, that was more to do with the *other* properties of unicorn horn. Worked into the tips of arrows or the blades of knives or the edges of swords – hell, probably into *bullets,* for all I knew – powdered unicorn horn created weapons that could cut through troll hide, freeze the watery blood of sprites, even pierce dragon scale and stop the heart of a basilisk. It could end all nine of a cat's lives in one go, too. That was not something the Watch would tolerate.

"Not so much unicorn dust," Callum said. "It was expensive, and we were kids. It was mostly imp dust and gnome-made liquor and swamp grass."

"Urk."

"Yeah, well." He took a hard drag on the cigarette and stared at Art. "I got out. And I've no desire to go back."

"I'm not dealing," Art said, his voice flat. "As if I would, after everything. Even if it hadn't been for the

Watch, as soon as the herd had been mine, I'd have stopped."

Callum just watched him.

"Not all of us got to run away like you," Art said. "Some of us didn't get that luxury."

Callum's mouth twisted. "You could have come. You *should* have."

"Sure, and leave Kara there?" Art shook his head. "It was fine for *you*. You were the youngest. Your brother and sister were already in the business. If I left, Kara would've been dragged in, and I couldn't let that happen."

"We could've helped her get out, too."

"We were sixteen. She was *twelve.* What were we going to do?"

Callum ground his cigarette out with a sigh and said, "I know. I'm sorry."

"So will you help?"

Callum opened his mouth, but before he could say anything I said, "Hold your unicorns, dude. Let's get the full story here. What happened after the Watch raid? I mean, surely they didn't let you just keep the unicorns? Especially when you were trading."

Art blinked at me. "Yeah. I did think they'd wipe out the herd, and do for me and Kara, too, but this one cat stepped in and said she had a better idea."

"Claudia?" I asked. "Calico, different-coloured eyes?"

He shook his head. "No. Black cat, seemed kind of in charge."

"Black cats are the best," I said, and Callum snorted. I glared at him, then said to Art, "So what did they want you to do?"

"She said there was no point letting the herd go extinct. Kara and I were to stay on and look after them, and we had to keep the horns ground down, both so they couldn't stab each other and so no one tried to steal the horn."

"And what do you do with the dust?"

"Destroy it. A couple of cats come by every month and check the herd's there and we're disposing of the horn properly. You know, silver buckets and apple cider vinegar and moonlight, that sort of thing."

I looked at Callum. "You believe this?"

"Hey," Art protested. "Why would I lie?"

"It's weird, is all," I said. "I mean, since when do the Watch care about stopping species going extinct?" They'd made it pretty clear with the whole zombie outbreak thing earlier in the year that human extinction wasn't an issue for them. I didn't see unicorns being *that* different.

Callum ran both hands back over his hair, getting his fingers stuck in the tangle left by the imp. He wiped imp dust off on his jeans, nose wrinkled in distaste, then said, "Anyone left in Dimly? Norths, I mean?"

"We don't go there anymore," Art said. "We moved the herd out. The cat showed us a place."

"What's her name, this cat?" I asked, and he shrugged.

"She never said."

Great, he was one of *those* humans. The ones who saw Folk but still somehow thought there were levels to them. That it was worth getting an elf's name, but not a cat's. "Awesome," I said. "So *some cat* gave you responsibility for a herd of non-extinct unicorns, and now you've lost them and are freaking out because she's not going to be best pleased. How the hell do you lose them, anyway? I mean, they're kind of big."

"Extant," Callum said.

"What?"

"Extant. It's the opposite of extinct."

I narrowed my eyes at him. "And this changes the question of hippie-pants here losing them how?"

Art shook his head. "I didn't lose them. They've been stolen. And it's not the Watch that's worrying me as much as Kara. I mean, *anything* could've happened!"

Callum sighed, and looked at me. I shrugged.

"Was she taken at the same time as the unicorns?" Callum asked.

Art nodded. "It was just the other night."

"And how many unicorns did you have?" I put in.

"Eleven," he said. "Just had the first foal in about five years. Cute little thing, even if you don't want to be in the paddock with it."

I looked at the ceiling. There was a blue smudge of imp dust up there in the exact shape of a small, winged body splatting into the plaster at great speed. "You lost eleven stroppy, horned horses and one human all at once. Careless, dude."

"Unhelpful," Callum said, and poked his cigarette packet.

"Just stating facts."

Art rubbed his face. "Look, I don't know how it happened, okay? I just know that my sister's missing, and I have to get her *and* the herd back before the Watch check in again. They can't be the ones to find her. I'll take responsibility for the loss. It *can't* be on Kara. I can't have the Watch do … well. Whatever the Watch do to people they don't like."

A shiver corkscrewed its way down my spine. I knew what they did. I'd had it done to me in every one of my previous three lives, and I hadn't even deserved it. Well. I *mostly* hadn't deserved it. Most of the time. Anyhow, it had ended my last life. Ended it screaming in the Inbetween, the space that runs between all worlds and realities.

Callum gave up the fight and lit another cigarette. He blew smoke toward the open window, his face set in unhappy lines. "I don't know, Art. I mean, I'm really sorry to hear about the whole thing, but Gobbelino's got some issues with the Watch that mean we don't want to get caught up with them. And I can't go back to Dimly. You know that."

Art sighed. "I know. Well, about you, anyway. But there's no one else I can ask, Callum. No one's even meant to know we've still got the unicorns. And it's not like I can go to the police."

Callum rubbed his forehead with his cigarette hand, the smoke wreathing him for a moment, making him unfamiliar and distant. "I can't go back."

"You'd wouldn't have to go to Dimly," Art said. "I can't see anyone taking the unicorns there, anyway. Where would they keep them?"

"Dimly's that pocket over near the canal, right?" I said.

"Yeah," Callum said.

"You don't have to go near it," Art said. "Just come to the house. Please. Have a look. I *have* to find the unicorns.

I have to get Kara back. I can't ... I've lost everything else. Every*one* else. Please, Callum."

Callum scrubbed his face with his hands, the movement rough and angry, and swore as the makeshift dressing slipped off his hand.

"Oh, that looks nasty," Art said, leaning over the desk. "Let me see."

"No." Callum got up, shoving the chair back roughly. It clattered into the wall behind him. "No, just go, Art. I'm sorry about Kara. I'm sorry about *all* of it. But you have to go."

Art stared at him for a moment, then his shoulders sagged and he nodded. "Alright. Sorry." He leaned over the desk and picked up one of the surviving pens, then scrawled an address and phone number on a torn scrap of a book page. He put the pen back, looked at both of us, and left without saying anything else, his back stiff with anger and grief and something I couldn't quite taste.

WE LISTENED to his footsteps scuff down the threadbare carpet in the hall outside, and the screech of broken hinges on the door to the stairwell. Callum ground out his cigarette, picked up the biscuits, put them down again, tried to run a hand through his hair, then just stared at the imp-inflicted puncture wounds, still oozing blood.

"You should put some peroxide on that," I observed, and nibbled on a cat biscuit.

He grunted, and prodded the ball of his thumb, making it bleed more.

"Gross," I announced. "And you just cleaned that floor."

He sighed, wrapped his hand in the filthy T-shirt, and looked at me properly. "You're quiet."

"Nothing to say."

"That's a first."

I narrowed my eyes at him, but didn't argue the point.

He flicked ash into the dish on the windowsill that served as an ashtray, then said, "I can't go back there."

"That's fair enough," I said.

"And it could get you tangled up with the Watch again."

"No one wants that," I agreed.

"And I've been gone for *ages.* Why come to me? He didn't even say how he found us!"

"He didn't."

Callum frowned. "Should we be worried about that?"

"Probably."

He rubbed his face with his good hand. "You're not helping here, Gobs."

"I'm being very agreeable."

"That's what's worrying me."

We looked at each other for a moment, then I said, "Look. You might've left Dimly, but you didn't leave the north, did you? You didn't even leave *Leeds,* and it's hardly a long way from here to Dimly."

Callum shifted uncomfortably. "I didn't have any money."

"I'm not judging. It took me three lives to get out of London, and in the end I got in the same trouble up here as I did down there. Location's not all it's cracked up to be."

"You're saying I *wanted* to be found?"

"I'm saying maybe you've got unfinished business. First Ifan in that zombie case, now Art? The past never lets us go entirely."

Callum looked at his cold tea rather than at me. "I think I prefer it when you never shut up than when you get all thoughtful."

"Yeah, well, bite me. I'm not telling you anything you don't already know."

"So you say we take the case."

"I say we see if he can pay us first."

Callum snorted. "That sounds more like the Gobs we know and tolerate. What about the Watch?"

I shrugged. "We're not doing anything wrong. Finding them their lost property is all."

He watched me for a moment, then said, "You do know that saying about curiosity killing the cat, right?"

"Dude, I've been killed three times already. Curiosity had *nothing* to do with it."

"And this?"

I wrinkled my nose. "Ifan the magician's son. Art the unicorn keeper. Your family. *Your family.* I'm basically *all* curiosity right now."

He'd been smiling, but when I mentioned his family it faded. "Yeah, well. If there's any of my family left, and we run into them, the Watch really will be the least of our problems." He stubbed the cigarette out and picked up the scrap of paper with Art's address on it.

"You never checked? After the Watch went through?"

"No."

I watched him, the questions itching at the base of my

skull like a flea bite you just can't reach (look, even the cleanest cat gets fleas sometimes. Don't act like you've never left your hair dirty for a week). But I didn't ask. Partnerships are built on agreements and compromises, both negotiated and not. Spoken ones, like *don't bite me and I won't throw water at you*. And unspoken ones, like the knowledge that both of us had pasts that were best left behind us. Pasts that didn't need to have questions asked about them.

Pasts that maybe we didn't even know how to answer questions about.

So I just groomed one faintly sudsy paw, and after a moment he said, "Let's get that pasta salad from Mrs Smith, then we'll head over."

"We'd best take some supplies," I said.

"She said she had tuna for you."

"Not for lunch. For the trip."

He wrinkled his nose. "It'll take us half an hour, tops. And I'm certain there's still some treats in the car, as *someone* has an absolute phobia of running out."

"Can't be too careful," I said. "What if we break down?"

"Half an hour," he repeated. "I think we'll manage."

"With that car, half a *mile's* a risk," I pointed out, and he got up with a sigh.

"Fine," he said, and went to dress his hand.

I stayed where I was, watching the sun slanting through the grimy windows and wondering if the unicorns would be the most dangerous things to come.

I doubted it.

4

THE UNICORN FIELDS OF LEEDS

IT'S ALWAYS STRANGE TO FIND THESE LITTLE FORGOTTEN scraps of farmland, encircled by houses and bundled up on the outskirts of cities, like patches of earth someone forgot to sprinkle buildings on. Pockets of a more green and rural magic than Folk pockets, I suppose. All sorts of scraps are left behind as cities advance, fighting back in their own wild and furtive ways. I'm not saying they're great rolling fields or anything, and the woodlands are usually home to as many broken bottles and secret human plantations as they are rabbits and foxes, but still. There they are. Little remnants of wilderness and greenery that have resisted the onslaught of lawnmowers and pavements and corner shops.

We wound our way out of Leeds, heading west toward where the sprawl of the city and its attendant towns would eventually give way to high clear skies and the hulking backs of the fells, all stone walls and old cairns and secret places and bewildered sheep. But we weren't going as far as that. Instead we trundled past terraced houses and rundown shops, mills reworked into posh apartments and wine bars, second-hand car yards and leafy schools and the ugly sprawls of supermarkets. And finally, as the long summer afternoon edged into the start of a long evening, we found smaller lanes lined with semis and bungalows and the odd detached house pushing their back up against the forgotten stretches of fields and trees.

Callum chose one of the skinnier streets, puttering down it as it gave way to something that was more driveway than lane, barely wide enough for the car and penned in by the low garden walls of houses to either side. Then the last of those petered out, and the tarmacked strip turned to a pitted track scattered with loose gravel and dandelions. Before long we found our way barred by a gate with a *Private Property No Thoroughfare* sign on it, and another that read, *Almost Knackered Pony Sanctuary*.

"Nice," I said. "Real subtle."

"Well, if anyone fancies rescuing a pony, they're unlikely to choose an almost knackered one, are they?" Callum asked, swinging himself out of the car to open the gate.

"True," I said, and watched him wrestle with the latch then drag the thing open, having to lift it on its sagging hinges. I didn't think many people would be coming out here anyway. There was a whiff of charms about the place, low-level background magic that would keep the whole place *faint*, beneath the notice of most humans.

Which made sense. Even if the unicorns were hornless, there'd be nothing wrong with their hooves. Nothing like a few trampled walkers to draw attention to a pack of bad-tempered, formerly extinct magical horses with teeth on their foreheads.

The track didn't improve once we were through the gate. If anything, the potholes became more like ravines, and the car started lurching about like a particularly disoriented camel, making nasty scraping sounds as it dragged along the ground between the ruts.

"Can't be far now," Callum said, wrestling with the wheel as the car made it clear it'd rather plunge nose first down the grassy slope to our right than persist with the horrors of the track.

"It'd better not be," I said, hooking my claws more tightly into the cracked vinyl of the seats. "I'm more worried about the trip back, though."

Callum didn't say anything, just nodded at another gate ahead of us. Not that it meant anything, necessarily. I still hadn't seen a house.

We made it through the second gate with the car making the sort of noises you normally hear on rubbish collection day, and came through a thin stand of trees to find a small cottage squatting comfortably behind a low dry-stone wall, roses nodding over the top. A slightly scruffy vegetable patch stood to one side of the cottage, along with a tiny, grimy greenhouse and a couple of dilapidated wooden sheds. A broad field rolled downhill from the garden gate to another stand of trees that probably hid the canal. I could smell the green, slightly metallic tang of the water on the shifting breeze. There was a barn not far from the house with a couple of goats standing on top of the hen house outside it, and a dejected looking donkey wandered up to inspect us as we got out of the car. He stared at us mournfully, then gave an enormous bray.

I jumped backward, banged into the car, and swore roundly. Callum just grinned at me, gave the donkey a scratch on the nose, and let himself through the little wooden gate to the house.

"That's why you're called an ass," I told the creature, and followed Callum. The donkey waggled his ears, but didn't reply.

"Ass," Callum said.

"That's what I said."

"Not the way you pronounced it."

"Yeah, well. *You're—*" I stopped as Art swung the door open ahead of us, beaming through his scruffy beard.

"You came!" he said, and threw both arms around Callum. Callum made a funny *urk*-ing noise and waved his hands as much as the embrace would let him, as if not sure what to do with them. "I *knew* you'd come," Art said, releasing him. "I knew you wouldn't leave me in this mess."

Callum had gone a shade that almost matched the roses, but now he frowned. "This is a job, Art. I'm not doing this for old times' sake or anything."

"No, no. Of course not," Art said, and ushered us out of the late afternoon sun and into the house.

Callum had to duck his head to avoid cracking it on the low door frame, and we stepped straight onto the stone-flagged floor of the kitchen, all white-washed walls and low ceilings cut through with exposed wooden beams. It smelled of herbs and wood smoke and, weirdly, sheep. Well, not so weirdly, as I saw once we were in. There was a large sheep with a black face and black legs lying in front of one of those enormous, ancient wood stoves, yellow eyes half-closed against the heat. The rest of the small room was taken up by a chunky wooden table and a collection of mismatched chairs.

The sheep looked up at us and bleated in an offended sort of way.

"She fell in the stream behind the house," Art said. "And it's going to be cold tonight. I didn't want her catching a chill."

The sheep and I stared at each other, and I said, "Humans."

The sheep didn't say anything, and Callum snorted.

"Um, tea?" Art suggested, rubbing his hands on his T-shirt.

ART MADE EVEN MORE of a performance of the tea than Callum usually does, heating a fat green pot and fussing with sieves and milk from a jug and honey, which he said was better than sugar. Callum made a face as he stripped out of his ancient charity shop coat, the one he thinks makes him look like a professional PI and that I think makes him look like a professional flasher.

"Who else knows about the unicorns?" I asked, as Art put a tin of fruit cake on the table, as well as a bowl of milk for me. I eyed it suspiciously – it didn't smell like the milk we got from the corner shop.

"Just the Watch," Art said. "As far as anyone else

knows, when they took out the Norths and the rest of my family, they took out the unicorns, too."

"And no one else has been around since then? No nosy neighbours?"

"None," Art said, setting the teapot on the table. "The whole place has hiding runes on it, and is shift-locked so no cats can shift in. Even the Watch have to walk when they come to check on things."

"I'm surprised they put up with that," Callum said.

I was, too. Shifting is how cats appear in places humans think they have no right being, behind locked doors and inside your halls of power. It's also how we get *out* of places you think we can't. It's an exceptionally handy ability, only thanks to the Watch, I can't do it. To shift, you have to pass through the Inbetween, and the beasts that haunt that not-place have my scent. I can't get in there anymore, not unless I want to step out again in pieces.

"That cat insisted on the shift locks," Art said.

"That cat." I snorted, and he gave me a puzzled look, like he couldn't see what was so wrong. "Right. So no business dealings? No little back door trade in unicorn horn?"

"No." He slammed the mugs down on the table, sploshing milk over his hands. "*Of course* not."

I narrowed my eyes at him, and Callum raised his eyebrows slightly. Neither of us said anything, though.

Art frowned at both of us, then topped the mugs up with tea. "I told you, I'm out of all that. Just like you, Callum."

"*Hmm,*" Callum said, and accepted his mug. "That's good to know."

"I just couldn't leave, you know. Because of Kara."

"I think we've got that," I said, and stuck my nose in the milk bowl, then spluttered. "What *is* this?"

"Fresh goat's milk," Art said. "Much better for you than cow's milk."

I blinked at him. "It tastes *hairy*. Callum, I told you we'd need supplies, didn't I?"

"Just drink your milk," he said, although he didn't seem in any rush to try his tea. "When did you last see Kara, then?"

"It was the same day," Art said. "I'd gone to get some supplies in, you know, feed and some fencing wire and stuff, and I was gone most of the day. When I got back the unicorns were gone, and so was she. Just … *gone.* No note, no message. Just a couple of broken plates in here. It doesn't even look like any of her clothes are missing."

"Did she work with the unicorns, too?" I asked. "Do you think they took her so she could look after them?"

Art examined the cake as he nodded. "Yes, I imagine that's it."

I looked at Callum, but he just took a sip of his tea, made a face, and put it down again. "So we find one, we find the other," he said.

"The unicorns will be easier to track, I'd guess," Art said. "We should concentrate on them. I mean, much harder to hide them than one woman, right?"

"Right," Callum said, and took the slice of cake Art handed him. He sniffed it, and gave the other man a slightly worried look. "It's … what is this?"

"Fruit cake with hemp flour."

"Right." Callum handed it back and looked at me. "Check the barn?"

"Good a place to start as any," I said, and jumped to the floor as Callum got up.

Art looked at his tea. "We can take it with us, I suppose?"

Callum didn't.

THE BARN WASN'T BIG, just enough for half a dozen wide stalls, one inhabited by a big, elderly sow who watched us pass with thoughtful eyes but said nothing, the rest clean and empty. There was a hayloft above, and water in stone troughs near the door. The goats followed us in, bleating and bouncing about the place on stiff legs, and the donkey kept trying to nibble the back of Callum's shirt until Art grabbed a handful of his mane and led him around with us.

I hung back as the two men went outside again, Art pointing to the woods behind us and theorising about tracks and trailers and all sorts of other things.

I jumped onto the wooden beams enclosing the pig's stall. "Hey," I said.

She rolled her eyes toward me and said nothing.

"May your hay be fragrant and your mud be, um, muddy."

She looked back at the very un-muddy floor.

"Right. Don't suppose you know where the unicorns went, do you?"

She flicked one floppy ear and investigated an apple she was apparently saving for later.

"I'd ask the goats, but you know what *they're* like. Must be pretty boring, stuck in here with just them for company."

She grunted, which I took as encouragement.

"And the donkey, I suppose. He doesn't seem like a sparkling conversationalist."

She picked up the apple and carried it across the stall, stashing it under some hay.

"Not that I imagine the unicorns were amazing, either. Snotty things, from what I've heard. Probably thought talking to a pig was beneath them or something."

She sighed, and settled herself down in some sunlight edging through a high window.

"Right," I said. "Good chatting to you and all." I examined the barn. There were a few chickens pecking around the place, but there was no point asking them anything. Bird-brained is a term for a reason. "I suppose I'll try talking to the donkey," I said to the pig's back. "Maybe he's the actual brains around here."

She shot me a disdainful look, but still didn't reply.

"Vow of silence?" I asked her.

She grunted, laying her jowly chin on her trotters.

"Really?"

She closed her eyes. Great. Chickens, goats (who only ever really talked about what they'd eaten. I mean, that was *it*), and a sulky sow. I jumped back to the straw-strewn concrete floor and padded out into the early evening light, the shadows long and undercut with the chill of a clear night creeping in on the edges of the horizon. Art and Callum were standing halfway down the field, Art pointing in various directions like he was directing traffic, Callum standing next to him with his hands in his pockets. The donkey was chewing on a dandelion, looking bored.

I trotted up to him. "Hey," I said.

He blinked at me with long, graceful lashes. "No thanks," he said. "Dandelions are tastier. I try and eat fresh where I can."

"Right. Fair enough. You can talk, then. I was starting to wonder, with all that braying."

"I mostly certainly can communicate," he said. "Whether I choose to or not depends on the person I'm addressing."

I blinked at him. "Ah … Okay. Got a name?"

He regarded me through long dark lashes. "I have a word with which people reference me, yes."

I swallowed a sigh. "Which is?"

"Kent."

"Kent. Great. Look, you don't happen to know where the unicorns have gone, do you?"

"No," he said. "I don't interest myself in the doings of those beyond this yard. Our world is these fields. All other things are unproven to exist."

"Right," I said again. "Um, were you here when they were taken, then?"

He considered it, drooling green foam from the corner of his mouth. "In a manner of speaking, yes. All beings are everywhere within their worlds. Our molecules are interchangeable."

"So, in a manner of speaking, might you have seen who came and took them?"

"Perception's a tricky thing," he said. "How do I know that what I see is reality?"

I sat down and scratched my ear with a back paw. Maybe I'd do better asking the goats what they'd been eating when the unicorns were taken. It'd be about as helpful. "Well, could you tell me what you *did* perceive, and let me decide on the reality of it?"

"But how can I be sure my words will communicate to you the correct reflection of my perceptions? Your experiences are different to mine. Your reality is different. Miscommunication is the only certainty in a world of uncertainty." He found another dandelion and munched on it happily.

"My certainty is that you're talking bollocks," I muttered, then said more loudly, "Can you tell me *anything* about when the unicorns vanished?"

"Oh, yes," he said cheerfully. "The moon was almost full. Or I perceived it to be so, the silver light painting the trees in dream shades of what I call blues and greys, but you may call another colour. The sheep engaged in that state of consciousness we may call sleep, but which—"

"Do you know *anything* about who took them?" I demanded. "Did you *see* anyone? Yes or no?"

Kent gave me a hurt look. "That's a very reductionist approach."

The whiskers on the left side of my face were twitching. "I'm starting to see why the pig doesn't speak, if this is what she puts up with. Although I'm not sure why she won't speak to *me*."

"She's questioning her existence in this reality, the significance of her corporeal body and the importance – or lack thereof – of her spirit. If we indeed have one. Such things are, of course, always open to debate. We may be no more than a fleeting dream in the mind of a figurative, hibernating dormouse."

"What?"

"Or maybe *we* exist, but the dormouse is the dream."

"Oh, Old Ones take you," I said, and stalked away as Kent called after me, "Don't you want to hear about that night?"

I met Callum on the way up the field. "Let's go," I said. "This is a bust. It's all figurative dormice."

"What?" he said.

"Never mind. Just don't talk to the donkey."

Art shook the dregs of his tea out of his mug and said absently, "That's kind of a curious thing to do, anyway. What would you talk about?"

"More than you'd imagine," I snapped. "Callum, are we going?"

"I think we should stay," he said. "Get an early start tomorrow. The car can't take that trip too many times anyway."

"Ugh. Really?"

"You'll survive a night without your heatable bed, if that's what you're worried about."

"Well, I'm not eating goat's milk, or talking to any more donkeys," I said. "Let's be clear on that."

Callum just snorted, and gave Kent a scratch on the snout as he passed.

5

LOCAL SOURCES OF DUBIOUS INFORMATION

After a very questionable dinner involving far too many vegetables and weird grainy things (although Art did find some sardines in his pantry, so that was something), our host showed us to a guest room complete with a faded floral quilt and a dusty green jug with matching tumbler on the dresser.

"I wouldn't use that," Art said, drawing flowery curtains that clashed violently with the quilt. "I'm pretty sure there's a brownie that swims in it."

"Noted," Callum said, and sat on the bed to kick his boots off. We listened to the creak of the stairs as Art headed back down to the kitchen, then Callum looked at me and said, "Anything other than dormice?"

"*Figurative* dormice," I said. I jumped on the bed and tested it for softness. It wasn't bad. "I'll try again. Talk to the goats if I have to, but unless the unicorn thieves left some really unusual snacks behind they probably won't remember anything."

"You pick up anything from Art?"

"Other than him being a bit of a species-ist, you mean?"

Callum snorted and pulled the covers back on the little bed, exposing daisy-patterned sheets. "He talks to you."

"He has to. Doesn't bother talking to the animals on his own farm, though. Just treats them like any human would."

"I know. But we were kind of brought up with that – you know, animals are still animals. Some Folk are worth knowing, others are just a nuisance."

"Nice," I said, although cats aren't exempt from that sort of behaviour. Just look at how many ignore rat treaties. "So why are we taking cases from *imps*, if you know all about them?"

He poked at the books stacked under the nightstand. "I figured if I'd been taught the wrong things about one kind, I might as well assume I'd been taught the wrong things about all of them."

I snorted. "Well, you can just listen to me in the future. I'll steer you right."

"Sure you will," he said, sitting back on the bed and grinning at me. "I mean, you're totally free of prejudice, right?"

"I *am*," I insisted. "Cats are just quantifiably more awesome than any other kind. Well, most of us, anyway." He just laughed. "Ugh, whatever, you turnip. You believe he's not dealing?"

Callum shrugged, still grinning. "I'd like to believe he's not."

"You're his long-lost whatever. Is it the sort of thing he'd do?"

Callum shook his head. “It’s been a long time. Things change.”

I watched him for a moment, then said, “Well, I can’t tell if he’s out-and-out lying or not. But there’s more going on than he’s telling us. If he’s dealing, might be whoever’s buying decided to cut out the middleman and just take the unicorns. If he’s not, maybe he just hasn’t been as careful about hiding as he says. Loose lips, tongue shall be split and all that.”

Callum stared at me. “What?”

“It’s a saying.”

“Loose lips sink ships, you mean?”

I thought about it. “No, that doesn’t seem right. What have boats got to do with it? And there’s definitely a tongue in there somewhere.”

Callum started to say something, then just shook his head. “Well, we’ll see what we can find out tomorrow.”

“Try the dimple thing on him,” I said. As well as projecting an oddly harmless air for someone I’d seen battle big cats with nothing more a spray bottle, and take on hordes of the undead with a can of air freshener, Callum has dimples that seem to work a very particular magic on certain people. They’d tell him anything, and top it off with a cup of tea, when he used the dimples.

“There’s no dimple thing. I just ask nicely. You should try it sometime.”

I lifted my nose. “I work more in the fields of stealth and cunning.”

He snorted. “Yeah, you’re a regular Mata Hari.”

“Who’s that? Is that like James Bond? *Better* than James Bond? That seems reasonable.”

"Sure. Although you bear more than a passing resemblance to Johnny English, now I'm thinking about it."

I huffed at him and jumped off the bed. "You obviously need your sleep. I'm off to snoop around. Open the door, will you?"

"Of course, sir. Anything else you need? Whiskers cleaned? Claws polished?"

I lifted my lip to show him one of my fangs, but he just scritched me behind the ears as he padded across to the door and opened it enough that I could slip through. "Leave it open," I said to him.

"Well, I'm hardly going to shut it and have you scratching to be let in at three in the morning again."

"Look, that very rarely happens. But you just never know when you're going to meet some nice young she-cat who's new in town. You should try it sometime. It might cheer you up."

"One cat is plenty," he said, and nudged me out into the hall with one bare foot.

THE LANDING WAS dark and a little chilly, the tatty carpet silent under my feet as I wandered down the hall. I found a bathroom with the light of the moon captured in a tarnished mirror above the sink, and a bedroom smelling of incense and bad dreams, clothes piled on a chair in the corner and the bed empty. I nosed around, my ears twitching for any sign of Art on his way back up the stairs, but all I found was a pile of books with titles like *More Eggs With Fewer Chickens* and *101 Things to Do With Goat's Milk,* an empty bag of peppermints, and a dusty collection of weights. Nothing exactly screamed, *I'm a drug lord!* And judging by the clothes on the chair he frequented the same shops Callum did, so if he was a drug lord he was a pretty unprofitable one.

I jumped onto the chest of drawers to inspect some pictures crowded into a frame. There were some old postcards, and a couple of flyers advertising bands with long hair and glassy smiles, as well as some actual photos. One showed Art, an older couple, and a young woman I guess had to be his sister. Art looked younger than he did now, his beard even more patchy, and Kara wasn't much more than a girl, all blowing dark hair and a pretty smile. Their parents were offering stiff smiles, the mother with a firm grip on both her children, as if pinning them in place. Only Kara looked happy.

I was about to give it up as a bad job when another photo caught my eye. It was older than the others, and it showed four boys at the age when everything's going gangly and no one's clothes seem to fit right, all of them leaning against a grimy-looking wall as if they didn't know whether to act tough or start laughing. One was Art, in a green jumper with a hole in the side. A shorter boy with the same rough hair and long nose leaned next to him, caught with a smirk on his face and his hands in his pockets. Next to him, a boy with dark skin and a luminous smile was whispering something to the fourth boy, who was looking off beyond the frame, his hands in his pockets and dimples stitching his cheeks above half a smile. His thicket of brown hair was as messy as it was today, and I put my paws on the wall to peer at the whispering boy.

I was almost certain he was going to grow up to become the dead man who had set us off on a zombie hunt earlier in the year.

I jumped back to the floor and slipped out of Art's room, wondering who the shorter boy with Art's nose had been, and why he wasn't in the later family photo. Wondering if it mattered. But somehow it felt as if *everything* mattered now, as if Callum's past was circling us like dogs scenting an injured beast. I didn't like it.

THE FINAL ROOM had to be Kara's. It was tidy, a stuffed bear resting against the pillows and the walls adorned with cutesy prints of uplifting quotes. There was a yoga mat in one corner and the whole place smelled of perfume and candles and a quiet undercurrent of healthy sweat. The most suspicious thing I discovered was a large jar half-filled with miniature chocolate bars. And they were only suspicious because I'd seen how quickly Callum could eat his way through some discount chocolate.

I sat back on the deep white rug in the centre of the floor and scratched absently at the scars on my shoulder. The room hardly suggested someone who loved living on a fake pony sanctuary, but I could smell old clothes and hay from behind the closed wardrobe doors, so she obviously did her share of the work, like it or not. And as bland as the room was, nothing about it suggested she was about to swipe the unicorns and head off to live the high life somewhere.

I poked around for a little longer, wondering if she had a diary or something, but all I could find were a couple of books of poetry and a handful of printouts from travel websites, all dated last year. The whole place had a resigned, wistful air, and I felt weirdly as if I were intruding. I mean, I was, but in my line of work it's called investigating, and it's perfectly legal. Well, it's perfectly acceptable. To me, anyway.

I padded back into the hall and down the stairs, hearing Art talking to the sheep in the kitchen, and the clink of a teaspoon in a mug. I nosed into a cold dining room filled with haphazardly stacked filing boxes, two broken chairs, and some garden furniture, all smelling faintly musty and neglected. Next to it was a living room with two big, soft sofas and a large TV next to the fireplace, the heavy wooden coffee table in front of it piled with magazines and marked with rings from mugs and glasses. There was a heavy population of spiders in one corner, but nothing else very interesting.

I slipped across the hall and poked my nose around the door. Art was sitting at the table, a mug clutched in one hand and his phone in the other. He hadn't been talking to the sheep after all.

"I know," he said, his voice tight and almost choked. "I *know.* But I haven't found them yet." He waited, then took a deep, rough breath. "I *am* trying! I've even got help—" He broke off, and my ears twitched as I strained to hear the other side of the conversation. "No! *No!* Of course I didn't tell them! They're just looking for the unicorns, I promise! Please don't—" He stopped again, and this time he pulled the phone away from his ear and stared at it, then put it down on the table and dropped his face into his hands. I could see him shaking. "I'm trying," he said, to no one in particular, and the sheep bleated anxiously.

I WATCHED Art for a little longer, until he got up and switched the light off. He headed upstairs with a heavy, plodding tread as I retreated into the shadows and watched him go. Then I slipped into the kitchen, following the scent of cold fresh air seeping in from an open window somewhere.

I found it in the pantry, a small window held open on a metal arm, and I sat there scenting the night for a moment before sliding my paws down the outside wall and jumping into the whispering shadows of the garden. A couple of mice gave shrill screams and fled out of the veggie patch, dropping their plundered tomatoes, and somewhere a night bird called, the sound dropping like liquid through the dark, setting my tail shivering to attention.

I padded to the garden wall and jumped to the top of one of the gateposts, glancing at our car leaking oil and leaving a lingering stench of burning rubber on the drive. It had a funny angle to it, and I hoped we'd just stopped in a pothole and nothing important had fallen off. Like a wheel.

Reconnaissance done, I dropped to the drive and headed across it to the unicorn-less field beyond, the night drawn in velvet grey and luminous black around me. The stars were pulling out of a thin covering of cloud, battling the light leaking from the unseen city, and the thin moon threw uneasy shadows among the trees. I eyed it, wondering what old Kent had been talking about with his *moon was almost full* bollocks. But that's what you get with donkeys. Especially philosophical ones. I ambled on. There was no wind, and I could hear the whisper of my own breath and the panicked racing of small feet as a couple of rabbits bolted across the grass.

Across the drive I sat down and watched the empty field for a little, ears flicking at the small noises of secretive life around me, wondering who Art had been talking to. Someone else was chasing the unicorns, or forcing him to, which meant their existence wasn't the secret he claimed it was. And I had an idea that was only the first of the things he was lying to us about. Which I suppose didn't change the job, but I had an idea it might change how Callum felt about taking it on.

"Whatcha doing?" a warm voice asked just over my ears, and I shot sideways, crashing through some nettles and fetching up flattened against a fencepost. I scrambled around to face a pointed nose and two bright eyes. "Dude," the owner of the eyes said. "Sorry. Didn't mean to scare you."

"I wasn't scared," I said, trying to get my fur to settle back down as I eyed up the visitor. I'd run into the odd urban fox before. They were unpredictable, full of loss and dislocation and a strange, cruel humour, and I was never sure how likely they were to try cat for dinner. There didn't seem to be any guidelines regarding the eating of cats among foxes. This one stood taller than others I'd seen, sleek and young and sharp-toothed.

The fox cocked its head. "Is that some city greeting, then? The backflip?"

"Okay, so you startled me."

"Ah. I see the distinction." His eyes glittered as he looked around. "So whatcha doing? Stargazing? Philosophising?"

"Phil— No. Had quite enough of that with the donkey."

"Oh, yeah. Kent. I had a really long conversation with him one day and it took me about a month to think straight again." The fox thought about it. "I don't like his sort of philosophising. It makes your head hurt. But I do like to just find a nice place and sit and *look,* you know? Wonder about the lives that have stood in the same spot, and what they thought, and what we're all made of, and how it can be fair that shrews are both cute and tasty. It's a dilemma, that one."

"I can imagine," I said. "I prefer my food to be neither cute nor chatty, personally."

"Oh, chatty's the worst," the fox said. "I have to bite their heads off quick-like, before they get talking. Otherwise I get indigestion for days."

That was promising. I never had a problem with being chatty.

"I've even tried," the fox continued, "to only eat things that don't talk, like frogs and birds. But then I realised that they *may* talk, and we just don't understand them. These questions are difficult."

"They are," I agreed, starting to think the fox might make my head hurt as much as the donkey. "That's why I got a human. Hunting for food's a bit passé for the modern cat."

"Now, I have wondered about getting a human. Are they as slow and smelly as everyone says?"

"Well, you want one that showers regularly." I picked my way out of the weeds and sat down next to the fox. "You come around here a lot?"

"Most nights."

"You happen to notice anyone unusual around? Before the, uh, horses went missing?"

"You mean the unicorns?" the fox asked, giving me an amused look.

Of course. Glamours were for creatures that see what they expect to see, like humans. They don't work on creatures that see what's really there. It's a lot harder to hide things from them. It can be done, but it takes extra care and different charms. "So, not exactly a big secret, then?"

"You won't find a squirrel this side of the city that didn't know about them."

"What about humans? Or any non-animal Folk? They know about them?"

The fox shrugged. "Maybe. If they asked us. But no one really asks animals, do they? We're just here to be chased, and hunted, and blamed for trying to hold on to the land they're stealing from us."

"Fair point." We watched the quiet field for a little in silence, the fox's brush curling over his toes. Finally I said, "Have you seen anyone new about, by any chance?"

The fox looked at the sky, lip curling back off his teeth. "Not new, exactly. There's a troll family down by the old Middling Road bridge that turned up a few moons or so ago. One of the young ones comes creeping around, feeding carrots to the unicorns."

"Trolls, huh? And she knew they were unicorns?"

"Maybe. She feeds the donkey, too," the fox said. "Odd sort, those trolls. They have flowers."

I blinked up at him, but he didn't elaborate further. Maybe it was some fox-philosophy reference. But trolls were interesting. A family of trolls could polish off a herd of unicorns for Sunday lunch, although that didn't explain the missing sister. Unless she'd been the appetiser, which was always possible with trolls. Their species-for-eating rules were pretty loose and flexible.

"Anyone else?"

The fox thought about it. "Not really. Plenty of humans, but there's always plenty of those. I've not seen them come up here, though."

"Alright," I said. "Thanks."

"Sure," the fox said, and gave me a speculative look. "Have you considered dormice?"

"Only figurative ones," I said, and ambled back to the house before he could tell me what I should consider about them. It seemed wise.

6

CROSSING THAT BRIDGE NOW WE'VE COME TO IT

I WOKE UP TO CALLUM POKING ME IN THE RIBS, AND opened one eye to stare at him. "What?"

"Why're you sleeping on me? It's weird when you sleep on me."

"*You're* weird," I muttered, and tried to go back to sleep, but he pushed me off his belly and I flopped ungracefully onto the bed as he sat up. "Look, I was cold after all my investigating last night. You were tucked up in here all nice and warm while *I* was out interviewing witnesses."

"Which somehow involved you waking me up and demanding second dinners," he pointed out, getting out of bed and crossing to the window to push the curtains open, his arms looking cold and bumpy.

"I had to keep my energy up," I said. "And it wasn't much of a second dinner. Biscuits and goat's milk. I told you we needed supplies."

"Gobs, you think we need supplies when we're going to the cafe for breakfast."

"Ugh, the *cafe*. I want to go there for breakfast now," I said, stretching. "I really think I need bacon and sausage if I've got to get up at such an uncivilised hour."

"Yeah, well, we need to do some poking around before we go anywhere. The car's not going to get up that drive too many times." He struggled into his jumper, getting caught up in a hole in the sleeve. "Go on – what'd you find out last night, then?"

"I've barely slept," I said, snuggling my nose into the covers.

He sat on the edge of the bed to pull his boots on. "Come on, Gobs. Sooner we get this sorted the sooner we can go back to being attacked by imps and having a ready supply of fried food."

"You make it sound so appealing." I sat up and examined him. He looked paler than usual, and was already pawing through his jacket for his cigarettes. "You not enjoying the trip down memory lane?"

"Not especially, no."

"Saw an old photo of you last night."

"Did you now." He stood up and shrugged into his coat, cigarettes clasped in one hand.

"Yeah. You, Art, and someone who looked a lot like Ifan, your undead buddy."

He gave a one-shouldered shrug. "Ifan was around. He wasn't from Dimly, but he hung out with us."

"And someone else," I said. "Didn't recognise him. Looked a bit like Art."

Callum crossed to the window and pushed it open, resting his elbows on the sill as he lit a cigarette. "He was

Art's brother," he said to the pale morning sky. "Rory. He died."

I watched the stiff line of his back, waiting. We were silent for a moment, then Callum said, "So? What did you find out?"

It looked like that was all the reminiscing he was going to be doing.

CALLUM LISTENED CAREFULLY while I told him about the unhidden unicorns, the trolls, and Art's one-sided conversation with someone who didn't seem too happy that we were involved. He finished his cigarette, waved a pillow around the room for a bit to clear the smoke, then said, "Let's sit on the phone thing for now. Hit him with the trolls first."

"That seems a bit excessive. And dangerous. What if they hit us instead?"

He looked at me blankly for a moment, then snorted. "Not *hit* him with the trolls. Ask him about it."

"Oh. Right. That makes more sense." Humans and their weird language.

We ambled downstairs and found the kitchen empty of both humans and other creatures, although a woolly smell still lingered. There was a mug set on the counter next to a rough loaf of unsliced bread, with a note that said, *Back soon! Help yourself!*

"Handy," I said, jumping onto the table.

"He won't have gone far," Callum said, filling the kettle

and setting it on the big iron range. "You want some more biscuits?"

"Not really."

"Well, it's that or lentils."

"No more sardines?"

"Don't think so." He wandered into the pantry and started digging through shelves of rusting tins and unlabelled jars, asking me if I fancied pickled onions or preserved peaches. I was demanding if he thought I was a goat when Art clattered through the door, stamping his feet on the mat outside and pulling his wellies off as he stepped in.

"Good morning!" he said, far too cheerfully for the hour. "It's beautiful out there. One of those right crisp mornings that makes you happy to be alive."

I personally thought that sitting in front of the range with the heat baking my black fur made me happier to be alive than being out there in the cold thin air, but Callum just made an agreeable noise and took a second mug off the side of the sink.

"Sleep alright?" Art asked, pulling his woolly hat off and sending his hair into erratic directions.

"*I* didn't," I said, before Callum could answer. "All sorts of disturbances, there were."

Art stopped with his jacket half off. "Were there?"

"Yeah. Turns out half the county knows you had unicorns."

He gave me a puzzled look. "But they can't have. No one even knew we were here!"

"Every squirrel this side of Leeds did, apparently," I snapped.

"He means all the animals," Callum said.

"Oh." Art finished hanging his coat up and went to wash his hands. "Well, that hardly matters, does it? What's a pack of rabbits going to do with a herd of unicorns?"

I looked at the ceiling. "Gods save us from humans and their human-centric little lives."

"Which I think means that if anyone cared to ask, they could've found out about the unicorns," Callum said.

"But who's going to ask a rabbit?" Art asked. "I mean, really?"

"You've heard of familiars, right?" I pointed out. "That's not a myth. Familiars are just animals that choose to hang around sorcerers and magicians. And they talk plenty."

"Oh, they do," Callum said, almost under his breath. I shot him a dirty look.

Art sat down rather abruptly. His joy-to-the-world smile had vanished, leaving dark shadows under his eyes. "I didn't … I mean, I never thought animals would be bothered about the unicorns. And I don't even know how to do the charms to hide things from *animals*. How am I supposed to know that sort of thing?"

"Dude, you're a *unicorn-keeper*," I pointed out. "I'd have thought it was in the job description."

"So *anyone* could have them?" Art asked, looking at Callum rather than me.

"And Kara," Callum said.

"Yes. Them. Kara and the unicorns." Art fiddled with his hat. "I thought – I didn't think it'd be this hard to find them."

"Well, we have only just started," Callum said, putting a mug of tea in front of Art.

Art was silent.

"Oh, you soggy potato," I said. "You didn't call us straight away, did you?"

He examined his tea a little more carefully.

"Art?" Callum said, in his patented patient tone, and sat down across from the other man. "Why don't you tell us what's actually going on?"

"What's going on is this celery-brained incense stick of a—"

"Gobs."

"There's not even any breakfast! How can I be calm when I've got no breakfast?"

"There's some kippers in the fridge," Art said, his voice low. "I found them in the freezer last night."

"There we go," Callum said, getting up. "Now will you calm down?"

"Maybe a little," I said. "Although, *kippers*. It's hardly Scottish salmon, is it?"

"Do you want them or not?" Callum asked.

"*Yes*. But how're we supposed to do a proper job when amateurs are DUI-ing all over our case?"

"I don't even drink," Art said, and we stared at each other, puzzled.

"What?" I said

"Well, not much, anyway."

"He means DIY," Callum said, tearing bits of the fish into a bowl. "Why don't you tell us what you found out, Art, and what else you actually know, then we can start looking into things properly?"

"I haven't found anything out," he said, and sighed. "I thought I could. I thought there couldn't be that many people who'd know about the unicorns, and that it was probably someone who thought they were horses just stealing them for pet food or something. And they wouldn't have got far if that was the case. The unicorns would have busted out of pretty much any trailer at the first traffic lights."

"Yeah, I can see that going well," I said.

"Exactly. But they didn't turn up at any of the other rescues, and there were no reports of horses on the loose. I couldn't even find any sign of trailers having been here, or that they'd been hurt. Not even a broken fence. They just *vanished.*"

Callum put the bowl in front of me and said, "Could cats have shifted them?"

I gnawed on a mouthful of smoked fish while I thought about it. "Possible. It'd take a fair few cats to shift something the size of a unicorn, though. Probably a dozen per shift, and it couldn't be the same cats all the time. The beasts would get their scent, and we all know what that leads to." Me. It led to me, unable to shift, and always aware that the walls between this world and the Inbetween were thin, and things in there were sniffing for me.

"How long since it happened?" Callum asked Art.

"About ten days," he admitted, and I choked on my kipper.

"Ten *days?*"

He stared at his tea. "I spent a week trying to find them, then I started looking for you."

"And how often do the Watch check in?" Callum asked.

"Once a month."

"And when are they due back?"

Art took a deep breath. "Next week."

"Fantastic," I said. "So we've got a week to find your unicorns and your sister, and get them back here so you can pretend you never lost them."

"More like five days," he admitted.

"Amateur," I hissed, and Callum poked me in the side. "Stop that. And this fish has freezer burn."

So all Art could tell us was that, after bumbling around for a week, he had nothing to show for it but a complete lack of evidence. And considering we'd had some good Yorkshire summer rain since then, it wasn't like we were going to find anything by sniffing around the field.

Which meant a visit to some trolls seemed a reasonable next step.

Art knew the bridge, part of a disused road about five kilometres away. Far enough from the nearest houses that the only passers-by were the odd dog walker braving the nettles, close enough that the trolls could scavenge in the evening. Fox had his info right on that.

It wasn't anywhere we could drive to, and even if I had been inclined toward a walk, time was suddenly feeling a lot tighter. Callum packed up a dozen eggs and a frozen ham, the remains of the weird fruit cake and three jars of preserved peaches, and Art rolled a quad bike out of one of the rickety outbuildings. I examined it doubtfully. The odds were good, with such slim pickings as bribes, that we'd be running from trolls before lunch, and the bike didn't exactly fill me with confidence regarding its suitability as a getaway vehicle.

"Does it actually run?" I asked.

"Starts first time," Art said, turning the key. The bike did indeed start first time, with a roar that sent the chickens squawking for cover and a cloud of exhaust smoke that made me screw my eyes shut.

"Great," I said, and scrambled up to Callum's shoulder as he climbed on behind Art.

"Don't fall off," he told me.

"Eh," I said, and Art opened the throttle. We jolted forward so hard that I pitched straight off Callum's shoulder and slid down his back, claws still embedded in the collar of his coat, and wound up standing on my hind legs behind him, which was neither dignified nor comfortable.

We bounced and jolted our way across the field, skirting the band of trees that masked the canal, and headed through a gate to another empty field, houses pulling away and leaving the country to creep in. By the third gate I'd figured out that sitting on the seat between the two men was both warm and less likely to land me in a pile of fox dung, although I had to put up with Art's hippie stink. He was grinning wildly as he gunned the bike over the fields, letting out the occasional whoop as we went airborne off a rise, sending rabbits scattering in panic. Callum was slightly less enthusiastic, but even he burst out laughing as we tore across a shallow ford, scattering water into prismatic rainbows in the mid-morning sun. Humans.

SEVERAL FIELDS and some scrappy woodland later, we stopped upstream of the bridge. Well, *a* bridge. You can normally tell a troll bridge by all the discarded car parts and old boots and empty beer kegs and bones piled up like flotsam around it, stacked in some strange order of importance that only a troll can determine. Instead there was a weather-bleached log, its branches festooned with random bottles hanging from string. They clinked together softly in the faint breeze. There were also piles of river-smooth stones, stacked in carefully diminishing size, and some geraniums planted in old saucepans.

I blinked at the rocks, and Callum said to Art, "You should stay here. Trolls can be tricky."

"It doesn't look too scary," Art said.

"It doesn't look right, either," I said. "I don't like it when things don't look right." Although, admittedly, the troll version of *right* tended to involve a lot of bones and rotting skin.

"Maybe they're nice trolls?" Art offered, and shrugged when I looked at him. "It's possible, right?"

"It's also possible that there's a pile of tuna at the end of the rainbow, but I've never found it."

"Gold," Callum said.

"I can't eat gold," I pointed out. "Besides, you get gold, you get leprechauns. No one wants leprechauns."

"I suppose not," Art said, and Callum just shook his head.

We wandered closer, careful not to bump into the tree

or disturb any of the stone art, and I said to Callum, "Can you see a door?"

He shaded his eyes against the sun and peered into the shadows under the bridge. It was old grey stone, the years breaking over it like so much persistent tide, crumbling and softening its edges but never washing it away. A walking track or bridleway ran over the top of it and vanished deeper into the woods, but it was merely a suggestion among the weeds. This was another place humans turned away from, the mere presence of Folk forming a glamour that pushed them away the same way one magnet pushes another.

"Well. There *is* a door," Callum said, sounding unsure.

"And?" I said. I couldn't see much at this distance. There was a shadow among shadows in there, but for all I knew it was moss on the old stone.

"It's got a wreath," Art said. "With flowers in it."

"And a knocker," Callum said.

"And a doormat," Art added.

I looked up at them, wondering if they were joking, but they just kept staring at the bridge. I trotted forward, picking my way over the soft grass of the bank and spotting crowded flowerbeds penned in with stones, a riot of colour and smells. Bees buzzed heavily among the blooms, and there were no weeds I could see. Well, they could all have been weeds, for all I knew, but, you know. They looked tidy. And they didn't quite mask the smell of troll, but it wasn't the usual fetid stink I expected, rotting food and unwashed skin. It was diluted, more *eau de troll* than the pure stuff.

I stopped in front of the door and stared at it. It was

wooden, painted a blush pink that was very fetching against the old stone, and there was indeed a wreath and a knocker. The wreath was heavy with pollen and scent, and the knocker was a brass ring polished to a rich, warm lustre. I looked down at the mat beneath my paws. It looked like it had just been vacuumed, and it said *Welcome Home, Stranger!* There was a smiley face in the *O* of *Home.*

I looked up at Callum and Art as they joined me. "Dude, I don't know," I said. "No one who wants you to come in this much is ever up to any good."

"You mean they might eat us?" Art asked, looking around nervously.

"Well, given that they're trolls, that's always a risk. But look at this place. They might preach at us or something. *Sing* at us, even."

"Trolls don't usually eat people these days," Callum said. "Not unless they're really hungry."

"Not usually," I agreed. "But this is hardly usual."

"But is all this," Art waved vaguely at the door and flowers, "eating people sort of unusual? I'm not getting that feeling."

"So they might be some kind of born-again trolls. In which case there may be singing."

"Is singing such a big problem with trolls?" Callum asked.

"I don't know. It's more the flowers and pink paint giving me a *we'll sing at you* vibe."

"It's definitely not a people-eating vibe," Callum agreed, and we both stared at the mat as we considered this. As we did, Art leaned past us and grabbed the knocker, rapping the door briskly. Inside, I heard the sort of echoing *boom-boom-boom* that was better suited to a castle dungeon. Or troll's eating lair. Callum and I looked at Art in horror.

"I *knew* we shouldn't have brought you," I hissed at him.

"Well, we're not getting anywhere like this, are we?" he asked.

Callum grabbed Art's arm and took a large step back as someone yelled, "Coming!" from behind the door in a rocks-in-a-tumble-dryer voice. Slouching, heavy footsteps accompanied the voice, and I caught a whiff of pure troll, animal and hungry and endowed with that peculiar, permanent rage. The hair on my spine stood to attention and my tail bushed out, and as the lock rolled behind the door I whispered, "Hairballs."

7

A DANGER OF SINGING

I'VE COME UP AGAINST THE ODD TROLL.

Well, *across* rather than *against*. Even a pack of Watch brawlers, all *look how hard I am* muscle and missing teeth tend to avoid going *against* trolls. One svelte (Callum says skinny, but he can talk) PI cat on his lonesome is best to exercise discretion and take a tactical detour at the first whiff of troll stink.

I've talked to a few, though, always from well outside grabbing distance, getting what information I could out of creatures for whom *information* has about three too many syllables. By which I don't mean they're thick, exactly. Just that they tend to use all their brainpower for figuring out what they can put in their mouths and what they may as well just sit on. There's not a lot of processing space left over for niceties such as chit-chat and personal hygiene.

Given all that, knocking on a troll's door – even one with a wreath and a welcome mat – seemed like a shortcut to having your tail removed. But even as I considered the wisdom of a rapid retreat, the door swung open (noiselessly – I'd expected creaking hinges, but apparently someone knew their way around a tin of WD-40) and a troll stared at us, blinking myopically in the low light under the bridge.

He had the triple-plated forehead of a full-grown male, and the heavy green tattoos that marked an experienced fighter swirled and coiled over his cheeks, down to his shoulders, and presumably over his massive chest and thick arms. I say presumably, because his arms were covered in a woolly brown cardigan with leather elbow patches, the stitching stretched so thin I thought one well-placed claw could set the whole thing unravelling. He had a double string of glossy, pinkish pearls looped over the area his neck would've been if he'd had one, and matching earrings dangled from his cauliflower ears. He was also wearing a yellow corduroy skirt with red flowers on the hem, and a pink apron adorned with so many ruffles I half expected him to break into a flamenco.

We stared at each other for a long moment, and he finally said, "Can I help you?" None of us answered, and after a moment he added in that earth-mover voice, "I wasn't expecting anyone. I've still got me curlers in!"

We looked almost helplessly at the tuft of his tail, which was indeed adorned with six pink curlers. I opened my mouth, and Callum gave me a not entirely gentle nudge with one boot. Unfair.

"Good morning," Callum said, and did the dimple thing. I had no idea if it'd work on trolls, but this was no ordinary troll. The whiff of baking cake drifting from the depths of the bridge said as much. "Art here has the stables just up the river, and he's lost a couple of horses. We're just helping him track them down."

"We?" the troll said, and spotted me. "A cat. I see."

"May your tail be curly and your ears stay clean," I said, as the usual troll greeting of *May your teeth rend the flesh from your enemies' bones* seemed a little out of place.

"I don't suppose you've seen anything?" Callum asked. "It would've been about ten days ago."

I growled at the back of my throat and Art shuffled his feet.

"*Hmm,*" the troll said, then gasped and threw his hands up, sending the three of us staggering back a few steps in fright. "Where are my manners? Do come in. I've just put the kettle on. Tea? Earl Grey? Or I've got a lovely Lapsang Souchong."

"Um, well," Callum started, but the troll grabbed his arm and pulled him inside.

"Just wipe your feet, dears. Come in, come in! We're all in the salon." And he vanished, dragging Callum with him.

Art and I stared at each other, and he made some wild gesture that might have meant, *What do we do now?* Which was a great question, but had only one answer. Callum had been taken to the *salon,* which I assumed was a newfangled troll term for *the room where we boil you alive.*

So we were going too, obviously.

I BRACED myself for the usual troll stench of old, half-cleaned bones and stale bedding made from the skin of dead things, for half-cured hides and forgotten corpses trodden underfoot and gone to rot. Instead we were enveloped in gusts of air freshener and scented candles and room sprays, assaulting my nose and setting me sneezing.

"Oh dear," our host said, glancing back at me as he hustled Callum inside. "You're not getting a cold, are you? Terrible things, are summer colds. I'll bring you some nice lemon and honey, shall I?"

I shook my head in alarm, wondering if that was the modern troll's go-to marinade, and sneezed again. It was worse than a pedigree Persian's boudoir.

"Wow," Art said, as we emerged from the hall into a room bathed in warm light. "Your place is ... pink."

"And pretty," Callum said hurriedly, one arm still lost in the troll's grip. "Really ... homey. Cosy. Right, Gobs?"

I blinked around the room. There were no windows – trolls may not turn to stone at the slightest kiss of daylight, but they burn badly, and no one needs a sunburned troll. It does nothing for their temperament. Despite the lack of windows, though, frou-frou curtains flanked white window frames on the stone walls, and idyllic woodland scenes featuring frolicking animals had been carefully painted into the frames. You know the sort – deer snuggling up to birds and bunnies nuzzling skunks like some cross-species lovefest. A frankly enormous sofa was pushed up to one wall, half-hidden under a cascade of throws and lacy cushions, and three big armchairs faced it, two occupied by trolls in button-down shirts and immaculate denim dungarees. One of them, for reasons that escaped me, was wearing a small white sailor's hat.

"Yes," I said, staring in awe at a set of shelves crowded

with porcelain cherubs and glass birds and painted plates in stands. "Cosy."

"Why, *thank* you!" our host exclaimed, releasing Callum and clasping his huge hands together lightly. "We don't get many visitors, but we like to keep the place nice. Don't we, dears?"

One of the other trolls nodded enthusiastically and said, "Yes! Always nice! No nasty troll house!" He had the forehead plates of a male as well, but they were still forming, hardening out of the crevassed grey skin of his skull, so he was only a juvenile. He was also struggling with some enormous knitting needles, a tangle of multi-coloured wool spilling over his knees and onto the floor. Sailor Hat just grunted, staring at me with three bulging eyes. A young female, then.

The big troll pushed Callum into the sofa in a manner that was probably meant to be friendly, but which sank him into the drifts of cushions with a strangled yelp, his feet swinging clear of the floor.

"Oh dear – I do forget my own strength sometimes," the troll said, and chuckled. "You're alright though, yes? Yes. Now you sit down too. Sit!" He waved at Art, who just about dived onto the sofa. Neither his nor Callum's legs reached the ground, and they looked like dolls propped up among the cushions. The troll gave me a snaggle-toothed smile. "Do you need a lift, puss?"

I wrinkled my nose. "Nah, you're good." I jumped to the arm of the sofa and surveyed the room. Sailor Hat was still staring at me, and she seemed to be drooling. Funnily enough, although that was more the troll behaviour I was used to, it didn't make me feel particularly reassured.

"William, dear, go and put the kettle on," the big troll said, settling himself into the free armchair. "Use the good cups."

"And cake have?" the young troll said, laying his knitting carefully aside.

"That's not quite it, William. Try again. You know how we can be judged by our diction."

William thought mightily, his soft forehead plates clashing together. "Will … *shall* we can have cake?"

"*Much* better. *Shall* we have cake?"

"Why asks me?" the young troll said, frowning. "I asks you."

Callum and I exchanged glances, his eyebrows raised and my whiskers arched, and after a momentary confusion William toddled off to what was presumably the kitchen, muttering "*Shall* we, *shall* we," under his breath as he went. The big troll leaned forward, heavy forearms on his knees, and said, "It's *so* important to speak well if we wish to be valued as members of society."

Callum made an agreeable noise and I considered the fact that plenty of humans didn't bother with it too much.

"Now," the troll said, leaning back. "That was William. This is our lovely Poppy." He indicated Sailor Hat, who wiped drool off her chin and gave us a broken-toothed grin. "And I am Gerry."

I wondered briefly if that was short for Gerald or Geraldine, but it hardly mattered. People place too much import on such things. More interesting was the fact that none of them were called Skullcrusher or Bonemuncher.

"So, what," I said. "Are you new age trolls or something?"

"New age," Gerry mused. "That's a rather nice way to put it. We are indeed working to break stereotypes and redefine trollness in the modern world, so yes. Perhaps we are new age trolls."

"Cool," I said, because there wasn't much else I could say. I couldn't spot a single skull goblet or femur flute on the shelves, so who was I to argue with some pretty classy needlepoint (*Troll hearts are big to hold all the troll love,* one read above me) and a line-up of bunny rabbit dolls in Victorian dress? "So what do you eat these days?"

"Gobs," Callum said, poking me in the ribs. I lifted my lip at him, and he said to Gerry, "Sorry, he's not a new age cat. I'm Callum. He's Gobbelino, and this is Art."

Gerry stretched a huge hand out and very carefully shook hands with both men, and nodded at me. "We're terribly pleased to meet you. It's so neighbourly of you to stop by!"

William reappeared in the doorway while I looked expectantly at Callum to see how he was going to go about reminding a large troll that we weren't being neighbourly, just conducting investigations. The young troll was cradling a cup in his hands like an injured bird, and he crept to the coffee table to put it down, holding his breath as it touched the glossy wood. Gerry *tsk*ed, making him jump, and he hurriedly put a cork coaster under the cup, then trundled back to the kitchen.

"To answer your question, Gobbelino," Gerry said, "we're vegetarians."

Poppy gave a strangled sigh and wiped some more drool from her chin. Vegetarian trolls. Well, why not. "Cool," I said again, watching William creep back with another cup. "So you wouldn't have any use for a herd of bad-tempered ponies, then?"

"No, indeed," Gerry said, then clashed his forehead plates as he frowned. "Do you mean the unicorns?"

"Dude," I said, glaring at Art, and Callum pinched the bridge of his nose. "You weren't even shielding them from *Folk?*"

Art waved vaguely. "Well, I *was*, but the charms might have been left a bit long. I mean, no one really comes around there but humans, anyway. It just seemed like a lot of faff to redo them *every* month."

"So you didn't bother *at all?*" I asked Art. "Gods, how'd they even survive this long, you cabbage?" Callum poked me again, and I hissed at him. "Stop that."

"You stop it," he said, and looked at Gerry. "Sorry. Like I say, not a new age cat."

"I'll new age you," I mumbled, and jumped out of poking range.

Gerry just nodded. "Cats never are," he said, in a tone that seemed to ignore the fact that it was one of our better qualities. "I'm very sorry about your unicorns."

Poppy made a snuffling noise as William brought the last cup in, wiped his forehead, and left again.

"Thanks," Art said, and sighed. "They've been in the family for like, ever. My mum would be so disappointed."

"Should've thought of that—" I stared, and Callum threw a cushion at me. I jumped off the arm of the sofa with a snarl.

"I don't suppose you've noticed anyone unusual hanging around?" he asked Gerry. "I realise it's not exactly your backyard, but we heard you had been around a little."

"Well, I haven't been there personally," Gerry said. "But Poppy loved the unicorns. Just like any young girl, you know? She was always up there taking them treats." He shifted his bulk in the chair. "Did you see anyone unusual, dear?"

I personally thought Gerry might have misunderstood her affection, given the drooling, but I decided to keep my mouth shut. And, to be fair, one juvenile troll would be hard-pressed to eat ten full grown unicorns and a foal in one night and leave no trace. Of course, she could have had accomplices, although I doubted it was Gerry. He seemed pretty invested in the whole new age thing.

Poppy took a deep breath. "I … I … Poppy … I no. I have no seen. Them." She grinned triumphantly.

"Well *done,* Poppy," Gerry exclaimed. "Excellent pronunciation. But *not.* I have *not* seen them."

She nodded, her sailor hat tipping over her third eye. She pushed it back into place. "I have not seen them go. But I … am sadness. Sad. I am sad. I likes them."

Gerry opened his mouth, presumably for more language lessons, and I said hurriedly, "Did you show anyone else the unicorns, Poppy? Any friends, maybe?"

Callum sighed, but if we were going to wait for the trolls to tell us in perfect English we were going to be here for even longer than the tea was taking.

"She doesn't have any friends," Gerry said, before Poppy could answer. "None of the other trolls in the area are working to improve themselves, which is why we moved out here. They're a bad influence."

Poppy sighed, and I wondered just how much she agreed on that count. William appeared, carting an enormous tea pot, which he set next to the milk jug, sugar bowl, cake tin, plates, and some napkins the size of hand towels.

"Tea," he announced. "Earl Grey. With the lost leaves."

"*Wonderful!*" Gerry cried. "*Loose* leaf, though, William." And he set about pouring tea and serving cake, while I wondered if I preferred new age small talk trolls or traditional trolls who just grunted at you and occasionally tried to tear your head off.

I couldn't decide.

IT TOOK ALMOST AS PAINFULLY long for the tea and cake to be served, consumed, and complimented as it had taken William to make it, and it was all accompanied with some equally painful small talk about weather and vegetables. Art and Gerry discovered a mutual passion for kale, which said everything, really. No one had anything more to say about unicorns, and Poppy kept snuffling and wiping her nose on her napkin. I wasn't sure if she was really that sad about the unicorns or if it was all the air freshener. It was certainly making me sneeze still.

Eventually, Gerry got up and showed us to the door. "It's been a most wonderful pleasure having you here," he said. "We don't get quality company often enough. I do hope you come again soon."

"Oh, definitely," Art said, shaking Gerry's hand enthusiastically. "I'll bring you some of my purple kale. It's a revelation!"

I tried rolling my eyes, not for the first time. This is what you get for hanging around humans. A hankering for roll-able eyes.

Callum rubbed the back of his head and said, "Let us know if you hear anything about the unicorns. You can just pop a note through the door at the house or something."

Gerry nodded and lowered his voice. "You should look in Dimly," he said. "Limestone Road area. I didn't like to say anything with the young ones about – I'm not the troll I was when I used to frequent that place, and I'd rather they didn't know too much about that part of my life."

"Limestone Road," Callum said, his voice oddly flat. I couldn't tell if he was trying to commit the name to memory or stop it from lodging there.

"Yes. An unpleasant part of an unpleasant town," Gerry said. "But in my day you could get anything there. Including unicorn dust."

"Thanks," Callum said, and shook hands with the troll. I was mildly surprised he emerged with his hand intact, and contented myself with a nod.

"Laters, Gerry. Cheers for the cream. Top stuff."

"You're most welcome," he said, and closed the door behind us.

We stood there under the ageing bridge, looking at the clear, meandering waters of the stream and listening to someone gunning a car on a road beyond the woodland. Closer, someone was screaming at a kid or a dog, and it all seemed a little raw and harsh after the cosy confines of the troll house. Although at least I could smell something other than lily of some artificial valley.

"Well," I said. "That was about the weirdest bloody thing I've ever seen."

"They were nice," Art said cheerfully, and kicked his way across the grass to the quad bike.

I looked at Callum. "Dimly, huh?"

"Yeah." He put his hands in his pockets and followed Art.

"We might have to check it out."

"I hope not."

"Care to share some details?"

"No." He lengthened his stride so that I had to trot to keep up. Then Art was there and I couldn't ask again. Which was odd. We might not talk about the past much – we both know it bites, and sometimes sharing is less caring and more shoving your arm willingly back into its maw. But we don't keep secrets where it matters. Not when it comes to jobs and walking into places we'd be better forewarned against.

But I left it. Some things come in their own time.

8

ALL ROADS LEAD TO DIMLY

THERE WAS NO LAUGHTER OR WHOOPING ON THE WAY BACK to Art's ramshackle farm, just silence of different varieties from the two men. I kept my mouth shut, too – I could feel something coming, that same sense of circling predators, and some stray's instinct told me not to draw attention to myself.

We rattled up to the house in silence, and Art stopped by our car to let us climb off.

"I'll just put this girl to bed," he said, patting the bike like a friendly dog.

Callum didn't reply, just took his cigarettes out of his pocket and wandered over to the gate where I'd met the fox the night before. He rested his forearms on it and looked down over the field, his tatty coat hanging from his hunched shoulders. I jumped to the fencepost next to him and watched some small bright bird scatter in fright.

Callum lit his cigarette, put his lighter away and said, "Trolls were nice."

"Positively charming," I agreed.

He flicked ash into the grass, and said, "I don't think they ate the unicorns."

"Gerry didn't," I said. "Or William. Poppy I'm not so sure about. She seemed maybe a little less committed."

"Could a troll that size eat an entire herd of unicorns in a night?"

"No," I admitted. "But maybe she does still have contact with other trolls. Or she's stashed them somewhere. I'm sure she could make quick work of a human."

"I suppose," Callum said, scratching his chin. Two-day stubble rasped under his fingertips. "It doesn't feel right, though."

I watched him for a moment, then said, "So, when were you going to tell me about the family business?"

He didn't look at me, but I caught the twitch in his jaw. "I probably wasn't."

"Might be handy to know some details, if we end up in Dimly. Background, you know."

He sighed, rubbing his face with one hand. "My family dealt pretty much everything, to anywhere and anyone who wanted it. Relics. Weapons. Pixie juice. Faery bones. Cheese graters. If you had the money, they'd find it."

"Sounds like a successful operation."

The corner of his mouth hitched in a half-smile. "Profitable."

"But you left."

"Let's say I didn't agree with their business practises."

"And they weren't too happy about you quitting the firm?"

He did look at me then. "The Norths had certain ways of doing things. It was all about keeping secrets and holding power, and people leaving was not an option. Not even North kids got that option. *Especially* not North kids. Getting out almost killed me." He shrugged. "What I got into when I was out almost killed me, too. You know that."

I did know that. And he'd got out of that as surely as he'd got away from his family. I took no credit for that. Yeah, having a scrawny young cat biting your dealer and trying to steal the product was unhelpful, but it wasn't the sort of thing that stopped anyone. Some evolutions can only be taken alone.

I twitched my ears against a small breeze and said, "We don't need to take this job. We could drop it right here."

He smiled that slightly crooked, familiar grin. "Protecting yourself is one thing. Turning down an old friend who never had a choice in things is something else entirely."

I thought about it, then said, "Is his sister hot, then?"

He flicked my ear, and Art called from behind us, "Shall I put the kettle on?"

Callum turned around, leaning against the gate in a way that made me think of the photo on Art's wall. "I've had enough tea for now."

I almost fell off the fencepost.

"Who knows I'm here, Art?" Callum called.

Art had stopped by the gate to the house, and now he took a small step toward us, smile fading. "No one. I mean, I didn't even know you were in Leeds at first. Everyone thought you went down south or something. If you were even still alive."

"That was pretty much the impression I was hoping for. So how'd you find out?"

"I just . . . I asked around."

"Asked who?" Callum's voice was friendly, casual, but Art looked as if he wanted to retreat inside and lock the door against us. "And who was on the phone last night?"

"Phone?"

"Yeah, that plastic thing you were flapping your gums on in the kitchen last night," I said.

Art shot me a look that was part distaste, part fright. "No one. No one important."

"But whoever it was knew we were here," Callum said. "Gobs says you were telling them not to worry, that we were just looking for the unicorns. What about Kara?"

Art wiped his mouth. "I meant Kara too. He got it wrong."

Callum nodded thoughtfully. "Gobs gets plenty of things wrong, but what he sees and hears is rarely one of them."

"Hey," I said. "I get plenty of things *right*, actually."

"Well, he misunderstood, then," Art said. "It was a friend, is all. I told them I hired a PI, and they were just worried that the Watch might catch wind of it."

Callum and I looked at each other, then Callum said, "So it wasn't the dealer wondering when their next shipment of horn's coming in, then?"

"What? No! No, I told you, the Watch check up—"

"Horn grows quick," I said. "If they're only coming once a month, all you have to do is show them your buckets of vinegar or what have you, maybe have a bit on hand to throw in if they want to see you do it. You'd still have three weeks' worth to sell on."

"No," Art said. "No, no, I *haven't.* Callum, you have to believe me!"

"I'd like to," Callum said. "Especially after Rory. After what the horn did to him."

Rory. Art's brother. The smallest of the boys in the photo, smirking in that young teen, the-world-is-mine way. I shifted my paws.

"He didn't get it from me," Art said, and there was a new hardness in his voice. "You know who he got it from. Where we got *all* our gear from."

"I do," Callum agreed. "And my sister might have dealt it to him, but it was your family's herd it came from. Your herd that supported the whole damn thing. So I bloody hope you're not dealing again, Art. Because the Watch can have you if you are."

The words hung between them, Art with one hand in his hair, his ridiculous *I went on an overseas trip and bought a hippie top to prove it* jumper hanging baggy as a tent around him. Then Callum ground his cigarette out on the fencepost and dropped the butt back in the packet.

"Let's go, Gobs."

"Where?" I asked, as he swung his lanky frame over the gate.

"A little stroll along the canal."

"Will there be refreshments?" I asked, trotting after him.

"It'll be bloody refreshing if you fall in," he said.

"I hope that's not a threat."

CALLUM HEADED down through the trees to the canal at an easy pace, hands in his pockets, and I loped after him. He still had the hessian bag with the frozen ham in it that we'd taken to give to the trolls. Gerry had been very happy to take the eggs and peaches (and had made polite noises about the weird fruit cake, although I think even for a vegetarian troll hemp flour was a step too far), but he'd sent us back with the ham. Art didn't follow us, and once we were wandering down the towpath, the sun warm on my fur, I said, "Where to now, then?"

Callum nodded along the path. "You can walk all the way to Dimly along here. There's a river joins the canal, and if you follow it, it'll take you right into the pocket."

"Which we're not doing, right?" I said.

"Not right now. Hopefully not at all." He shrugged out of his coat, pushing a hand back through his hair. "Even with my family gone, I might get recognised. Maybe."

"And that's assuming they're all gone."

He glanced at me. "The Watch are usually pretty thorough."

"Yeah, but they left Artful Dodger there and his sister, didn't they?"

"Fair point."

We walked in silence for a little longer, passing the odd jogger or dog walker. Their gaze drifted over Callum without pausing, and other than a terrier that stuck his nose in my face and got a slap for his troubles, no one bothered us. The path crossed over to the other side of the canal on a metal-framed bridge, but Callum kept along on our side, the packed earth of the towpath giving to softer dirt as the trees drew down around us to admire their reflections in the water. His feet were muffled by fallen leaves, and I could smell the quiet wariness of small creatures as they watched us pass.

The tow path across the canal veered inland, leaving us alone with the still water, and a hush crept down around us. There was a broken-down old canal boat moored up not far on from where the path vanished, rust seeping down its hull and its roof sprouting weeds and flowers. Someone watched us pass from inside, but I couldn't see them, only feel the scrutiny of eyes as wary as those of the mice and birds.

Only once the boat was out of sight around a bend did Callum stop and step to the edge of the canal, peering down into the opaque green depths. It could have been half a metre deep, or have gone halfway through the earth. The trees leaned in around him, and the still surface of the water was littered with fallen leaves, as well as a couple of crisp packets and an empty can of lager.

Callum unslung the bag from his shoulder and took out the ham, which had gone a bit sweaty and gunky in its bag as it defrosted. He pulled it out and held it over the water, stuff dripping from it and setting up little fatty dimples on the surface.

"River spirit," he said. "Take this offering as a mark of our respect, and grace us with your presence." He dropped the ham as he finished speaking, and it *gloop*ed loudly into the water, setting ripples running in every direction.

I looked up at Callum. "River spirit? You're looking for a sludge puppy, aren't you?"

He snorted, fishing a cigarette out as we watched the ham bob gloomily on the green. "I probably wouldn't call it that to its face."

Well, fair point. Sludge puppies were, technically, river spirits. Sort of. They were bottom-dwelling creatures, as ancient as the waterways they patrolled, and they'd live on forever if they weren't trapped by bridges or choked out by pollution and run-off and land reclamation and what have you. *Land reclamation.* How human. All land began under the sea, but no. They had to say they were *reclaiming* it, not stealing it from those that needed it.

Whatever. It was best not to call on a sludge puppy empty-handed, and it was best to address them with respect. Not even the Watch had any sway over creatures like them, old as the world itself.

"I wouldn't have thought you'd know how to talk to them, given your family didn't seem to think much of less human-ish Folk."

"Eh. I didn't learn *everything* from my family."

"That sounds sensible," I said, and set to grooming my paws while we waited.

"THERE WE GO," Callum said finally, and I sat up from where I'd been dozing. He'd been squatting on the canal wall, and now he stood up and nodded down the length of the water. I followed his gaze, spotting a V-shaped ripple pushing itself toward us, sending the rubbish and fallen leaves swirling in its wake. It stopped beneath us, and I could feel scrutiny from below the water, sharper and more thoughtful than that of the canal boat. After a moment a head raised itself slowly above the surface. Barbels descended from its chin and its eyes were the yellow-green of sunlight on stained water. The head blended as seamlessly into the body as a fish's does, and translucent eyelids slid sideways across its eyes as we stared back at it. Then its pursed mouth split into an enormous, toothy grin, and it waved four webbed limbs at us, scattering water everywhere. I ducked behind Callum with a hiss, and he grinned, waving back like a kid at a fairground.

The sludge puppy held up the ham in two webbed paws. It looked about snack-sized for the creature. "Hey, cheers," it said. "All the damn birdseed and bread everyone drops in here these days, I'm starved for some variety."

"Pleasure," Callum said, still grinning, then recovered himself. "I mean – may the sun shine sweet on your waters and the rain glut you with strength."

"Ah, yeah," the sludge puppy said, examining the ham. "Right on. Back atcha, dude."

I looked up at Callum and said, "I think your greeting book might be a bit out of date."

"You remember what I said about refreshments? It can be arranged."

"Dudes, it's cool," the sludge puppy said, taking a nibble of the ham. About a quarter of it vanished. "Some of the older rivers would totally dig the formalities. But, you know, they're kind of stuck in the mud. *Heh.*"

We *heh*-ed, since that seemed to be required.

"So, you like, wanted counsel? Only I'd go to a professional for that. I'm a good listener, but I'm not qualified or anything."

"Not that sort of counsel," Callum said, while I huffed laughter. "We just wanted to know if anyone had dumped any … animals in here over the last ten days or so."

The sludge puppy sighed. "*All* the time, my man. Puppies. Kittens. If I'm quick enough I can sometimes get them out, but people seem to hang around to watch, which is seriously sick."

I shuddered. I'd met the type of people that do that sort of thing, and had the cigarette burns scarred into my flanks to prove it. I was quite open to the idea of feeding that sort of person to the sludge puppy, now I thought about it.

"That's awful," Callum said. "But we were actually thinking of something bigger. Maybe even eaten already. Bones, I guess."

The sludge puppy scratched an ear flap. "I had a couple of human bodies last month. They were whole, though, not eaten. All wrapped up and weighted down, they were. It was interesting, actually – they had the police down and everything, even divers." He grinned hugely, exposing snaggly black teeth. "I snuck up on one and spooked them. I just couldn't resist. They were so *serious.*"

"Unicorns," I said, swallowing my laughter. "Ten adults, one foal. They're all missing, and we just wanted to … well, we thought they might've been munched."

"*Dude,*" the sludge puppy said, clutching the remains of the ham to his chest. "The *unicorns?* Oh, that sucks."

I looked at Callum, who was shaking his head. Art

really hadn't hidden the damn things from *anyone*. He may as well have put a sign on the river saying, *Unicorns This Way!*

"I haven't seen them," the creature added. "I'll keep a look out for you, though. That's a really bad scene."

"Thanks," Callum said. "At least we know they're not bones, right?"

"Well, not in here, anyway," the sludge puppy said. "But you should check Dimly. I cruise up there now and then, keep an eye on the creeks. It used to be my buddy Hayley's territory, but she just up and vanished. I think it was the condos in her favourite reeds that did it. She *loved* those reeds. All the moorhens nested there. Can't find scale nor tooth of her these days, so I keep an eye on things, just in case she comes back."

"I'm sorry," Callum said.

"Happens all the time," the sludge puppy said. "I mean, usually it's a hibernation that just never ends, you know? But sometimes someone gets caught in some new foundations, or trapped on the wrong side of a lock. Progress, huh?"

Neither of us answered, and the sludge puppy tossed the ham from one paw to another.

"Why Dimly, though?" I asked.

"Oh, yeah. Unicorn dust in the run-off. Hadn't been any for a while, but it's been back in the last couple of years. It's around."

Callum ran both hands back through his hair, and nodded. "Alright. Thank you, um ...?"

"Call me Dustin," the sludge puppy said. "Cool, huh? Hayley and I both got new names. The whole, *Hallowed*

River Spirit of the Upper East by North-East Fifteenth Sector by the Moon thing was *so* boring."

"Harder to remember, too," I said.

"Totally." Dustin gave a gurgle that seemed to be some sort of chuckle. "Come back anytime, okay? No need for ham. I mean, not complaining, but it's nice just to chat, you know?" He gave us another enthusiastic wave, then swept off down the canal, bobbing on his back as he tossed the ham between all four front paws, four back legs and tail sweeping him along.

We watched him go, then I looked at Callum.

"I know," he said. "Dimly again."

"No," I said. "I was going to ask why we've never met a sludge puppy before. I *like* them."

Callum snorted. "City centre canals are hardly sludge puppy central. Want a lift?"

"Go on, then." I scrambled to his shoulder as he turned back the way we'd come, the shadows short and deep as the long Yorkshire summer morning rolled toward the longer afternoon, and somewhere around a turn in the canal I could feel Dimly waiting for us, a blight on a sunny day.

9

THE WELCOME IS A LITTLE LACKING

CALLUM HEADED BACK ALONG THE CANAL AND VEERED through the trees to climb the field to Art's house, which was a relief. I'd half-expected him to insist that we head straight for Dimly, even with the tension I could feel reverberating in him.

He paused halfway up the field, shifting his coat to his other arm and pushing his hair off his forehead.

"Your fitness age is much older than your actual age, you know," I told him. "It's all the smoking. You're probably about ninety in fitness age."

"It's carrying your extra weight that's doing it," he said, and I huffed, jumping off his shoulder to the soft grass. "Plus, it's hot," he added.

"You just keep telling yourself that," I said, and peered up at the house. I couldn't see anyone outside from this distance. "What now?"

"We're going to have to check out Dimly," he said, rubbing his chest as if was paining him.

"We could drop it," I said. "Arty there's telling sausage rolls."

Callum stopped rubbing his chest and stared at me. "What?"

"He's telling lies."

Callum thought about it for a moment. "Pork pies, not sausage rolls."

"Well, I don't know. Some sort of meat product." I licked my chops. "I could go for a sausage, though."

"Yeah, we need some food." He fished his cigarettes out of his pocket, and I arched my whiskers at him.

"Seriously?"

"Look, my life expectancy once I head back to Dimly might not be all that high anyway. Depends who's there and if I'm seen."

"Even with your family gone?"

"Even with my family gone. It wasn't just that I left. I was that I knew the business, knew who was in it and what was being moved and how. Plus, I left."

"You were just a kid, though. How much could you really know?"

He smiled as he lit his cigarette. "We didn't exactly have a regular education."

I considered it. "Then we don't go. It's too risky."

He shook his head. "I can't just leave this. I left Art and Kara behind once, because I had no choice. I've got a choice this time. I can help."

"*If* Art's telling the truth. What if this is all some sort of set up?"

"For what reason?"

"To get you back here? Maybe someone's still looking for you."

He thought about it. "No. Art found me easy enough. If anyone wanted to come after me, they would've."

"Something's still not right about all this. *Someone's* dealing unicorn dust, and it's not like they can be getting it from many places."

He shrugged. "Maybe it's an old stash."

"That seems supremely unlikely."

"It does." He sighed, glanced at the house, and looked back at me. "I know it's not all adding up. But Kara *has* been taken by someone. My best guess is whoever's running the trade in Dimly these days found out about the unicorns and has been forcing Art to pay them off in unicorn dust. Now the unicorns are gone, they've taken Kara to make sure Art does his best to get them back. And he's not going to admit *anything* to us, not while they've got her."

"So you're just going to put us in the middle of it all."

"Just me. You don't need to come to Dimly."

I looked at my paws, then back at him. "No. *You* don't need to. I can be all quick and quiet and cat-like, and we can try to see what's really going on here."

"You're in no better shape to go in there than me. It's a pocket, and a rough one at that. Cats aren't welcome. We know about cats in pockets, and no one trusts them. At best, no one'll talk to you. At worst, they'll run you out. Or … well, there is worse than that, actually."

I examined him. "If they know it's you—"

"I'll be careful," he said. "I'll just go in as a customer." That strange flatness was back in his voice, and in that moment I'd have cheerfully left Art and his unicorns to be pulled apart by Dimly's latest enforcers, or the Watch, or pretty much anyone who fancied it. Callum shouldn't have to do that. He shouldn't have to go back to those days of endless, gnawing hunger, a hunger that won't be sated, that tears at the very bones of your soul. He shouldn't even have to pretend.

"I've got a better idea," I said. "Let's get Gerry to sit on Art until he spills his guts. You know, figuratively or literally. Either will do."

He snorted. "What, after Art offered him purple kale? I think we'd struggle to top that."

"Yeah, I suppose." I stretched. "Well, come on, then."

"Come on what?"

"I want lunch before we brave the mean streets of Dimly. Plus we need rat bribes. I reckon that's our way in. Rats are *always* the best way in anywhere."

"Gobs—"

"Actual lunch. Not biscuits or some ancient fish scraped out of freezer ice." I turned and started picking my way up the hill to the house, and after a moment I felt Callum follow me. He stooped to scritch my ears as he caught up to me, his touch cool despite the sun, and I shivered. Predators everywhere.

WE WENT STRAIGHT to the car, Callum kicking one of the tyres doubtfully then declaring it should get us to the nearest garage. I didn't much like the *should*, but given the oil slick I could see on the drive I wasn't sure the tyres were going to be our make-or-break anyway.

Art came out while Callum was trying to persuade the ancient engine to fire up. It was coughing a lot and wheezing exhaust everywhere, but didn't seem too keen to do much else.

"Callum?" Art called, his face drawn in anxious angles. "What're you doing? You're not going?"

Callum winced as the engine gave a particularly nasty belch, and said, "We're going to follow up a couple of leads."

"Well, I'll come," Art said, hurrying around to my door.

I pressed my paws on the lock thingy, which was so stiff it did precisely nothing. Art opened the door, and I swiped at him. He jumped back with a yelp. "Back off, you hippie lentil," I told him.

"You what?"

"Don't mind him," Callum said, leaning over me to look at Art. "But you can't come."

"Professionals only," I said, and bared my teeth.

"But where are you going?"

"Tell you later." The engine finally growled into reluctant, chugging life, and Callum smiled. "There she goes."

"You're not going to Dimly, are you?" Art asked, still leaning in the door. "Like Gerry said? You can't go there!"

"Shut the door," Callum said.

"Callum, it's not safe!"

"Your face isn't safe," I said, popping my claws out at him. "Shut the door, you tangerine."

"I'll call you later," Callum said. "Thanks for dinner and all that."

"But—"

"Shut the door, Art."

Art stared at Callum for a long time, then shut the door and stepped back. We left a smokescreen behind us as we rumbled up the drive, but through it I could still see Art watching us go, his hands in fists at his sides and his face pale.

WE MADE it to a garage as much by willpower as by any particular mechanical ability on the part of the old car, and Callum topped the tyres up with air and did stuff under the bonnet that hopefully meant we wouldn't end up having to escape Dimly on foot. Then he went into the little garage shop and came out with a wedge of cheese, a packet of chopped ham, and a sandwich, folding himself back into the drivers' seat and opening the packet of ham to set in front of me.

I examined it. "Hey, what if I wanted tuna?"

"Then you can go in and get yourself some," he said, taking a large bite of his sandwich.

I sniffed at him and tried the ham. It wasn't terrible. "So what now? Limestone Road?"

"I think we start by just taking a look," he said, firing the car up again. "See how Dimly feels these days."

We pulled out into the road, and I watched Callum as he ate his sandwich with one hand and drove with the other. There was a muscle twitching in his jaw, and I thought he was in that let's-get-it-over-with mood. You know the one, like when you build yourself up to run into a rainstorm, knowing your fur's going to be plastered to your back all but instantly, and the wind's going to cut at your eyes and near-enough blind you, and it'll be pure misery for as long as you're out there, but it's that or cower under a parked car with wet paws all night. Or how you feel when you know the lead tom in a rough part of town is coming for you, and you walk straight down the centre of the street like a gunslinger, ears trembling with the tension of it all. Maybe both of those put together, the fear and the discomfort all at once. But the longer you leave it the worse it gets, so you just have to step out there into the wild and the danger, set your tail and get it done. That's what it felt like.

GETTING to a pocket is neither as simple nor as complicated as you'd imagine. They sit there, on the blurred edges of towns and cities, in the folds of distant valleys, at the ends of roads that councils forget to fix, or name, or even survey. They're not on maps. They don't get visitors. The eye wanders away from them, and so do the feet and tyres. No one ends up in a pocket, no matter how lost they get. You have to set out for them with great determination, and ignore the whispers of glamour as they rise up and try to push you away.

First things get increasingly dismal. We're not talking a bit of graffiti and litter. We're talking houses beyond neglect. They look like they're rotting, being eaten from the inside out by a malaise that drags down the odd person (and they can be *very* odd) who shuffles down the street. It feels infectious, that rot. It drains the colour from the cars and shutters the murky windows of the stores. It gilds the trees with fungus and blight, turning them twisted and ugly, the weeds too poisonous for even a dog to wee on. It's the sort of rot that'll make you hesitant to even clean your own paws.

Not that it's like that on the inside, of course, otherwise no one'd live there, Folk or otherwise. On the inside, with the protective glamour left on the borders, pockets are whole towns squeezed into one neighbourhood. There are affluent streets where the legitimate and not-so-legitimate rich live, all strange cupolas and fanciful garden rooms. There are cottages behind gardens full of flowers you won't find in any reference book, and tottering blocks of flats with strange lights in the windows. There are slabs of land given over to creeping, jungle-like wilderness and tiny farms where the cows are unionised. Not all the doors are human-sized. And none of the shops are familiar. There's no Boots the chemist or Greggs the baker. Sometimes the language on the signs will be unfamiliar. Some of the products will be *very* unfamiliar.

Pockets are strange and complicated places, where even the Watch tread lightly. But for the Folk and the humans who slip through the cracks of the world, they're places of safety. The glamour pushes away outsiders, and they have no need to hide the reality of themselves. They can uncover their gills and their fur, their extra eyes and wings and limbs and spines. Judgement tends to be withheld unless someone gets eaten on an overenthusiastic night out or dismembered in a quarrel over a sports team. I mean, there's got to be limits.

So pockets tend to reverberate with their own quiet, joyful life, but as we eased past the edge of the glamour and deeper into Dimly, that wasn't what I could feel or smell. That sense of pervading rot followed us, as if it had been set too deeply, and was creeping to the core of the town itself. The streets were all but empty, and the people we did see barely glanced at the car, just hurried on with their heads down and their parcels clutched to their bodies. Curtains were drawn on windows, and the birds weren't singing.

"Cheery place," I said, as Callum found us a parking spot where a small green ran down to a waterway and cut the engine.

He frowned at the patchy grass and empty benches. There was a playground in one corner, but no one was using it. A woman with spiky arms hurried two horned children past, none of them speaking. She shot us a glance that was more fear than curiosity, and hissed, "*Hurry*," to the kids.

"This is weird," he said. "It wasn't like this before."

I put my paws on the dashboard and watched a man edge out of a shop across the road. He checked both ways, his face tight and glossy as a doll's, then rushed off with the clattering, sideways gait of a crab. "I think blending in might be a challenge. You know, given that there's no one to blend in *with*."

"Something's happened. It shouldn't be like this."

I looked up at him. "We're not here to save Dimly.

We're just here to see if we can track down some unicorns."

He rubbed his mouth. "What do we do, Gobs? We're going to be spotted straight away." There was a harsh, anxious edge to his voice.

"I'll go and see if I can scare up some rats," I said. "You stay in the car, stay out of sight. I've never felt anything like this place. It's like everyone's waiting to be rounded up for interrogation or something."

"Or already has been," Callum said. "I don't think you should go."

"And if I don't? How're we going to get any info on this place?"

He shook his head. "You're a *cat*—"

"And way less obvious than your scrawny self." I pawed the door. "I'm going straight down that alley across the road. There's a bunch of bins in there. There'll be rats. I'll ask my questions and be out again, quick as you like."

Callum examined the alley. "I don't like it."

"We're here. We may as well use the opportunity."

"I could—"

"Just open the gods-dammed door, Callum."

He looked at me for a long time, then said, "Be careful, okay? Even with the rats. Dimly's always been a bit different. And it feels *very* different now."

"No baby goats," I said, and jumped over him as he groaned and opened the door. The tarmac was warm beneath my paws, and a soft breeze rumpled through my fur, carrying with it the scent of old, deep magic and secret places and fried food.

Callum leaned out and gave me the cheese, which I picked up in my teeth as carefully as I could.

"Now, while you can't answer back – don't hang around, alright? If you don't find any rats in that alley, come straight back. No detours." He considered it. "Also, it's *no kidding*, not *no baby goats*. And your breath stinks."

I growled at him, then turned and ran low and silent into the streets of Dimly.

THE ALLEY RAN between a cafe decorated with pastel bunting and little blackboards with lots of exclamation marks on them (*Today's specials! Come on in! Home-cooked food!*), and a shop that seemed to live up to the name *Dimly Emporium*. The display windows were hung with black curtains and beaded with condensation, and as I scooted past something lunged at the glass, hitting with a hungry *thwock* and leaving dribbles of grossness running down the inside.

I wrinkled my nose above the cheese and slowed to a more careful pace, ears flicking as I examined the stained brick of the alley. There were big, overloaded bins crowded against the wall where the alley came to a dead end, and the walls to the sides held a couple of stained doors and frosted windows. Cardboard boxes slowly collapsed on the ground, and there was a whiff of rotting eggs and ancient tomatoes lurking above the drains, as well as the dank scent of stale water. The cafe's extractor fan huffed hot greasy air over me, making me narrow my eyes, and I picked my way toward the stacked veggie crates and wheeled bins by its back door. There was a low-level whiff of magic permeating the whole place, an undercurrent of spent power that might've been to do with the town's glamour or might've been more personal.

None of it seemed recent or urgent, though, and the doors stood closed and silent, so I ignored the magic and started scouting for rats. Above the rot was a hard stink of dog pee, among others, and I caught the thin scared smell of mice. No rats, though. I padded deeper into the alley, toward the bins at the end, my jaw starting to ache from holding the cheese. I checked the drainpipes on the walls and the grates set into the tarmac, but I'd never come across anywhere with less trace of rat in my life. There was nothing, despite the full bins and the quiet shadows, and after I'd circuited almost the whole alley I set the cheese down and worked my jaw for a moment. Weird. But there'd be other alleys. There were always rats *somewhere*.

I picked up the cheese again, intending to head back to the car, but as I turned a flurry of fast, feathered movement surged around me. I dropped the cheese with a hiss, jumping back as I found myself far too close to an alarmingly sharp beak. Shiny black eyes examined me, then inspected the bribe, and I took another couple of steps backward, not wanting to be within pecking distance. More birds were dropping into the alley, four, five, six of them, silent but for the hungry rustle of feathers. They settled to the ground behind the first crow, watching me with glittering eyes that reflected the sky above the alley.

I was blocked in.

10

OLD ACQUAINTANCES & NEW

WE STARED AT EACH OTHER, ME AND THE BIRDS WITH THEIR sharp hard beaks, the cheese sitting on the ground between us.

The first crow looked at me finally. “Cheese?” it said. “Hardly species appropriate.”

Gah. Crows give me the creeps. Regular birds are bad enough, little brainless dinosaurs. Brainy dinosaurs were much worse. “I was expecting someone else.”

“Oh? You came into *our* alley, expecting someone else?”

“Didn’t see the sign for Corvid Corner.”

The crow turned its head so it could examine me out of its other eye. “Are you attempting wit?”

I wasn’t sure what passed as wit in the crow world, but apparently it didn’t align with the feline version. “Not really,” I said with a sigh.

“So who was this someone else? A member of *Rodentia,* perhaps?”

“Is that a new band? Haven’t heard of them, myself.”

The crow shook its feathers out. "Again it tries for the humour."

"Not an it, dude."

"Not a dude," the crow said, its tone mild. "Let's try again. What did you hope to buy with this cheese?"

"Nothing. Just a gesture of good will. I'm new in town."

"Oh, I'm quite aware of that. Cats are not welcome in Dimly."

"Even bearing cheese?"

The crow pecked the lump of cheddar, then jerked its head. One of its buddies hopped forward, grabbed the cheese, and took off with one pull of powerful wings, heading out of the alley. "Gesture accepted. Now explain yourself, cat. Why are you here?"

"I'm accompanying a friend."

"No one in Dimly is friends with cats. Cats are nosy, sneaking creatures."

Well, there was unfriendly and there was just plain rude. "My friend's been away a while."

"Maybe they should be away longer, if they associate with cats." The crow took a step toward me, and my gaze kept going to its beak. It really was *very* sharp.

"What are you, the Dimly Corvid Crew?" I asked, my voice overloud and my tail bristling. "Are you actually trying to run me out of town?"

"Not trying," the crow said, taking another step. "No cats in Dimly. No *friends* of cats."

"And no rats either?" I asked, more for something to say while I tried to work out how I was going to get around a whole murder of birds without losing an eye. The crows all hissed.

"Nasty," one said.

"Vile little claws," another added.

"Bearers of disease."

"Awful teeth."

"And the tails. *The tails.*" A collective shudder went through the birds, which I almost joined. I wasn't a huge fan of rats' tails, either.

The head bird clicked its beak. "Tasty, though."

"Oh, tasty."

"Soft little bellies."

They were shifting excitedly now, eyes flashing toward me. "Like cats."

"More meat on a cat than a rat."

"Bigger eyes."

"More on the inside."

"Wet and red and warm on the inside."

I took a step back. "You lot are some seriously sick chickens, you know that?"

They chattered at me. "We are crows!"

"We are the best of birds!"

"We are darkness!"

"We are the heavy wing of the guard!"

"We are—"

"You are five feathers short of a boa," I snapped, and charged.

Well, there wasn't any other way I was getting out. There were walls behind me and to either side, and with no way to shift I'd just end up a perforated kitty. So I plunged forward, catching the lead bird one hard, claws-out blow across the head and sending it screeching into its fellows as I barrelled through them, heading for the street. One lunged for me, beak flashing, and I leaped to meet it, slamming both front paws into its feathery chest and tumbling free again. I landed hard and broke into a sprint, pain flashing up one leg as one of the over-inflated budgies caught me with their beak. Wings thundered behind me, cut through with caws and squawks, and I wished I had the breath to waste on flinging insults. I really wanted to.

I made it to the alley mouth still on my feet but minus some fur from my tail, and veered wildly left as I spotted the cafe tables. I dived beneath the nearest one, the crows crashing into the wooden frame behind me, sending a sugar bowl flying as faces popped up at the window, round and shiny and gawping.

"No cats!" the crows screeched, crowding into the table and onto the ground, darting beaks and claws at me as I kept a chair frame in the way. "No friends of cats!"

"Get out, get out!"

"Wet and red and tasty!"

"Gross," I mumbled, and dived for another table as the weight of the crows set the first teetering on the edge of balance.

"We are the guard, the darkness, the word!"

"This is not your place! Never your place!"

One of them scored a direct hit on my haunches, and I spun around with a snarl, raking my claws across its face and driving it squawking back as another took its place. I backed under a chair, trying to keep an eye on the birds in front as well as behind me, and heard the latch rattle on the cafe door.

"A little help here!" I called, and the latch made the

firm, unmistakable sound of a lock being turned. I swore, slapped another bird, and yowled as one plucked my tail. "Old ones *take* you!"

"We are the ancient ones! The birds of yore!"

"We are—" There was an alarmed squawk, and the thud of something solid hitting a feathered body. The bird in front of me leaped skyward, and others followed as there was another feathery thump and a chorus of outraged *caws*.

"Fie! Fie, he attacks the guard!"

"Treason!"

"Murder! *Murder!*"

"Shut *up!*" I yowled, and ducked out of cover to see Callum waving a chair about wildly as the birds ducked and dived, tearing at his hair and ripping a line of blood down his cheek. He abandoned the chair, the birds too close to swing it properly, and started laying about with a menu on a wooden clipboard instead. I threw myself at him and scrambled to his shoulder, lunging at the birds darting for the back of his head. "Let's go! We're going to get Alfred Hitchhiked!"

"Hitchcocked," Callum said, catching a crow with the menu and slapping it to the ground.

"I really don't care!" There were more birds now, a steady stream of furious dark shapes swelling from roofs and trees and rushing to join the fight, their eyes bright and hungry and eager. One bulleted out of the sky, dropping toward Callum's head with its claws spread wide, and I leaped to meet it, earning a scratched foreleg and a mouthful of feathers. It screeched in alarm and veered away, and I tumbled to the ground with two more bombing toward me. Callum grabbed his abandoned chair again and hurled it at them, then snatched me up in one hand, his other arm over his head to protect his face. The place was so thick with birds I could barely see the car across the road, and he staggered as they hit his upraised arm and back. He lunged for the cafe door.

"It's locked! Try the Emporium!" Even the unseen drooler in the window was better than this, although I kind of doubted we were going to get any sort of welcome anywhere.

Callum took a stumbling step toward the Emporium, kicking cursing birds out of his way as he went, blood smearing his forehead and running down his hand. Birds were pouring from everywhere, a feathered, oily tide studded with beaks and claws and fury, tearing at his coat and battering his head with their wings, and he could barely keep his feet.

"Put me down!" I shouted. "Put me down, I'll be okay!"

He just hugged me closer, fighting to move forward, and over the thunder of wings and caws and rage a new voice yelled, "Here! Here, get in, quick!"

A furled purple umbrella accompanied the voice, sailing through the throng and thwacking a bird that had been heading for my nose. It vanished with a squawk, and Callum veered toward the voice. A beach ball followed the umbrella, then a bicycle pump, a doorstop shaped like a hedgehog, a bright red frying pan, a mop head, two throw cushions, a toilet roll, and finally, as Callum took a last half-blinded step, one of those U-shaped travel pillows covered in long fluffy pink fur.

He stumbled up a doorstep, still fending off birds, and

hands grabbed him, hauling us through a door as someone hurled apples and potatoes from a nearby window at our attackers. The door slammed behind us, setting off a staccato of beaks and claws on the old wood, and shutters clanged shut on the window, and we were plunged into murky, fusty gloom.

Callum was breathing hard, and I could feel the stutter of his heart against my side. To be fair, my heart wasn't exactly tranquil, and my tail was the size of a toilet brush. We peered around, the room swimming slowly into focus as someone near the window said, "Are they alright? Are you alright? Is everyone alright?"

"I think they're alright," someone said from the door. "Are you alright?"

"I'm alright," window-voice said. "Are you alright?"

"I'm alright," door-voice said, then they chorused, "Are *you* alright?"

There was silence for a moment, then Callum said, "Oh. Us? Um, yes. I think. Gobs?"

"Yes," I said, still dangling from his hand in an undignified manner. I wasn't sure I wanted to go anywhere just yet.

"Oh, they're alright!" window-voice said. "Do you hear that, Marie? They're alright!"

"Oh, *that's* alright, then," door-voice – presumably Marie – said. "If everyone's alright, I mean."

"You *are* alright, aren't you?" window-voice said, moving closer. "You're not just saying that?"

"Um, no," Callum said. "I mean, yes. I mean, we're alright."

I blinked around the room. As my eyes adjusted to the

gloom I could see shelves running away into the dusty depths, curving around corners and reaching up to the roof, lined with books in a haphazard wilderness of bindings and sizes, spilling into piles on the floor and climbing in stacks on side tables. Little three-step ladders pocked the aisles with more books balanced on them, and the shelves bowed dangerously from the double and triple-stacked volumes they carried.

There was a deep, cushioned seat under the shuttered window, its frame made of old, faded hardbacks, and the table in front of it was an ancient scarred door laid across the top of still more books, with tattered *Reader's Digest*s and *National Geographic*s piled on top of it. Where the old wooden floors were visible they were printed with text and library stamps, as if the stories had seeped out of the books while they slept and had stained the very fabric of the world.

Marie left the door and padded closer, revealing herself as a small woman with a primly set helmet of grey hair, wearing a fetching lavender twin set that I thought Gerry would have envied. She wore glasses on a gold chain, worn-down biker boots, and two flasks slung at her hips like a gunslinger's holsters. Window-lady wandered over to join us, blinking up at Callum with wide, bright eyes. Her hair was cropped short and dyed pink, and she was wearing torn jeans and a hoody advertising a heavy metal band, but her soft features and diminutive frame were identical to Marie's.

"Um, thanks so much," Callum said, scratching his nose. His hand lingered, touching his injured cheeks, obscuring his mouth. "Is there a back door or something? Anywhere we could sneak out?"

Pink Hair pointed at him. "It's what's-his-face."

"No, I don't think so," Callum said from behind his hand.

"Ooh, I think you're right," Marie said.

"Of course I'm right," her sister said, flapping her hand at Callum. "You know the one."

"We should go," Callum said to his palm.

"With the books," Marie said. "Cherie, it was him with the books, wasn't it?"

"Of course it was him with the books," Cherie said, tossing her pink head. "Why else would we know him?"

"We know other people."

"Not to remember." They both stared at him, and he blinked nervously over his hand.

"Wouldn't think he'd read that much, not with his family," Marie said.

"Oh, but he had to know everything," Cherie added. "Hungry for words, hungry for worlds."

"Not like the others. Not like that sister of his."

"Oh, no. Oh, she hated it. Hated books. Hated him reading books."

"Give you ideas, books do," Marie said, sounding smug. "Make you think."

"And no one wants that." They both giggled, a conspiratorial little sound, and Callum stared back at them for a moment, then heaved a sigh and dropped his hand.

"Hello, Misses Silverfish," he said.

"Oh, call us Marie," Cherie said, pointing at her sister.

"And Cherie," Marie said, pointing back. "You're too old to be miss-ing us."

"Okay. I'm Callum, and—"

"We remember," they chorused, and Marie tapped the side of her nose. "We always remember the bookish ones."

I twisted so I could glare up at Callum. He pointedly ignored me, but I twitched my ears in a way that I felt indicated that this was what all his compulsive reading did for us. Got him recognised five minutes after setting foot in the place, and completely ruined our street cred.

"You have a friend," Cherie said, nodding at me.

"Hi," I said, a little breathless from Callum's grip. Okay, and maybe the whole corvid showdown. "Gobbelino London. Charmed to make your acquaintance."

"Oh," Marie said. "You're very polite. We thought all cats were a bit, you know."

"Socially inept," her sister said.

"Oh, he is," Callum said.

"I am not," I snapped. "I'm charm personified when I want to be."

"That doesn't happen much, does it?" he asked, and put me down. I huffed, and examined the printed floor beneath my paws, smelling the rich musk of universes packed in old paper, of magic spun from nothing.

"Nice place," I said. "Callum must've loved it." I side-stepped his boot before he could nudge me.

"Oh, he did," Cherie said. "He couldn't take the books home, so we let him read as many as he wanted right here."

"Sometimes he even slept here with them," Marie said, standing on her tiptoes to pat his cheek. "Books are escape hatches and life rafts and fortified castles, aren't they, boy?"

"Yes, Mi— Marie," he said.

"Do you still read?" Cherie asked.

"Of course he does!" Marie exclaimed. "Don't you, Callum?"

"So much," I said, before Callum could answer, because even without touching him I could feel a feverish sort of heat baking off him, some memory of fear and shame and defiance. "It's a pain. We've got this tiny little place, and it's just all books. He buys them by the box. *I've* had to sleep on them before."

Marie clapped her hands in delight, and Cherie grinned. "Well, it was inevitable," she said. "You read enough, the words get into your blood, and your heart will just plain break if you don't come back to them."

I didn't look at Callum. I could still feel that heat in him, and I didn't want to. I didn't want this glimpse into his past. What he had given me had been enough. This felt stolen, and painful, and unwelcome, this boy Callum who couldn't even take books home because they'd be torn from him, his peace stolen, his lifeline destroyed. This boy who slept among books because they were more welcoming than his home. "Well, fair enough," I said. "But I'd appreciate him leaving room for a few cushions, you know?"

The sisters laughed delightedly, and ushered us through the winding stacks and shelves, threading a maze of words and worlds until we popped out into a sunny little kitchen, painted yellow and crowded with so many plants it was like stepping into a greenhouse. A heavy wooden table held piles of cookbooks and paperbacks featuring an alarming number of bloody knives, and there were two plates and two cups draining by the sink.

"Sit down, sit down," Cherie said, hurrying to fill the kettle.

"And let me see you," Marie said, all but pushing Callum into a seat and fussing over his bloodied face and dishevelled hair. "Just scratched, but so many of them! Nasty, nasty birds."

"They suck," I declared, and jumped to the table, bumping Callum's hand with my nose. He gave me a half-smile and rested his hand on my back, and I could feel that painful fever fading, retreating behind the years again and leaving in its wake his usual steady scent of silence and old books and a quiet, endless magic that filled my soul.

11

A TACTICAL RETREAT

WE SAT AT THE KITCHEN TABLE IN HIGH-BACKED WOODEN chairs while Cherie made tea and Marie decorated Callum with bits of gauze and disinfectant. I'd been scolded for being on the table and relegated to a pile of cookbooks on one of the chairs, where I could still reach a bowl of chicken broth and a small plate of tuna. Both were fancy enough that I was starting to regret scoffing the corner shop ham. The whole place was warm and bright and *weird*. The one thing I hadn't expected to find in Dimly was hospitality and long-lost bookshop owners.

Marie finally capped the bottle of disinfectant and offered Callum some homemade shortbread. "So why are you back, Callum? It's been a long time. And your family …" She trailed off, glancing at Cherie, who just clicked her tongue and poured milk into the cups.

Callum took a biscuit and set it on his plate, staring at it as if it might answer for him. "I'm helping out a friend," he said at last.

"Nothing to do with the old business?" Cherie asked,

swirling the teapot. In the bright yellow light of the kitchen the women's skin was fine and pale, etched with age. Their eyes were bright, though, and I had an idea Marie's glasses might be more for effect than necessity.

"No," Callum said, his voice firm. "I was done with that when I left."

The sisters examined him for a moment longer, their gazes evaluating, then Marie nodded. "Good," she said. "But then you shouldn't be here. The Norths might be … well, not around, but that doesn't mean you won't be recognised. Strangers in general aren't welcome these days. You'll be even less so."

"I heard the Watch took them," Callum said, playing with the shortbread. "What's happened since? The whole town feels off."

The sisters looked at each other. Cherie handed out the cups, and Marie topped hers up from one of the flasks on her hip. She offered it to Callum, who shook his head.

"The Watch did come," Cherie said. "They took away a lot of people who were involved in the old things. The trade. Running the town. Even some of those who kept the borders. And they broke up the Norths."

Broke up. That was a strange way to put it. Although humans do love their euphemisms.

"And then there was what one might term a power shift," Marie said.

"With the Norths no longer running the town, someone had to step in," Cherie said, nibbling on a biscuit.

"*Slither* in," her sister said, adding a little drop more from her flask.

"Now, she's not been so bad for us. She likes books."

"She *ruins* them," Marie said, taking a gulp of spiked tea and wincing. "They come back all warped and damaged!"

"At least she reads." Cherie nodded at Callum. "He was the only North who read, and he left."

Callum gave a sort of apologetic shrug, and said, "Who's *she?*"

"I think she just looks at the pictures," Marie grumbled. "That's why she always wants the undersea photography books. For the *pictures.*"

Cherie flapped her hand at her sister and said, "She's the mayor. Elected by a landslide after the Watch went through."

"And do we know anyone who voted? *No,*" Marie said, giving up on the tea and swigging straight from her flask.

"Marie." Cherie's voice was sharp, more alarmed than reproving, and she glanced at the window over the sink, resting ajar on a minuscule back garden.

Marie followed her gaze, and her shoulders slumped. "Of course, she's done so much good for the town," she said, her voice too loud. "Cleared out all the ... undesirables. Made it safe."

Cherie looked at Callum. "Not safe for you, though. You need to leave now. And don't come back."

Callum nodded. "I know it's not safe. And thank you for helping us. But my friend really needs help, too."

"Tell them to sort it out themselves," Marie said. "This town isn't safe for you. It never was, really, but things are worse now. If it can't rot you slowly it'll just swallow you whole."

I shivered, licking chicken broth off my whiskers and

glancing at the window, looking for signs of feathered movement, but the garden was clear. "You're right," I said. "Will those vicious chickens still be about?"

"Probably," Marie said. "Do you have a car?"

"Just over the road," Callum said.

"Be quick and you'll be fine. But don't come back, understand?" She leaned forward to put one small hand on his arm. "Not for anything. Not to this place."

Callum rubbed the back of his head with his free hand, the scratches on his face standing out like brands. "Well—"

"Dude, we just about got *eaten* by a flock of bully-birds. If not for these lovely ladies we'd have been corvid crudités. So can we just go before we get them in any bother?"

"Oh, God," Callum started, and Cherie waved impatiently.

"Don't worry about us. We do what we need to do to stay in the mayor's good books." She flicked a look at her sister that I couldn't quite read. "Mostly, anyway."

"And crows won't bother us," Marie said. "There's not many that will."

A whisper rose around us, a surge of underlying power, and I peered from my perch at the wooden floor with its curls of prose and poetry. The text twisted and writhed, floating to the surface and sinking away again, reforming into new words and old quotes, breaking apart and rebuilding into charms and wards. I looked back at our hosts curiously, and spotted a lick of ink emerging from under Marie's prim neckline, curling to her hairline and retreating. Cherie smiled at me, a little knowing and dangerous, and I suddenly knew why Callum had always been safe among the books. Not many people would go up against magicians who had harnessed the power of this many words.

People underestimate them. Books, I mean, but little old ladies who live and breathe them, too. I might not have much need for books, but I don't disregard them, either. You do that at your peril. There's more than paper and ink in a book.

Why else do they drag you in, tear at your heart, rob you of your sleep and demand time and thought, and, sometimes, blood? Only magic things do that. Hungry things.

Callum took a final sip of tea and pushed his chair back. "Thank you," he said. "We'll go."

"I think it's best," Marie said, and the ladies got up to usher us through the living, breathing heart of the bookshop and out into the treacherous streets beyond.

THE STREET WAS clear when we peered out the door, no birds on the overturned cafe tables, none haunting the rooflines of the buildings by the little park. Our old car sat quietly across the road, a dozing life raft.

"Be careful," Marie said, reaching up to give Callum another pat on the cheek.

Cherie checked the road, her mouth pulled down in anxious lines. "And don't come back," she said. "We can only do this once." Then she all but pushed us out the door, and we heard the lock turn as it closed behind us.

"Do what once?" I asked, but Callum was already hurrying across the road with his head down and the collar of his tatty coat up. I bolted after him, my spine prickling. I wished I'd asked the ladies what the crows had meant when they'd said *We're the guard.* They weren't just some band of avian thugs. They were organised, somehow, and I wanted to know how. And I wanted to know more about whoever the hell the mayor was, too.

Callum was already at the car, hauling the unlocked door open and waving at me impatiently. I dived in, running across to the passenger seat, and Callum scrambled in after me, slamming the door and scrabbling for the keys. The car ground and groaned, refusing to catch, and Callum swore. He leaned back in the seat for a moment, pressing his hands flat against the steering wheel, his breath shaky, and I said, "You okay?"

"Sure," he said. "Peachy."

Then a crow plunged out of the sky and crash-landed on the bonnet, talons screaming on the metal, and both of us shrieked. Callum grabbed for the keys again as more birds started to appear, plummeting down like feathery cannonballs and hitting the car roof with ugly thuds, fluttering at the windows and pecking the glass with their ugly beaks, eyes amused and glittering in the afternoon light. The engine scraped over once, twice, and finally caught in a guttural roar, spewing exhaust fumes everywhere. Callum jammed the old Rover into gear, hauled the wheel over, and we lunged out of the parking space without any thought for other traffic – not that we could actually see anything through the windows anyway.

Feathers flew and birds screamed in fury, and the

crows on the bonnet went sliding off, catching the air and spinning away from us with enraged *caws*. Callum changed up through the gears, coaxing some bellowing speed out of the car, and as we roared down the deserted streets I stood up on the seat to peer out the back. The park behind us was thick with crows, crowded on the grass and the trees, lining the pavement and hurling abuse after us. No one else was moving. The town could have been deserted, some unused movie set, but I could feel eyes on us, peering through blinds and around curtains.

None of them felt too friendly.

WE WENT HOME. Callum sent Art a message saying we'd check in the next day, then we drove back through the messy, complicated, and desperately human roads as Leeds sprawled up around us. Callum cursed the after-school traffic, and I tried to get his phone to play some decent music, and he complained that I was getting snot on it because I was using my nose, and also that I had terrible taste. I pointed out that he couldn't accuse anyone of that when he went all gooey over acoustic guitars, and somewhere in the middle of the argument the phone fell between the seats and I couldn't get it out. So we had to listen to a rather muffled rendition of Guns'n'Roses all the way home, which neither of us really wanted to do.

But there were no crows, and no prying eyes, and Callum sang to the songs he did like, making up the words where he didn't know them, and I yowled when he hit the high notes, just to show willing. So by the time we found a space in the alley near our decrepit apartment building he had about as much colour in his face as he ever had, the scratches looking less violent on his cheeks, and I could almost believe that the past didn't have his ankle in its teeth. Well, for now, anyway. Reality is exhausting. Sometimes you have to just turn your back on it for a while if you want to survive.

Callum changed his scruffy shirt for a slightly less scruffy one, and we collected Mrs Smith from across the hall and took her to our favourite Turkish restaurant, the one where the waiters ignored me and the light was low enough that other diners never even noticed I was there. Neither of us were hungry, but it was nice to just sit in the warm, mellow-lit normality of it all, to wait for the food to arrive and to watch the little dishes be slid onto the table. To steal cheese pastries off Callum's plate when he wasn't looking, and to have Mrs Smith sneak scraps of fish to me.

I didn't even mind having to pretend I didn't talk. In a way, I liked it, being a normal cat for a while, passing beneath the attention of the humans and offering a few purrs to anyone who'd slip me treats. Things are a lot less complicated when humans think you're just a dumb animal. You get more scritches, too.

OUR APARTMENT still smelt of spilt washing up liquid and imp rage when we let ourselves back in after our early dinner, Callum waving to Mrs Smith as she closed her door. He picked up a couple of broken books, petted them gently, then went to put the kettle on. I jumped onto the desk and Green Snake lifted his head out of my bed, looking at me in a way that said very clearly he had no intention of relinquishing squatter's rights. I showed him one tooth, then took Callum's chair instead.

Callum came back in with a cup of tea, looked at me and Green Snake, grunted, and sat on the armchair that folds out into his bed. He shook a cigarette out of the packet, lit it, and said, "Now what?"

I jumped back to the desk and said, "Smoke that out the window. Me and Slither here don't want your second-hand smoke."

He sighed, but got up and reclaimed his chair, wedging the window open with a book. It let in a draught that carried the smoke to the ceiling and let it gather there instead.

I tried to evict the snake, but he wasn't having it, so I just sat down and said, "If you're actually asking my advice, then I say we drop the case. Stay the hell out of Dimly and away from bloody crows, and let Art find his own unicorns."

"And just let anything happen to Kara?"

"We don't even know she was actually kidnapped. We only know what Art told us."

He took a sip of tea and made a face. "I can still taste imps."

"Gross. You're not going to get all high on it, are you?"

He tried another sip. "Eh. It might be washing up liquid, actually. Look, I believe him. He wouldn't lie about something like that."

"Why not? He's lied about everything else, far as I can

tell. *Someone's* been dealing horn with Dimly, and he's saying he not only would never deal, he never goes near the place. He certainly lied about hiding the unicorns, as he apparently meant, *hide them from humans and never mind anyone else*. And the Watch were going to tumble to that one day, at which point they'd have his guts for giraffes."

Green Snake stared at me, and Callum snorted. "Garters."

"What about them?"

"They'd have his guts for garters."

I blinked at him. "Have you ever seen a cat in garters?"

"No," he admitted. "But why would a giraffe want Art's guts?"

"Look, no one ever said your language made sense. And that's also gross. Why would *anyone* want garters made from guts? Is that like a North family thing?"

"We're not the Hannibal Lecters," he protested.

"Who's he? Did he wear garters?"

Callum shook his head and took another sip of tea. "Never mind. Look, I know Art wasn't doing a great job. But that's just him. He's a bit …"

"Dog-brained? Rabbit-headed?"

"No. He just doesn't have great attention to detail. He means really well. And he'd do anything to protect Kara and those unicorns."

"Anything except hide them properly."

Callum sighed. "Yeah, I know. But if whoever's running Dimly now – the mayor or whoever's actually in charge – already knew about them, he probably didn't feel there was much point hiding them."

"Alright," I said. "So if the Dimly lot took the sister, then they don't have the unicorns."

"Makes sense."

"But we have zero leads on the unicorns being anywhere *but* Dimly. Unless you count the possibility of them being troll dinner, in which case they're long gone."

Callum shook his head. "I really don't see Gerry doing it. And Poppy couldn't have done it on her own. Plus, Dimly's a pocket. They're bigger than they seem. And the way the place is locked down … It's possible they have been taken there, maybe by someone moving in on the trade. That was always an issue when I was there – it's why no one was allowed to leave once they were in."

"Cool. So now we've got *two* dodgy Dimly gangs."

"Maybe."

"Are you sure we can't just leave this?"

"No." He stubbed his cigarette out. "Even if we can't find the unicorns, we need to get Kara out."

"Great. And we *still* don't know if she's actually been kidnapped. What if she just got sick of living with her hippie brother and took her chance to get out?"

The phone binged, and Callum rubbed his face. "There's only one way to find out."

"Well, you can't go back to Dimly. That's obvious."

"Neither can you."

I took a deep breath. "Can. You drop me on the outskirts. It's absolutely impossible for there to be *no* rats in Dimly. I'll find some, and I'll get the info we need. If Kara or the unicorns – or both – are in there, it's the best option for finding them. But you don't go near the place."

"I don't like it. It's too dangerous."

"Yeah, well, this whole case is making my skin crawl. I'll do it, and it'll be our last shot. See if we can find any hard evidence. If not, we're done with Dimly, and we can start looking elsewhere."

He ran a hand back through his hair and picked up the phone. "Maybe we need to look elsewhere first. See if we can find out if there's unicorn dust coming in the market from somewhere else."

"I guess it depends how impatient these kidnappers are."

He didn't reply, just stared at the phone.

"Callum?"

He looked up at me. "Pretty impatient, looks like," he said, and turned the phone so I could see it. It was open to a message from Art.

I JUST GOT THIS JESUS CHRIST CALLUM WHERE ARE YOU HELP I DON'T KNOW WHAT TO DO CALL ME PLEASE CALL

Beneath the text was a photo of a wooden chopping board. There was a finger on the board, blood smearing the wood and the pair of shears resting next to it. The dark-haired young woman from the photo on Art's wall stood next to the board, her hand wrapped in a bloodied tea towel and tears streaking her face. Her lips were contorted in pain.

"Ah," I said. "Hairballs."

12

TROLLING FOR INFORMATION

THE NEXT MORNING, AFTER THE WORK TRAFFIC HAD calmed, we slogged our way out to Art's cottage in the poor abused car. There were heavy clouds rolling in from the north, and a hungry little breeze had snatched at my tail as we hurried from the apartment to the car.

"None of this feels right," I said to Callum.

"I know," he said. "But the way Art was on the phone, he'll be heading into Dimly to tackle things himself if we don't get there and calm him down." He considered it. "I. If I don't calm him down."

I sniffed. "It's too convenient. We visit Dimly, and the next thing Art's getting fingers on his phone? Either those crows or your bookshop ladies are telling tales."

"Or the kidnappers are getting impatient."

"I don't like any of this, Callum. It's like that bloody town's trying to suck you back in."

"I'm not going to let that happen. Now can you just try not to be too rude to Art?"

"I'll be the picture of politeness."

"Why am I not reassured?"

I growled.

Art rushed out of the cottage as we clanked and clattered down the drive, the old Rover belching black smoke in even greater quantities than usual. He stood by the gate, twisting his hands together as if he could get juice out of them, and as soon as we ground to a halt he rushed to open Callum's door, looking like he wanted to throw his arms around Callum again.

Callum patted Art's shoulder a little awkwardly as he climbed out.

"I'm so glad you're here," Art said, his voice wobbling. He stank of fearful sweat and guilt and pain, with a dash of hippie soap over the top.

"Let's go in," Callum said, grabbing an old backpack out of the passenger footwell. He'd listened to me on the supplies this time and we'd stopped on the way to buy custard, real milk, tuna, and cigarettes.

"I just … I can't believe this, Callum! I can't! I said you shouldn't go to Dimly, and now look!"

"Hey, rhubarb-face," I snapped. "We went there to try and find your manky ponies. And we almost had our eyes pecked out. So don't be blaming us for this."

"But why now?" he wailed. "Why do this to her *now?* They must have seen you!"

"Maybe. Or it's just a reminder that they want the unicorns back," Callum said. "Or their horn, anyway."

"It's only because they saw you," Art started, then stopped, blinking at him like a pixie in a spotlight and still twisting his hands together. "What? But they *have* the horn. The unicorns, I mean."

"Sure. And I have the Taj Mahal in my back pocket," I said.

Art turned his blinking on me. "In your pocket …?"

"Oh, gods save us from clueless parsnips," I muttered, and Callum clicked his fingers at me irritably. I bared my teeth.

"We know there's unicorn dust being dealt in Dimly still," Callum said, his voice level. "There's only one place it could've come from."

"No, I didn't," Art said, his voice cracking at the edges. "I wouldn't."

"Let's try this a different way," I said. "The people who have your sister want you to get the unicorns back, don't they?"

"Yes," he said, then hurriedly added, "I mean, no. No, I told you! They want me to stay away. They took her as a … a warning. To make sure I didn't chase them. And that's why I called you, because you're meant to be professionals. But you went to *Dimly!*"

"So we should just leave then, yes?" I said. "You actually meant to tell us to keep clear when you called us, right? Don't get involved, or there'll be more fingers in your inbox?"

"I … No …" He covered his face with both hands, squeezing so hard I was worried he was going to scrub his scraggly beard clear off. "God*dammit!* I can't do this! Why did they *do* that to her?"

"Who has Kara?" Callum asked.

"I'm not … I'm meant to say it's whoever got the unicorns, but … they're *hurting* her!"

I opened my mouth, and Callum held a hand out to me.

"Is she in Dimly?" he asked.

Art scraped his hands down his face. "Yes."

"But whoever took her doesn't have the unicorns. They're holding her to make you *find* the unicorns."

"Yes," he said again, the word hopeless.

"You've been dealing."

"No," he whispered.

"Dealing, supplying, same difference," I said. "You've been selling horn."

He shook his head, a violent, panicked gesture.

Callum sighed. "Let's have a cuppa. Think this through."

I bared my teeth at both of them. "Sure, that'll fix everything."

"It's as good a start as any, Gobs," Callum said, guiding Art toward the door. He seemed to have shrunk, become bent and older.

I huffed and glanced around, spotting Kent the donkey ambling across the unicorn's field with his ears twitching softly. There was someone waiting at the far end, half-hidden in the shadows of the trees. I peered at them, but my distance vision kind of sucks, and all I could see were splashes of colour.

"I'm going to go and have a nose around," I said, and Callum waved me off. Well, fine. I knew what I was good at, and it wasn't holding hippies' hands.

I slipped under the gate and loped down the field, the grass still night-damp beneath my paws despite the fact my stomach suggested we were getting on for morning tea time at least. I could still smell the faint whiff of unicorn, horses wound about with muscular magic and arrogance, and over it the fusty scent of the donkey and whiffs of anxious goat. And I got a noseful of our visitor before I reached her, too.

"Hey," I said, coming to a stop a couple of metres from where she was rubbing the donkey's nose with heavy, creased hands. "Poppy, isn't it?"

She blinked her three eyes at me and grinned widely. Today's overalls were orange, with a green paisley shirt covering her long arms and a straw hat pulled down over her ears. A huge mountain bike with a reinforced frame and oversized wheels leaned on the fence next to her, a white basket on the front and streamers dangling from the handlebars.

"Kitty!" she exclaimed. "Poppy happy sees you." She frowned. "I happy to sees you."

"I'm happy to see you too, kid," I said, still keeping a decent distance between us. She was drooling again, and she wiped it away with one sleeve. "Should you be out in the daylight, though?"

"Gerry say Poppy uses hat and screeny, is okay."

I had no idea what screeny was, but judging by the white gunk slathered on her hands (and now on Kent's nose) it was cream of some sort.

"Cool," I said, and looked up at the field. "What're you doing here, Poppy?"

"Poppy – I – says hello to dinky."

"Donkey," Kent said, taking a carrot from her and crunching noisily.

"I says," she replied, frowning, then looked at me. "You finds unicorns yet?"

"Nope. Although I was hoping to run into you. Thought maybe you might have some information you'd like to share when Gerry wasn't around."

Her face scrunched in concentration. "Runs into me? No, kitty. I is heavy. You hurt nose."

Kent brayed amusement – and carrot – and wandered off, still munching.

"Bye, Dinky," Poppy called, and he flicked his ears. I mean, you wouldn't get much more out of me for a carrot, either, but it seemed a bit rude. She looked back at me. "Why you wants to runs into me?"

"It's a silly human expression. I just mean I wanted to talk to you more."

"Oh!" Her face split in an alarming smile, all teeth and heavy grey angles. "We has pickle-nicks?"

"Pickle-nicks?"

"With blanket?"

"A blanket? No, I don't think so."

"Oh." She looked in the basket of her bike. "I has the sandy witches, too. With cheese."

My head was starting to hurt.

"Poppy, have you seen the unicorns?"

"No," she said, still looking in the basket. "Is only cheddar sandy witch."

"No in the sandy— not in the sandwiches. I mean, have you seen where they went?"

She shook her head firmly, the brim of the big hat wobbling. "No."

"Are you sure? There's a human here who's in real trouble because the unicorns have gone."

She frowned at that. "Serves right. Humans mean. They no treat unicorns nice. Or others. No talk to dinky or goats. They not nice."

"Yes, but they were still looking after the unicorns. And now they're going to get hurt because the unicorns are gone."

Poppy scratched her jaw, not looking at me. "They not look after unicorns nicely. I sorry. I doesn't know."

I watched her for a moment, then sighed. Even if she did know anything, understanding what she told me would've been a whole other box of herrings. "Alright. Thanks, Poppy. You, um, ride safe."

"I does," she said, grinning again. "I safe biker." And she righted the bike, pointed it down the hill, and pedalled away, the frame creaking and her yelps of delight drifting back to me above the grumblings of the breeze in the tree.

"Cool," I said, and trotted back up the hill to the house.

THE KITCHEN DOOR WAS AJAR, letting out the smells of woodsmoke and soap as I nosed my way inside. Art was hunched over the big table, his eyes bloodshot and tired. I looked at Callum and said, "We off, then?"

"Off where?" Art asked. "You're not going back to Dimly, are you?"

"Dude, we've got nowhere else to look for the unicorns at the moment. All indications suggest that if *anyone* knew about the unicorns, it'd be someone from

Dimly. You want your sister to keep the rest of her fingers?"

"You can't go back," he said, shaking his head. "They'll be looking for you. And if they see you, they'll hurt Kara again. Never mind what they'd do to you."

"I'm not going in," Callum said. "Gobs is going to scout, see if he can pick up any information."

Art scratched his beard, his eyes wide and worried. "They watch all the approaches these days. And cats *really* aren't welcome. It's sort of a zero-tolerance thing since the Watch raid."

"Who's running things, then?" Callum asked. "Who's this new mayor?"

Art shrugged. "I've never met her. Folk of some sort. Apparently she's done really well at tidying the place up, and everyone loves her."

Callum and I looked at each other. Dimly hardly had the air of a town full of happy citizens.

"You really don't go there much, do you?" I said.

He shook his head, his hair moving stiffly around his face. "I never need to. Kara told me about it. She still has some friends there she stays in touch with."

"Have you talked to them?" Callum asked.

Art gave him a puzzled look. "She was *taken.* I got a phone call to tell me. Her friends aren't going to know anything." He shrugged. "Besides, I don't know them."

I opened my mouth, and Callum spoke over me. "They might have known you still had the unicorns, if she was still in touch with them. And that *might* give us an idea of who could've been interested in them. Are you sure you don't know any of them?"

Art thought about it for a moment. "Well. I mean, she used to hang around with Ez until the Watch raid. But now she's gone – I'm not sure. I suppose there might be a couple of people I can think of."

Callum drummed his fingers on the table. "She was hanging around with Ez?"

"Who's that?" I asked.

"My sister." His voice was flat. "Esme."

Art snorted. "Not that anyone'd call her *that* to her face."

Callum almost smiled. "No. But she's gone?"

"Gone in the raids." Art picked his tea up, put it down again. "I could ask around. But Kara's hardly going to be wandering around visiting people. She's a *prisoner*."

"If she's in Dimly, someone might've seen something," Callum said. "But if you normally never go in—"

"No, I can do this." Art looked up, his eyes brighter. "If anyone asks, I'll say I'm following a lead!"

"Oh, gods," I said. "More DUI-ing."

Art stood up, straightening his ancient fleece. "And I'll take you, too."

"Oh, no," I said. "I'm not going anywhere with you. For all I know you'll hand me off to the Dimly Murder Mob to score some points. They've probably got a cat bounty."

"Gobs," Callum said.

"What? He might!"

"He wouldn't. But you still shouldn't go, Art. Let us handle this."

"It makes more sense for me to," he said, his face pale. "You can't be showing your face, and no one's going to talk to a cat. Gobbelino can jump off on the outskirts, then I'll collect him later." He frowned at me. "Or you could just shift. That'd be easiest."

"Not an option," I said, ignoring his puzzled look. I wasn't explaining to some composted potato that the Watch had made sure I could never shift again. Or not emerge in one piece if I did, anyway. "But I might like this plan. Other than the obvious risk of you being a treacherous weed."

"I'm not," he said. "I know I should have told you about it being them having Kara, and not the unicorn thieves. But they told me not to. They told me this would happen if I did." He nudged his phone distastefully.

"Why even hire us, then?" Callum asked.

"Hire," I snorted. "Yeah, can't wait to see payment for this."

Callum waved me to silence, watching Art, and eventually he said, "I didn't think you'd do it if it was just the unicorns. And I didn't know anyone else who'd care enough about Kara to get involved. Who'd understand. There just isn't anyone."

We were quiet for a moment, then Callum looked at me. "Are you okay to go with Art?"

"Okay's a relative term," I said. "But I'll do it."

"I'll get my coat," Art said, getting up.

AND OF COURSE Art wouldn't take the ancient green Landrover from the shed, or even the rowdy quadbike. Instead he wheeled out a motorbike that looked like it had been dropped from an aeroplane in the war and no one had done much to it since.

"Where the hell do you expect me to go?" I asked him. "I'm hardly going to just sit on the back, am I?"

"I'll put you in my coat," Art said, unzipping the dead sheep jacket he'd pulled on over his fleece.

"Become a PI, you said," I complained to Callum as I jumped onto the bike and let Art zip the jacket over me. "It'll be fun, you said."

"Yeah, that one was your bright idea, if I remember right," he said, and tipped his head to the side. "Besides, you look *so* cute."

I hissed at him, and Art yelped. "Claws!"

"Sorry," I said. "Now let's go, before I die of either embarrassment or patchwork."

"Patchwork?" Art asked.

"Or whatever the hell this soap is."

"*Patchouli,*" he said. "It's very nice, actually."

I growled.

We rumbled down the drive, the engine throaty and rough but the bike managing the potholes better than our poor old car had. Art had a helmet of the same vintage as the bike pulled down over his ears, and once we were out onto tarmacked streets he opened the throttle into a harsh, hungry grumble. We stayed off the main roads and away from the worst of the traffic, leaning into the corners and ghosting down hills as we threaded the back streets toward Dimly. It was warm tucked into the jacket, even if it did still smell an awful lot like the original owner, and I tucked my nose inside to keep out of the wind.

Art pulled over where the rot was deep and ugly on the houses, the bins overflowing and the windows blank, hungry holes on the walls around us. He stopped the bike and pulled it onto the stand, muttering and poking the engine a bit, then crouched down as if to check the wheel.

"Oscar-worthy, that was," I said.

"Shh," he whispered, undoing the jacket and letting me slip to the ground. He set a packet of crackers in front of me (they may not be as enticing as cheddar, but they're a hell of a lot lighter to lug into enemy territory). "Be careful. They won't give you a slap on the wrist, you know."

"I don't have wrists," I said, and shivered in the fretful wind.

Art looked at me with his face held in tight lines and said, "I'll meet you back here in two hours, okay?"

"Sure. Shall we synchronise watches?" He just stared at me, and I sighed. "Two hours. Go easy, dude. You look like you'll pass out if someone sneezes." Then I picked up the crackers, slipped under the nearest parked car and hunkered down, wrapping my tail over my paws.

Art got up, started the bike, and left, and the street fell to silence, broken only by the wind playing with scraps of rubbish and rattling a window somewhere. I stared across the street, at the point where I could sense as much as see the border of Dimly, the line where magic bled camouflage out of the ground and realities blurred. The roofs were empty, the trees restless but uninhabited. No birds. No dogs. No people. Just the shifting, restless edge of glamour.

Eventually I crept out from under the car, my paws soft and wary, and ran low as a shadow across the road, plunging through the shivering lines of power, the hair on my tail lifting gently. Dimly flared up around me, and the sky pressed low and hungry and full of watching eyes above. I kept going, my chest tight and my breath fast, and left the world I knew behind.

13

MIND THE CERBERUS

I RAN THE LENGTH OF FOUR BLOCKS, PLUNGING STRAIGHT into the heart of Dimly, before I saw more than a sparrow. I kept to the shelter of cars and gutters where I could, flinching from crumpled paper bags and scraps of plastic as the wind rumbled them past me. My ears were flicking with the effort of trying to catch every shred of sound, and I was starting to pant from trying to smell everything at once. There was the usual whiff of dogs and birds and discarded food, old drains and stale water and the warm gentle rot of fallen leaves. There were trees and exhaust fumes and the frowzy, sweet scent of flower-stuffed gardens, and underneath it all ran the greasy stink of magic, flaring into something muscular and terrible outside a bland-looking house with white walls and a pretty, meticulously kept lawn, trailing off and becoming musical and sweet outside the rickety apartments down the street. I could have spent hours in one spot, just sorting through all the scents and making sense of them, but I was only interested in one.

Unfortunately it was the one I couldn't bloody well find, and that just made *no* sense, because rats get everywhere. It's one of the reasons I've always made an effort to befriend them, creepy tails and all. After all, for a cat who can't shift, and therefore can't do the appearing-in-places-humans-think-we-have-no-business-being thing, it's important to build up some allies. And especially when said cat is a PI.

I slowed to a trot, casting about more carefully as the outside world retreated and Dimly swamped me, all oddly shaped doors and leaning top floors, complete with cupolas and towers and weird rooftop platforms perched precariously on gables. There were areas of wild land too, thick with growth that whispered and shuddered as I slunk past, and the scents drifting out were feral and dangerous. Not unicorn-y, though, which was a shame. It'd be handy just to stumble on them in someone's backyard, but things work that nicely far less than they should.

A flicker of movement in the whispering trees caught my eye and I froze, belly sinking low in the shelter of a garden wall. I watched a bird wing past, high and distant. I couldn't tell if it was a crow or something less sinister, and it didn't stop, just swooped on toward the heart of Dimly. I put the crackers down and worked my jaw, my heart loud in my ears. My leg and tail ached from the birds' assault the day before, and I was starting to think Callum had been right. If I couldn't find any rats, there was no way I was going to be able to find the unicorns on my own. Not without being pulled to pieces by goth budgies or shoved in someone's stew pot, anyway.

I picked up the crackers again, wondering how long it

had been since Art dropped me off. Not long, I didn't think. Certainly not long enough to go back and get a lift home, so I might as well keep going. I took a step forward, and stopped. The fur on my spine was twitching even worse than before, and I turned my head slowly, looking over my shoulder at the house-lined street and its murmuring cover of green-clad trees. Nothing. But that twitching wouldn't stop. Maybe it was just someone watching from a window, wondering who the cat was.

I edged closer to the nearest car, some strange monstrosity of a thing that was all gleaning chrome and broken hubcaps, its wheels hunched up and curving over its back like a bird with its wings tucked back. I gave it a suspicious glance, not entirely certain it wouldn't open some metal maw and gobble me down like a horse's dessert or what have you, then snuffled the grate under the kerb without much hope.

There. I spat the crackers out and yelled, "Hey! Anyone home?" My heart rate had surged up again, and at this rate I was going to have a heart attack before I got eaten by anything, which I supposed was a better way to go anyway.

My shout echoed sharply off the ugly car, amplifying the *hey*, and I stuck my head out for a look at the sky. Still nothing, but my back was a mess of spiked fur. That sense of being watched was stronger than ever, and no matter how quick I turned my head I was convinced I could see movement at the corner of my eye.

I turned back to the grate and hissed, "Hello? I come bearing gifts."

Still no response, but now I had the feeling someone

was watching me from below as well as above. I just hoped Dimly's rats weren't some weird, cat-eating hybrid.

"Look, I don't mean any harm. I just want a bit of information."

Nothing, but I sensed movement.

"Please? No tricks, I swear. I—"

"Shut *up,*" a small voice hissed from below me. "Get out of here, you moth-eaten moggy!"

"Hey, it's not *that* bad," I said, glancing at my tail.

"Get *out.* You're drawing attention to us."

"Sorry, I know, but—"

"*Go away.*"

"I can't do that. I'm sorry, but—" I broke off as a small furred face pressed itself to the grate, little damp paws gripping the metal as a she-rat glared at me. A scar ran down her snout, reducing one eye to a pale, milky grey, and her nose twisted to the side, the lip pulling back from the teeth in a permanent sneer.

"You'll get us all killed," she hissed. "They're watching. They're *always* watching."

I glanced anxiously back into the street, then looked at the rat. "Please."

There was a scuffle below the grate, and the rat turned away, hissing something, then looked back at me. "Shadow-demons of Guthrey Hall take you. Will it shut you up and get you out of here?"

"Yes," I said, wondering where Guthrey Hall was.

"Gods' whiskers. *Fine.*" She pointed her nose across the road. "Down the side of that house to the south corner of the garden. *Move.*" Then she was gone and the grate was empty and silent, not even a whisper of movement to mark her passing. I crept to the street side of the car, peered around carefully, then bolted for the house across the road, my back itching wildly. I shot to the top of the gate amid a rush of whispering movement behind me, and glanced back to see a dozen or so crows crowding the wall above the strange car. One opened its mouth and screamed at me, a harsh and wordless *caw*, and the rest all chuckled in a way that raised the hair on my back even further. I looked doubtfully down into the garden of the house, wondering if the rat had set me up, and with a thunder of wings the crows surged forward.

I yelped, threw myself off the gate, and pelted toward the back of the house. Set-up or not, I wasn't waiting around to be plucked. I came to a screeching stop at the edge of a broad sweep of garden, wondering how in hell I was supposed to know which corner of the flowerbed-hemmed lawn was the south one. I wasn't exactly carrying my Boy Scout compass. I glanced back. The crows hadn't followed me, but had landed in a flock on the gate behind me, clucking to each other and occasionally breaking out in laughter. I looked around uneasily, wondering what they were waiting for. The yard looked clear. I had a sick sense of misgiving in my belly, but I couldn't exactly go back. I turned and followed the garden wall down one side of the lawn, figuring there were only four corners, so I'd just figure it out as I went. Hopefully.

Between keeping an eye on the chortling birds and trying to find a handy drain, I didn't even notice anything was wrong until a huff of hot air blasted across my spine. Hot, *sticky* air, like the owner had bad stomach hygiene to go with the bad dental hygiene.

I said something even I'd never said before, and all but levitated off the lawn. I ended up in the flowerbed, standing on some richly scented pink flowers and staring at the heavy breather. It stared back out of three pairs of slightly rolling doggy eyes, and three tongues flopped messily out from between three sets of unnervingly sharp teeth. Only four paws to go with the three heads, though. This is what you get in magical neighbourhoods. Someone always has to go messing around, and you end up with damn Cerberus dogs.

"Good boy," I said, and the three heads growled. One snapped in my general direction, sending a little scatter of drool everywhere. Ugh. Dogs are bad enough with one head. "Sorry. Good girl?" It growled again and took a step forward. "Good … good puppy. *Good dog.*" Drool-y head licked its chops, and one of the others watched a seven-winged butterfly stutter past. The third just kept growling. "Sit?" I suggested, and growly head barked. I tried a step back, and the other two heads swung around to glare at me. "No, right, sorry."

"South!" a tiny voice shrieked from across the garden. "I said *south*, you useless feline!"

"I'm not Captain bloody Hook," I yelled back, and the Cerberus' heads jerked away from me suddenly. It gave an enormous chorus of *whuffs* and charged across the manicured lawn away from me. Two rats were sprinting across the grass, pushing a tatty pink ball ahead of them, both squeaking wildly and jumping in the air when they weren't pushing.

"South!" the unseen rat bellowed again, and I still had no idea where the hell south was, but I bolted toward the

voice. One of the Cerberus heads caught sight of me and it tried to spin the body around, but the other two heads were intent on the rat-propelled ball, and the dog threw itself into a yelping, furious circle, all three heads snapping at each other hysterically and barking their displeasure. The rats abandoned the ball and took off in the same general direction as I was heading, and I swore off custard forever as the dog stopped arguing with itself and pelted toward me.

The rats made it to the drain a breath ahead of me and plunged out of sight. All I could hear was the laughter of crows and the thunder of massive paws gaining on me, the three heads just about yodelling with excitement. The grate yawned before me, the gap looking about big enough for a hamster on a skinny day, but cats are liquid. I hoped.

"*Incoming!*" I yelled, and glimpsed a scatter of furred movement below me, although any shrieks of alarm were drowned by the dog's roar of rage. I shot through the gap, scraping my sides on the way through and losing some fur, and hit the sludgy bottom so hard my forelegs couldn't take up the strain. I bumped my nose on the rough ground beneath the muck and tumbled into a helpless somersault as my hind legs overtook me, slamming onto my back with a squawk and sliding through the sludge for about half a metre before I finally stopped, staring back at the entrance to the drain with all four paws in the air. The Cerberus was lunging wildly at the gap, which I was still fairly surprised I'd squeezed through. Drool flew from its multiple chops and its barks echoed down the dim stretches of the drains.

"Graceful," someone observed, and I looked around to see the scarred she-rat watching me, little paws braced on the wall above the muddy bottom.

"Can he get that open?" I asked.

"Nope," an elderly rat with only one front paw said. "We've secured it."

"Only thing that can get through is a crow," the scarred rat said. "Not that they try it much. They don't get out again."

Soft laughter ran around me, and I realised the walls of the drain were lined with rats, all of them very still and poised, their dark eyes watching me with a calculating appraisal that seemed a long way from the rats I was used to.

"Cool," I said carefully.

"Current tally, twenty-five," the old rat said.

"Twenty-five crows? You've killed twenty-five crows?"

"No, teddy bears," the she-rat said, and the rats tittered. The hair on my spine twitched in alarm, despite being both under me and coated in so much filth I couldn't even bear to think about it.

"Well. That's impressive," I said, hoping I didn't sound sarcastic. I didn't want to sound sarcastic around a pack of serial killer rodents. Plus I supported the culling of these particular crows quite strongly.

There was a pause while the dog pawed at the grate, whining unhappily, stalactites of saliva dangling and twisting in the depths of the drain. The rats kept watching me. I tried to look harmless, which felt fairly easy given my undignified position. Then I heard feathered movement outside, and the dog gave a yelp as if someone had jabbed him with something sharp.

"Here, kitty kitty," a harsh voice called, and ugly laughter joined it. "Here puss puss puss." The sunlight was cut off as dark, feathered bodies crowded over the grate, and beaks tapped teasingly at the metal. "Come on kitty. Don't you want a saucer of milk?"

"I wouldn't mind pie," I called. "And a few feather dusters."

The crows cawed amusement. "Oh, such a brave cat, talking so big. Come up here and say that to us."

"Pass," I said, then took a deep breath and chanted, *"Four-and-twenty corvids, baked in a pie—"*

"Never mind," the crow shouted over me. "You'll keep."

"Shouldn't that be *nevermore?*" I called back, which earned me a round of rat laughter. The crows cursed and shouted insults, but they didn't seem keen to venture into the depths. Apparently the rats hadn't been exaggerating their reputation.

"Come on," the scarred rat said. "As entertaining as this is, we've got work to do."

There was a general surge of ratty movement, ordered and silent, laughter gone, no chattering or pushing or arguing or any of the usual things you get with a whole pack of rats – or anything else, for that matter. I rolled over and stood up, scummy water dripping off my tail and ears and pretty much everywhere else. It stank.

The she-rat looked back at me. "Coming, Moggy? Or you fancy joining your friends out there?"

"Well, no. Where're we going?"

"Away from the damn birds," the rat said.

I peered into the narrow depths of the tunnel. "Right. I mean, good. But I just had a couple of questions—"

"Time for that later." The rats were vanishing into the shadows, leaving me with just the scarred she-rat, her whiskers twitching with annoyance. "You can't get back out there, anyway."

I glanced back at the grate, hearing the birds chattering above it. "No, I suppose not. What's *with* those bloody birds?"

"Later, Mogs. You want to ask your questions, you come with us." She turned and loped easily after her pack, leaving me in the tight, dim silence by the drain. The Cerberus was still whining, and the crows were teasing it.

"Wait! I'm coming." I broke into a splashing run, racing to catch up with the silent pack. None of them looked at me, just kept pattering swiftly along the low curve of the walls just above the gunk that lined it, and I had the uneasy feeling that it wasn't just a matter of them not being afraid of me. I thought maybe they felt *I* should be afraid of *them.*

We marched into the darkness, the tiny rat army moving silent and swift while I trailed behind. The walls and top of the drain pressed down around me, cracked with roots and leaking dirt that gathered in the standing water at the bottom, turning it to mud that squished between my toes and jammed in my claws. Even for my eyes, it was dark between the erratically spaced drains, the light not reaching far enough to penetrate the underground gloom. It was only just deep enough for me to stand upright, and the whole place felt tight and trapped and enclosed, no escape from anything that might come barrelling down on us, crows or dogs or something worse. I wanted to stop and breathe and try to clean myself off, to ask where we were going and what work we had to do, or if I was even a part of it, but I stayed silent and kept going, shaking myself off occasionally. When in Rome, wear togas, or whatever.

We plunged on through the dark bowels of Dimly, magic seeping from the very earth around us, and time stole away as the world narrowed to nothing but heavy, unpleasant scent and desperate, racing movement.

14

A LITTLE ANARCHY IS GOOD FOR THE SOUL

I'M NOT SURE HOW FAR WE'D GONE BEFORE WE FINALLY took a break. As for where we were, in the maze of under-Dimly I was fairly sure I'd reached the point of being uncertain which way left was, let alone south.

We stopped just short of where our tunnel intersected with another, a drain over the meeting point shedding grey light. It had started to rain in the outside world, and water dripped softly through the grate. I hoped we weren't going to get flooded out.

I kept my head low, so my ears didn't scrape the roof, and said to the she-rat, "Thanks for helping me out."

"Well, you yelling about the place wasn't doing us any good. And you might be useful."

"Fair enough." I lifted one paw, shook it off, then put it back in the same muck with a sigh. "I did have some crackers, but I dropped them."

"We've no use for crackers," she said. "What're you doing around here, searching for rats?"

"My name's Gobbelino. May your whiskers be soft and—"

"Save it," she said. "We've no use for flowery greetings, either. I'm Patsy. Ernie's my second." She nodded at the three-pawed old rat, who nodded back comfortably. "Now, what were you about?"

"Well, I tend to have a pretty good relationship with rats," I said. "I always find rats know all there is to know about everything worth knowing, so I was looking for a little local knowledge."

Patsy just waited, looking at me with that involuntary sneer on her face, although I had the feeling she might have looked the same even without the scar. Apparently flattery does not get you as many places as you'd think. Not among Dimly rats, anyway.

"I tried to do a bit of poking around myself," I said. "But the no cats thing makes it all a bit difficult."

"So does the no rat thing," Ernie said. "We're the last pack left. But we won't let them run us out. It's a matter of principle." He nodded firmly, and there were a few supportive mutters from the other rats. I wasn't sure all of them were there for the principle. Some of them looked more like they were there for the scrap. They were a motley lot, some still with the soft unformed look of juveniles, others almost as doddery as old Ernie. One was heavily pregnant, and she lay flopped on her side while still giving me the hard stare. And there were more missing toes and scarred backs than you'd expect to see at your average neighbourhood dogfight.

"This is all of you?" I asked. "*All* of Dimly's rats?"

"This is it," Patsy said. "And the cat population just

went above zero for the first time in probably three years."

I blinked at her. "*Three years?* They've been keeping cats out that long?"

"The last one vanished around then. There haven't been any more."

"But that makes no sense. I know pockets are self-governing, but the Watch still like to keep their nose in. They wouldn't just let a pocket drive out all the cats and not look into it."

She shrugged. "We sent a couple of messages when ... well, you'll see."

"*You* contacted the Watch?"

She regarded me with her one good eye, reflecting the light from the drain. "There's more going on here than absent cats. I thought that the Watch might want to know about it, but it seems not."

"What sort of more?" I asked.

"We'll show you, Mogs. What were you looking for, anyway?"

"Unicorns," I said, waiting for them to laugh, but Patsy just nodded. Seemed like I was the only person who still thought they were extinct. Or had.

"They're not here," she said, and I said something that made the younger rats giggle.

"Sorry," I said. "It's just that we've been chasing this damn case. Stolen unicorns and missing sisters and all sorts. It's the only reason I'm here."

"The unicorn trade started up again around the time everything changed," Ernie said. "The herd isn't here, though. Just the dust and hair comes through."

"Dammit. Look, I'm sorry about this. I never meant to call attention to you like that."

"Well, you did," Patsy said. "And it's not like they don't know we're here. They just can't catch us."

"Can't catch us, can't scare us, can't buy us," a young rat with a broken tail said, and chuckled. "We're just *vermin.*" A cheer went up at that, and more delighted laughter, and I arched my whiskers at Patsy.

"This place," she said, and shook her head. "It all changed a few years ago. They got the new mayor in, and then it was all, oh, let's get rid of the *undesirables.*"

"Little things at first," Ernie said. "Move the cats on, because no one wants the Watch in their business."

"I still don't see how the Watch let that happen," I said.

"Well, they did," Patsy replied. "And the mayor's people cleared out anyone who disagreed with the new way of things. Brought in curfews. Taxes. All for the *protection of the town.*" Her sneer deepened. "The birds are everywhere, spying on everything. Any dissent, and if those feathered mutts can't deal with it, they send something that can." She raised a paw to the twisted skin of her face. "Most people stopped disagreeing after the first few protests were dealt with. Almost everyone's a part of the operation now. They're either producing, selling, or using what this town produces, and the rot's so deep it'll just keep spreading."

"Already started," Ernie said. "They're shipping product up and down river, and out in trucks."

"Drugs?" I asked.

"Among other things," Patsy said. "And no one does anything."

"Except us," Ernie said. "We do what we can."

"*Vermin,*" the young rat said again, earning himself a chant of *ver-min, ver-min* from the others.

"What do you do?" I asked.

"Sabotage, mostly," Patsy said. "We chew through wiring, bring down the lights in the storehouses and the mayor's precious humidifiers. Get into the warehouse and break bindings and nibble through seals. Whatever we can, really. It's not a lot, but it adds up."

"Anarchy is still anarchy, no matter how small," Ernie said, cleaning his whiskers.

I was even more certain than before that I wanted to stay on the right side of Patsy's anarchist crew. I also wanted to get the hell out of here and tell Callum the unicorns weren't in Dimly, but there was more going on here than just that. We'd dealt with zombies only a few months ago, actual, real, eat-you-alive zombies. And the Watch hadn't been interested. In fact, Claudia, the lovely but slightly alarming Watch-but-not-entirely-Watch lieutenant, had thought someone high up in the council might have had a hand in cooking up zombie juice. And the also lovely but even more alarming sorcerer, Ms Jones, had agreed.

I saw brownie points ahead if I could find out a little more. And given that Claudia was about the only thing keeping the Watch proper from flinging me back to the beasts of the Inbetween, brownie points seemed handy. The fact that Claudia's mismatched eyes gave me shivers was *nothing* to do with it. Plus, the happier Ms Jones was with me, the less likely I was to end up turned into a smoked haddock. So, win-win.

I licked my shoulder absently, getting a mouthful of Cerberus drool and drain scum. I spluttered and tried to wipe my tongue on my chest, not that it was in much better condition.

"You alright there, Mogs?" Patsy asked.

"Ugh. Yes. Just connecting a few dots."

"Well, connect them on the move. Don't want to sit in one place for too long down here."

"Do I want to know why?" I asked.

"Probably not," she said, and the rats started to move.

"Hang about – where are we going?"

She paused to look at me while the other rats moved on. "You want to find out more about your missing unicorns? I can show you what's being done with the horn. And then you can take it to the Watch. We're the only resistance this place has, and we need help. We'll show you what the town is dealing in, what it's building." Her lip twisted further. "But you'll need to get your paws dirty."

I looked at my filthy feet, then back up at her, deciding not to tell her that the Watch and I weren't exactly on speaking terms. It seemed unhelpful. "Well, they can't get dirtier."

"Come on then, Mogs. Welcome to the resistance." And she was gone, running so fast and light that I had to sprint to keep up, dirty water splashing into my lowered nose as my paws slid on the slimy bottom, and the way grew narrower and darker and more and more treacherous, and I was so lost there was no way I was getting out on my own.

PATSY TOOK THE LEAD, running fast and sure through the secret mesh of tunnels and drains that underlay Dimly. She shot around turns and hooked through bends without hesitating, never pausing directly under a grate, stopping at the occasional intersection to sniff the air and place her paws on the greasy stone, feeling for vibrations. Once we waited while a surge of sudsy, bloodied water rushed through a drain that crossed ours, and twice we hunkered down in silence as something slithered and panted its way through an unseen junction.

"D'wyrms," a broken-tailed juvenile whispered to me. He had a scar on his haunches and he limped, but it didn't seem to slow him down. None of them were slow, not even the pregnant queen, and my legs ached from too long in tunnels that forced me into a half-crouch.

"The worms?" I asked.

"*D'*wyrms. No eyes, lots of teeth. Fast. Follow scents through the drains. They made them to track us, but turns out they're not so good at differentiating between fresh and old scents. So long as you keep quiet, they'll go past."

"Oh."

"Yeah. You don't want them to hear you. They'll tear in one end and out the other, quicker than you can think."

"Oh," I breathed, and wondered if it would be a diplomatic breach to ask him to stop the nature lesson, then. A moment later we were running again.

I decided at least three times that I couldn't take it anymore, that I was just going to have to beg Patsy to point me in the right direction and I'd straggle back to

Callum with nothing to show for it but a nasty taste in my mouth and some matted fur. The first time I almost gave up was when my legs were screaming with oncoming cramp after a particularly long, low tunnel that I had to tip-toe through with my legs at strange angles. My next almost-breaking point came when we plunged into a sewer where I could at least run upright, but I missed the ledge on the side and fell into the stinking, flotsam-strewn water below. Something *totally* touched my paw, and the only thing that stopped me screaming the place down was the thought that the d'wyrms would all come flocking to me. Well, that and the snickering rats. I just hoped it hadn't been an eel. I *hate* eels.

And now I was seriously considering giving up again as we raced through increasingly low and narrow passageways, the floor rough enough to tear at the sodden pads of my paws, the sides wet and slick with moss and dark growth. It was too dark to see more than the racing, furry rump of the rat in front of me, and the air was so thick with stale humidity I could barely breathe. The gouges from yesterday's crow attack were stinging with the filth that had been rubbed into them, and my bumped nose hurt to breathe through, and all I wanted was a warm bed and a large bowl of custard, whatever promises I might have made about giving it up. I'd been under duress, after all.

Just as I was about to flop to my belly and declare they'd have to overthrow Dimly without me, light started creeping in from ahead of us, and I suddenly had my feet among the rats rather than behind them.

"Sorry," I whispered to a young female whose tail I'd

almost stood on. She just bared her teeth at me. We slowed more, then finally came to a stop. The rats weren't even breathing hard, and I tried to get my own breath under control. Look, cats are more sprinters than endurance runners, okay?

"Mogs," Patsy said, her voice low, and I shuffled past the rest of the pack to hunker down next to her. Blue-white, unnatural light crept around us, the sort thrown by fluorescent tubes, and she had her nose to a split in the plasterboard. She looked up at me. "Can you fit through here?"

I examined it, and pawed the edges. It crumbled easily enough. "I'll manage. What's out there?"

"Come see." She vanished into the stark light, and I shouldered my way through after her, having to scrabble on my belly while the plasterboard scraped my ribs and spine.

"Better knock off the chicken nuggets," someone said behind me, and there was a ripple of laughter.

I growled, pushed harder, and forced my way out onto a hard concrete floor, bringing a shower of dust with me. A pallet piled with a pyramid of fat orange pumpkins sat directly in front of me, held in place with netting and straps. Off to one side were more pallets, these ones piled with boxes that had been labelled in some sort of Cyrillic, with an English translation of *"Nappies"* underneath. I was willing to bet that the quotation marks were entirely appropriate, especially as one box had split and there were small, clawed footprints running away from it. Off to the other side were neatly stacked urns of the sort humans put their loved ones' ashes in, and in which, in a place like this, sorcerers stored the shrunken corpses of their enemies.

I took a couple of cautious steps toward the pumpkins, one of which snapped open pale eyes and bared some substantial fangs at me, which I was fairly sure wasn't usual pumpkin behaviour. I ignored it and joined Patsy, peering around the corner of the pallets into a cavernous warehouse. The roof soared twice as high as a regular ceiling, and huge racks of shelving stretched off into the distance, packed with things that smelled of strange places and curious power, of packing tape and preserving oils and dust.

"This place is *huge,*" I whispered.

"And there are four halls like this," she said. "They could supply the whole country."

"Supply them with what?" I glanced at a pumpkin that was straining a fleshy tongue festooned with seeds toward Patsy. "Carnivorous pumpkins?"

"Magic carpets. Living statues. Mixed herbs. Dead things in oil. Live things in jars. Also snacks."

"Snacks?"

"Dried earwax. Cheese straws. That sort of thing."

I wrinkled my nose. "And unicorn dust, I guess."

"Oh, sure. They've got a whole locked, airtight office for the drugs. Even we can't get into that one. But that's not what I want to show you." She waved at the other rats, who spread out and started clawing at packing straps and gnawing on boxes.

"Is that wise?" I asked, imagining an avalanche of snarling pumpkins and nastier things chasing us down the alleys between the pallets.

"We don't release anything. Just weaken stuff up so that when they get moved ..." she trailed off, her sneer deepening.

Well, I don't know what I expected from pocket-sized anarchists. "Cool," I said.

"Come on." She scurried off, racing across the broad, open floors and diving into the shadow of the shelving. I followed her at a sprint while things twisted and chattered above us, pushing desperately at their bonds. Once a basket tumbled off the stacks, bouncing past us with something hissing furiously inside. I hissed back, but Patsy ignored it, and we ran on through the harsh light and shadows of the underground warehouse.

It felt like forever before she came to a stop in the cover of a patchily shrink-wrapped pyramid of sarcophagi. Things were moaning waspishly inside them, and judging by the eye-watering stink the preservation technique hadn't exactly been up to the Pharaoh's exacting standards. I stepped over a desiccated finger and followed Patsy's gaze to a section of the huge shelving racks that were encased behind heavy metal bars.

"Is that for the really rowdy products?" I asked.

"No," she said. "Is the padlock on the outside?"

I peered across the aisle, spotting a heavy padlock as big as my head, firmly latched closed. "Yeah."

"Good. That means no one's inside. Let's go." And she raced across the floor and dived between the bars.

I followed her, my stomach tight and my matted tail doing its best to stand to attention. The whole place was a swamp of magic charms and ugly power, but what was seeping through the bars of the enclosure was blood-stained and ugly, full of hungry, pointless anger, like the stink leaking from our local pub late on a Friday night.

I slipped through the bars, my breathing shallow and fast, and gazed around at the shelves of racked boxes and the crowded hooks on the walls. The labels were stark as a wound. *UH knives. UH pellets. UH arrowheads. UH spear-heads. UH sabres.*

"UH?" I said, as if Patsy might tell me it meant *Ultra-Happy* or something like that, something that would contradict the crossbows hung on the walls and the banded forests of spears with heads that glittered and shone with a soft, self-satisfied luminescence.

"What do you think, Mogs? Can't you smell it?"

I was trying not to. I could smell grease and steel and leather and old blood that won't wash off, cursed blades and spears that ate your soul. It was enough. It was more than enough. But it wasn't all. There was a sharper, harder threat, an aching and urgent one. One that shimmered with rainbows and deadly beauty.

"Old Ones take us all," I said softly. "How much is there?" How many unicorn horn weapons, weapons that could kill anything you cared name, that could tear through a cat's nine lives in one stroke? How many weapons that could bring down the world as we knew it?

"I can't count that high. Lots."

"And you tried to tell the Watch?"

"More than once."

My vision was going a bit wonky with the assault of scents and the lingering traces of horn dust, and my heart was way too loud in my ears. "Soggy, hungover, Weetabix. With seeds in."

"What?" Patsy asked, giving me a puzzled look. "Are you alright?"

"Not so much."

And that was the moment when we both heard booted feet striding down the warehouse, and the clatter of heavy keys being tossed from hand to hand.

15

SEVERAL DRAGONS SHORT OF A BARBECUE

THE FOOTSTEPS ADVANCED STEADILY, THEIR ECHOES CUT short by the crowded shelves, and there was no mistaking it. They were coming closer.

Patsy rushed to the bars to peek out, then hissed, "They're in this aisle. We can't get out. Hide!"

"Oh, gods-dammed purple sprouting broccoli with hairballs," I mumbled, and dived under the nearest shelf.

The shelves in the enclosure ran out at right angles from the wall, in some cases forming a U with further shelves set flush with the grey stone, which was perfect for sneaking along unseen. Where I was, though, the wall had been left bare to house all the crossbows and other overly dramatic weapons on hooks, leaving a nasty, exposed stretch of concrete flooring between Patsy and myself. I scooted to where the end of the shelves met the wall, pressing myself against the cool stone and hoping no one was bringing any more Cerberus dogs with them. Or ordinary dogs, for that matter. Although, given the magical stench of the place, it was possible we still could've passed undetected. Patsy waved to me impatiently, but I shook my head at her – the feet were closer now, so I could hear softer steps among the steady bootfalls, and a strange sound that was both slithering and scratching. It made my claws twitch.

"Mogs, come on," Patsy hissed. "There's more cover over here."

I caught a glimpse of movement outside the lock-up, heading for the door, and I hesitated. There was no cover between my shelves and where Patsy crouched, and if they looked in, they'd see me. On the other hand, Patsy was right. Shelves lined the back walls of the aisles beyond her. We could work our way to the far corner and sneak out through the bars.

I crept to the edge of the shelving, the wall of hanging weapons to my left like a monstrous cliff of devastation, and gathered myself to sprint across the gap. Then the footsteps stopped, and a key rattled in the lock, and I backed up. The bars of the lock-up gave a clear view inside, and it wasn't like anyone in this town was going to say, "Aw, look at the kitty! Where did *he* come from?"

People knowing the truth about cats definitely has its disadvantages.

Patsy threw her paws in the air and made some gestures that I think were probably pretty rude in rat-speak, and I gave her a helpless shrug, then a little lifted paw that was intended to mean, *You go on, I'll catch up.*

She made more gestures that left me in no doubt of her opinion of my ability to get out of here on my own.

Which was insulting, but also reassuring. Never mind the warehouse – I'd never find my own way back through the tunnels if she left me.

The door swung open, and I dropped my chin to the floor so I could see as much of the people walking into the room as possible. Slithery-Scratchy didn't come in, which seemed like a good thing. Instead, a pair of beaten-up old trainers scuffed into the room, attached to skinny jeans with turned-up cuffs, and were followed by heavy, well-worn boots that looked like they'd been used for more unpleasant things than just walking. They walked straight down the gap between Patsy's shelves and mine, and I couldn't see more than denim-clad calves and thick khaki trousers pulled down over the boots.

The feet stopped in front of the wall, and Trainers said, "How far off are we?" Her voice was level, if a little tired-sounding.

"About three cases short on the knives, and two on the slingshot pellets. The elves are still being really snotty about those, too. Say they're too modern and there's no art to them."

"They're such bloody princesses, the lot of them," Trainers said. "Never complained about those iPhones I got for them, though, did they?"

"Yeah, well. Those are art, according to them."

Trainers snorted. "Well, we're not getting any further until we can get more dust, anyway. No more luck finding the herd?"

"None. We've been everywhere. We'd have caught them at the locks if they'd gone by boat, and the stupid things would kick a truck apart in five minutes. They're just *gone*."

"A herd of moody bloody horses doesn't just vanish. They've got be around here somewhere still."

"Not that we've found," Boots said. "No progress from the herd keeper?"

"Art's useless. I thought the finger might hurry him up a bit, but nothing."

Boots chuckled. "That was so dramatic."

"So Kara, you mean?"

"That's the one."

I tipped my head as I considered that, and a flurry of movement caught my attention. I blinked at Patsy, who seemed to be doing star jumps in the confines of the shelves.

I wriggled my ears at her. *What?*

She pointed her nose. *Behind you.*

I froze, the conversation of Trainers and Boots suddenly an awfully long way off as my sodden fur tried to go in any direction it could. From behind me came the clear, unmistakable sound of clicking claws. I stretched one back leg sideways, thinking I'd put my back to the wall again, and the clicking got louder. I stopped, then, breath harsh in my chest, I carefully twisted enough that I could see what dread thing the warehouse had conjured up. Over-sized earwigs, perhaps. Armoured stink beetles. It could be anything.

Googly eyes on stalks stared back at me, and a truly enormous claw clicked just next to my tail. A smaller claw tapped the floor thoughtfully, as if considering how best to skin me, and eight chitinous legs shifted softly, bristles giving them a fuzzy outline in the low light under the shelves. The thing was at least twice my size, and I wasn't entirely sure how it had managed to squeeze itself under here, but it wasn't the only one. There were two more to either side of it, staggered like backup dancers.

We stared at each other, the unicorn dust making my head swim, and I recited every human and Folk swear-word I could remember in my head. The crab clicked its big claw at me, the sound almost thunderous. Behind me, and a million miles away, Boots and Trainers continued their conversation.

"Has the mayor got wind of anything yet?" Boots asked.

"I don't think so. She's turning out to be a bit more perceptive than I thought, though. The other day she was asking why the town's so quiet, and why there's never any visitors." Trainers took a couple of steps back toward the door, pausing to look at something further along the shelf.

"Tricky," Boots said, following her.

"Yeah, I just told her it wasn't tourist season, but it's not going to last. She keeps saying we're not achieving the goals we agreed to when she was elected."

I curled my tail carefully away from the crabs. They watched it go, but didn't move.

"Doesn't have to last that long, though, does it?" Boots asked.

"No. Get this shipment in, then we can just take the town back. No one'll be arguing."

"Be a bit silly to," Boots said with a chuckle, and the crab poked my hindquarters with its claw, like a farmer checking the meat on a cow. I bolted, flinging myself out from under the shelf and sprinting for Patsy. The crabs scuttled after me, spiny feet clattering furiously on the hard floor, and I slid under the opposite shelf so fast I almost collected the rat in my front paws. She hissed at me and took off, keeping to the shelter of the shelves along the back wall.

"What the *hell?*" Trainers demanded behind us. "Crabs?"

Well, at least she hadn't said *cat.*

"They look like coconut crabs," Boots said. "I saw them in a documentary once. Freaky things."

"We don't have coconuts," Trainers said.

"We could," Boots pointed out. "When was the last time you checked the back rooms?"

Trainers didn't answer that, and I wasn't as concerned about the logistics of the coconut crabs as I was with how *fast* they were. I glanced back, and tried to push myself into a sprint. The monstrous things looked like they were gaining, and the shelves were forcing me to run in a weird crouch that made my muscles scream, Patsy pulling away from me as she headed for the end of the lock-up.

Patsy shot through the bars and looked back at me, her one clear eye bright and anxious. She waved me on, stealing little glances in every direction, and I put everything I had into a final burst of hunched, desperate speed. Patsy spun and pelted across the open floor, tiny and vulnerable in the vast expanse of the warehouse. I slipped through the bars, spotting a giant lizard by the door, straining against a leash that was tied to the gate. It hissed at us.

I sprinted after Patsy as the crabs clattered into the frame of the lock-up and forced themselves through the bars, and we put the pallet of stacked sarcophagi between us and them just as another enormous lizard appeared around the corner of the pallet in front of us. It stared at us, then lunged forward with its long tongue flickering hungrily over ragged yellow teeth. Patsy veered toward the sarcophagi, grimly silent as she scampered up the shrink-wrapped stack, and the lizard surged up on its hind legs as it snapped for her. I flung myself at the creature, hitting its face hard enough to send it off target, then jumped after Patsy. I reached her in two leaps, grabbing her by the scruff of the neck and carrying her with me as I raced for the top. I'd got a good look at the lizard's claws. Climbing was not going to be a problem.

We pelted to the summit of the stack and I dropped Patsy, spinning to confront the lizard I was certain was right on our tails. But the slope of our little refuge was empty. We peered down, and spotted the creature still on the ground, a coconut crab attached to each of its front paws and another in its mouth. It was alternately trying to flick the things off its paws and shaking the one in its mouth way a dog shakes a toy.

"Cool," I said.

"Not for long," Patsy replied, and nodded toward the lock-up. I flattened myself to the sarcophagus as a big man appeared with the lizard that had been tied up at the lock-up. It was tugging at the leash and sweeping huge front paws through the air as it tried to reach its buddy. Behind them was a tall, loose-limbed woman in skinny jeans and trainers, moving with a slouching grace that felt oddly familiar.

"Ugh. They really are freaky," Trainers said, examining the crab-beleaguered lizard below us. "Deal with them, will you? I need to go and make sure her swampy honour hasn't got bored and read some emails she shouldn't. Or ended up talking to Kara."

Boots snorted. "Good luck on that."

Trainers scowled at him. "How come you get to play with attack lizards and I have to people-wrangle?"

"Because you're the smart one," Boots said, and gingerly unclipped the leash. The lizard spun around, stood on its hind legs (making it almost as tall as the humans, who jumped back), *hissed,* then spun around to deal with the crabs.

"Seriously, ugh," Trainers said, as the lizard snatched a crab up with a crunch.

"Mogs," Patsy said, her voice soft.

"What?" I turned, finding that she'd crept away to the other side of the stack and was peering down. "Oh, tell me it's more crabs. Or bunnies. Cuddly, fluffy bunnies."

"Nope," she said.

I joined her, and we stared down at three more enormous lizards cruising around the bottom of the pallet like four-legged sharks. One looked up, hissed, and started to climb.

"Hairballs," I said. Even from here, I could see its teeth, and there was scratching coming from around the corner of the stack. I ran to check it. Another lizard there, and I was willing to bet that if there wasn't one on the third side already, there would be soon. We were surrounded.

"Demon snot of Anglesey," Patsy said in a conversational tone.

I looked at her. "Do you trust me?"

"Not really."

"That's fair," I said, and as the first lizard muscled its way to the top of the stack I grabbed her and jumped.

I LAUNCHED myself almost straight up, which isn't exactly an easy feat even without a full-grown rat dangling from your jaws. But the sarcophagi were stacked high, and I didn't have far to go. I snagged the hanging fluorescent light with my front paws, stomach churning as my claws screeched on the metal casing. I slid helplessly, straining to find a grip, then came to a precarious halt as my claws found a seam. I dangled there with Patsy in my jaws, my heart hammering while the hissing of a single lizard became a chorus below us, and hoped Trainers and Boots had gone. I didn't fancy anyone trying out their flashy new weapons on me. The light swung on its chains, scattering dust on my snout, and I tried not to sneeze.

"Genius," Patsy said. "Now what?"

"*Mmmph,*" I said, because if I said anything else I was going to drop her.

"Obviously," she said, and wriggled. "I'm going to climb up." She dug her paws into the fur of my forelegs, and a moment later the weight was off my jaw. I released my mouthful of rat fluff, and she scrambled up to the top of the light, her tail slapping my nose and almost making me let go. The hissing underneath was a good reminder not to, though. She found her balance and peered down at me. "Coming up?"

I looked past my splayed back paws at the sarcophagi stack. There were five lizards crowded onto the very top, and as I watched one slipped and fell into another, which turned on the first with snapping teeth and those awful, rending claws. The first returned the attack, and the two of them swayed together for a moment then plunged off the side, still tussling as they tumbled all the way to the ground. Trainers had vanished, but the big guard was trying to fend off the coconut crabs, who'd evidently decided he was an easier target than the lizards.

"Help!" he yelled, the shout deadened by the laden shelves. "Hey, help? Anyone?"

Well, at least he wasn't looking at us.

"Up rather than down, I think," I said, and kicked my back legs up.

But there was no grip for them. I couldn't get the same angle as I had with my front paws, couldn't snag the seam on the light casing, and there was nothing else to help me haul myself up. My claws felt like they were tearing from the beds, and a tremble of fatigue was setting into my shoulders. I glanced down again, hoping the rest of the lizards had suddenly fallen off or lost interest, but they were still there, all massive teeth and tiny eyes. One of them hissed at me hungrily.

"Old Ones take you, you overgrown skinks," I grumbled.

"Komodo dragons," Patsy said, peering down at me.

"They don't look anything like dragons, and none of them's so much as suggested a barbecue."

She narrowed her good eye at me. "It's a human name, not a proper one."

"Don't they remember what dragons look like?"

"Evidently not." She examined me again. "Are you stuck?"

"Well, I'm not hanging out just to build my front body strength."

"Huh." She put a paw on the chain, looking up to see where it connected to the ceiling. She shook her head and trotted to check the other one, her steps making the whole light swing. I tried another little pull-up, but it was even weaker than the first one. Patsy wandered back, looked down at me, and said, "Hang on."

I considered pointing out that I didn't have much choice in the matter, but I needed all my breath. I ordered my aching muscles to keep my claws digging in, and there was a rattle of ratty paws above me, galloping the length of the light. It rocked gently, and I wailed, "What're you *doing?*"

Patsy didn't reply, just kept running, one end of the light to the other, and the rocking grew more pronounced, starting to settle into a pendulum motion. It was small at first, but as she ran steadily the motion grew, moving into a low arc that almost threw me off as I was jerked through the change of directions.

"Patsy! You're going to throw me off!"

"Just don't let go until you're going *forward*," she called back, still running.

I had about half a second to decide which way forward was, then the claws of my left paw jerked free. I yelped, clinging on with my aching right paw until the end of the arc. And then I had no choice. The motion tore me off the light and sent me tumbling through the still, stinking air of the warehouse, the lizards hissing their fury behind me and my limbs splaying of their own accord as I rolled into the fall and hoped that whatever I landed on would be un-alive, un-toothed, and un-hungry.

16

A ROUT IS JUST AN ENTHUSIASTIC RETREAT

I ARCHED INTO THE FALL, TWISTING TO SPOT MY LANDING, the motion more instinct than thought. I was plunging toward an enormous stack of rolled carpets that steamed magic like a warm spring on a cold day, and I just hoped they were unshaped ones. The last thing we needed was to unleash a flock of flying attack carpets, and if they were home security ones I didn't fancy tumbling straight through into a prison made of stitching. Then the moment for thought was gone, and I hit hard enough that my joints shook and my belly bottomed out, the rugs less soft than one would imagine.

I huffed air and looked for Patsy, glimpsing a tiny blur of movement right before a faint thud came from higher up the stack. I scampered over the rolls and found her wedged between a fat, dull carpet that looked uncomfortably as though it were woven from the hair of unwilling donors (there were some nasty stains on it), and a slimmer, fluffy roll that was all the pinks of a princess party. The rat was motionless.

"Patsy?" I whispered. She didn't move, but I could see her sides flaring with urgent breath. I took a peek back at the warehouse. Big Man was shouting somewhere out of sight, someone answering him, and the Komodos had scrambled off the sarcophagi to the floor. They were hissing and clawing at each other as they cast about for our scent.

I pawed Patsy carefully out from the gap between the carpets, in case she suddenly got sucked in by one, and nudged her with my nose. She flopped like an empty glove.

A scamper of claws of the floor below made me look back, and I sighed. The lizards were scurrying toward us at a completely unreasonable speed, and Trainers was laying about the crabs that were still attacking Boots with what looked very much like one of the unicorn horn spears. Boots was shouting at her to be careful, and he shrieked every time she swung. She was swearing at him as much as at the critters. They hadn't even glanced at us, but we had the full attention of the Komodos.

"Hairballs," I said, to no one in particular, and picked Patsy up by the scruff of the neck again, my jaws aching in protest. She didn't react, and with a last look at the Komodos I headed down the opposite side of the stack.

I made the floor in two enormous bounds, and took off at a flat-out sprint – well, as close as I could get to one, anyway. A roar of excited grunts and hisses went up behind me, and when I risked a glance back the lizards were gaining fast. A couple of them were running on their hind legs with their forelegs flexed like bodybuilders, while the rest galloped rather more conventionally, their teeth on alarming, drooling display and their claws looking like they could tear a hole in the world. And they were *fast*. I wasn't going to outrun them, and Trainers was shouting for more guards to come, that something was in the building, while Boots screamed that he'd lost a toe.

A pallet of unlabelled boxes reared up in front of me, and I launched myself up it without pausing to think what might be in them. The cardboard shifted uneasily under my feet, feeling thin and untrustworthy, and I hoped the creatures followed me up rather than having the brains to circle the bottom. I mean, you can't have bad luck *all* the time, right?

I raced up the stack as boxes tore and crushed behind me under the assault of the lizards. I allowed myself a moment of triumph, and paused at the top to look back. The creatures were trying to reach me, but the boxes were collapsing under their weight, and as I watched one plunged through the weak cardboard like it was tissue paper. The lizard reared back, trying to pull its forelegs free, but something had hold of it, and an angry buzzing was starting to rise around us, humming in a way that shook my bones.

More human shouting was going up now, and a couple of men, one of them even bigger than Boots, appearing around the shelving and ran toward us. Trainers ran after them, stopping short as soon as she saw the torn boxes.

"Stop!" she yelled. "Jesus – don't go near that lot. Call off the lizards! Hurry!"

The men kept their distance, and started to yell for the Komodos to get down like they were trained dogs or something. Neither the humming nor Trainers' warning seemed like a good sign, and I scampered down the opposite side of the stack before anything could try to eat us, Patsy still swinging like a dead weight. I didn't pause again until I was well away from the boxes, then checked back to see two Komodos still struggling after us. One was all but lost under a web of fine, dusty strands, barely twitching, while the other fought on with minuscule insects spinning and roaring around it, singing the sort of soporific song that brings sweet and deadly sleep to every kind. A third lizard tumbled wearily from the top of the stack all the way to the floor, the insects surging joyfully after it to spin their cocoon. I had a feeling there wouldn't be a butterfly emerging from it.

Which got rid of a few lizards, but there were still several unaccounted for, plus the humans. And at least one of them was waving a unicorn horn weapon. I chose what speed I had left over evasive action and raced across the open floor to the shadow of the shelving. I sprinted straight down the edge of the aisles, not looking back, running as hard as I could while clawed feet skittered after me and my heart rose in my ears and my vision swam with exhaustion. I pushed harder as I reached the end of the racks of shelves, leaving them behind and plunging toward the pallets of toothy pumpkins, aware of the huge, bare space around me, bereft of shelter and defence as the feet behind me thundered closer.

Patsy shifted in my grip, and I willed myself not to drop her, not to stumble, not to fall. I didn't dare look back. If the guards had seen me, it was too late to do anything. And the clawed feet were so close now that I could smell the sort of breath that reminds you toothpaste is a foreign concept to many species that could actually do with it.

The floor stretched out empty and featureless, and I swear the pallets were drawing away from me. I stumbled, heard a hiss of delight that all but ruffled the fur of my neck, and Patsy bellowed, *"Drop 'em!"*

I just about dropped *her,* and someone shouted, *"Incoming!"* which was all very well, but unless they were incoming on time machines they weren't going to reach us before those reeking teeth did.

"Let me go," Patsy snapped. "Hurry!"

I didn't even protest. My mouth fell open almost of its own accord, and somewhere I found the energy to leap over her as she dropped to her feet. It wasn't pretty, and it wasn't graceful, but suddenly I was running faster and she was a sleek ball of pure speed tearing away from me at a right angle, making the Komodos stumble into each other as they all tried to go in a different direction.

And then the pumpkins fell. The netting floated down from the top of the pyramid, releasing an orange tidal wave of jack-o'-lantern fury, teeth sprouting in wide, hungry mouths and empty eye sockets flaring with hunger. They tumbled and cracked and sometimes smashed to bits on the floor as they washed toward us, scattering the place with seeds and pumpkin innards. Tendrils were sprouting from their stalks and skittering off ahead of their round orange bodies like spiderwebs. I squawked and swerved away, heading for the back wall and hoping Patsy was already there. Rats leaped down the intact netting at the base of the half-destroyed stack and poured across the floor, squeaking in furious triumph.

I skidded to a stop before I reached the hole in the wall, letting the rats go in first. The Komodos were spitting and snarling and uttering guttural, growling barks, still trying to struggle forward against the snapping flood. The pumpkins were rolling under their own power as much as the fall now, and they were using their tendrils to haul themselves along. As I watched, one wrapped a vine around a smaller pumpkin and flung it at a Komodo like a little shrieking missile. It hit the lizard's shoulder and latched onto it with whatever weird little pumpkin teeth it had, and as the creature tried to shake it off, more rushed in around its paws. The pumpkins were piling up into angry avalanches, swamping the lizards and bouncing off shoulders and heads and haunches with gleeful abandon. The guards had run up behind the Komodos but stopped before they reached the oncoming attack of the pumpkins, looking worried. I didn't blame them.

I peered around, looking for Patsy among the sleek brown bodies flooding back into the walls, but I couldn't see her. Ernie was huddled in the centre of the floor, halfway to the destroyed pallets, checking everyone had made it back. My stomach twisted, thinking of the size of her amid the onslaught of ravenous pumpkins on one side and the raging lizards on the other.

Ernie turned and loped back toward me.

"Patsy?" I called. "Patsy!"

He waved at me. "Get in, hurry up!"

"But—"

"*Hurry!* You're not helping anyone out here!"

I took a step toward the wall, still scanning the wreckage, and Trainers shouted, "Goddamn *rats!*"

No one was moving beyond Ernie but the pumpkins, and the Komodos were shaking them off now, tearing the vines with their talons and ploughing through the bouncing orange globes toward us, yellow teeth bare and furious.

"That's a *cat!*" someone else shouted, and I thought it might be Boots. Something whispered over me, and a crossbow bolt embedded itself in the wall just above my ears. I ducked with a hiss.

"Get *in!*" Ernie bellowed, nipping one of my paws.

I flinched, but didn't move, still scanning the floor, poised to jump forward and … and what? Collect a body?

Another bolt hit the wall above me, and a blur of furred movement broke from the pumpkin pallet and raced across the floor to us. Patsy, running hard with her whiskers flared and her ears back.

"What're you waiting for, you broken sausage?" she yelled. "Get in, go, go!"

Ernie dived past me, but I waited for her, unwilling to leave her out here on her own. She glanced at me out of her good eye as she went past and said, "Move it, Mogs. Unless you want to find your own way back."

I dived after her as a final bolt hit the floor where my feet had been, leaving the raging Komodos to their hungry pumpkins.

We didn't pause inside the tunnel. The rats headed off at the same hectic pace as before with me stumbling and splashing along behind, my shoulders aching and my joints creaking, too tired to even care about the muck splashing up in my face and squidging between my toes. The dark pressed down around us, and all was racing paws and quick harsh breath and the nagging worry over being spotted.

A cat, sniffing around unicorn horn weapons, which was bad enough in this place, but could it lead back to Callum? Not in theory, but it led to the other thing that was bothering me. Trainers' casual mention of Kara and her finger. She'd hardly sounded like a kidnapper talking about her victim – not that I had a lot of experience in how kidnappers talked, admittedly, but it still felt weird. Kara had begged Art to find Callum. And now Kara was on first name basis with the kidnappers. It didn't sit right. And that was without the fact that the mayor didn't seem to be as in charge as we'd thought. None of it was adding up, and I was too tired, anyway. I couldn't have solved a maze for cheese, let alone x for y, when x is who the hell knows what and y is why did we even take this case.

I struggled on, barely paying attention to where I put my feet, slipping on greasy lichen and wading through filthy water, bumping my shoulders on sharp corners and stumbling on unseen edges. All that mattered was keeping up with the rats. Everything else could wait.

I was so worried about not falling behind that I tripped over the closest rat as they came to a stop.

"Sorry," I said, and he gave me a disapproving look.

Patsy made her way back to me. We'd stopped at a

relatively large junction, dimly lit by the dull light from a grate a couple of metres away. Fresh water dripped from a cracked pipe, and the rats were taking turns drinking from it. I licked my chops and looked at Patsy.

"Alright?" I asked.

"Bit of a sore neck," she said, her tone mild. "Thanks for the lift."

"Thanks for the save on the light."

She inclined her head, then said, "I didn't expect company. You see why I've been trying to tell the Watch about it, though?"

"Definitely. I can't believe they don't care. That amount of weaponry ..." I couldn't even begin to describe it. That was a war waiting to happen, and it was all being made for some unknown buyer. Someone was stocking up.

"Well, you can tell them now. Being a cat and all."

I sighed, too tired to lie. "The thing is, I don't have the best relationship with the Watch."

"What?"

I was suddenly aware of all the little eyes and sharp teeth around me. "We've had some ... professional disagreements."

Patsy examined me. "So I just dragged you across half Dimly and through a lizard-infested warehouse *for nothing?*" Without seeming to move, the circle of rats felt a little tighter.

"Um. No. No, look, I do know someone. She's a lieutenant, actually. Watch lieutenant. Yes. I can tell her."

"Well, off you go, then."

The rats all looked at me expectantly. I licked my

chops again. "Ah, I can't do that. I mean, shift locks on the town, you know."

Patsy looked at Ernie, and they both gave that soft rat titter. "We *know,*" Patsy said. "We're in a pocket. Every pocket's shift-locked for privacy."

"Oh. Right." I was sure her sneer was more pronounced.

"You can't shift, can you?"

I sighed. "One of those professional disagreements ended badly."

"Never mind," Patsy said, and nodded at the drain. "Through there, and you're not far from the edge. There's a culvert that runs almost all the way out of town. You'll be fine."

I blinked at her, aware the tension around me had eased. I was starting to suspect that Dimly rats had a strange sense of humour. "Oh. Okay. Will you be alright?"

"We're always alright," she said. "And that really gave them something to clean up today."

A murmur of satisfied agreement ran through the rats, and a small chant of *ver-min, ver-min* followed it.

"Anarchy," Ernie said, shaking a small fist.

"Good for the soul," I said, and touched my nose to his paw.

"Watch how you go, Mogs," Patsy said. "And get word to your lieutenant. I'd hate to have wasted my time on you." She winked, and then they were gone, shadows fading into the deeper dark of the tunnels. I stayed where I was for a moment, then turned and padded toward the light.

I NOSED my way out from behind the grate and found it let directly into a culvert that ran along a skinny lane with backyards to either side. It wasn't entirely covered over, and my spine itched with the exposure, but there were enough walkways laid over it and weeds tangled above it that I could hobble along in reasonable cover, the grey day spitting drizzle. Not that it mattered. I was dripping wet, and caked in so much muck I felt about a kilo heavier than I had that morning. Which was surprising, considering how hungry I was.

The culvert ran a full block, and I paused as the alley intersected a larger road. I could tell from the deepening of the glamour that the edge of town lay to the right, and Patsy hadn't put me wrong. Well-foliaged gardens butted up to the pavement, and I stumbled out of shelter, scrambling up the first fence and doing a cursory check for dogs before dropping to the other side. Anything that tried to bite me right now would probably poison themselves, anyway.

I scaled four more fences before I dropped to the road at the end of the block, checking the sky and the trees warily. Every muscle in my body was screaming with exhaustion, but I didn't dare stop. I crossed the road and gave up on the gardens and their fences, using the parked cars for cover instead as I pushed on toward the edge of the glamour, trying to hurry. I wouldn't be safe as soon as I was out, either. It wasn't like the crows – or worse – couldn't chase me. I wondered how long I'd been. Longer than two hours, I was certain. Art better have waited, or I'd put some claws somewhere sensitive.

I crossed the last road, stumbling through the heavy grip of the glamour like a diver emerging from the sea. It felt reluctant to let me go, tendrils drifting after me and rendering the day hostile and unpleasant. But finally I was through, forcing myself to keep going, knowing I was only a few blocks away from where I'd left Art. It felt like an impossible distance. My jog became a hobble, then a stagger, and finally I stopped, swaying where I stood. I had to rest. *Had* to.

I flopped to my belly in front of a shop with bars on the windows, as heavy as the lock-up. I peered at it, wondering what they were protecting. Probably nothing as dangerous or valuable as what I'd just seen in Dimly. I swallowed hard. I was panting. My feet ached, and my scraped sides burned, and my tail stung, and there was blood on my paws. I stared at them, wanting to clean them, but my tongue was stuck to the roof of my mouth. *I'll close my eyes just for a moment. Just for a moment.*

Rain whispered down on my ears as my eyes drifted closed, and in a distracted way I imagined it might wash me clean. I waited for it to do its work, the world drawing away and becoming heavy and dark and warm, a promise of a peace that could never be.

17

MAD AS A WET CAT

HOT BREATH ON ME, RAW AND HIDEOUS, AND IT WAS THE Komodos, or the Cerberus, or something worse than any of those, something–

I woke with a yowl, leaping away from the toothed maw bearing down on me, and lashed out as hard as my exhausted muscles would allow. I caught a confused Labrador a belt across the snout and it gave a horrified yelp, diving behind a woman's legs. I swayed where I stood, blinking at them both in confusion, and the woman pulled the dog's leash taut, even though it had plainly decided that it was never going near me ever again.

"You horrible creature!" she shouted, and made shooing motions at me.

"Yeah, well, bite me," I said, forgetting we weren't in Dimly anymore.

She stared at me, and the dog whined. "What?"

"Hairballs," I muttered, and wondered how far I could run. Not far, judging by the fact that the ground wouldn't stay still underneath me. The woman took a step forward, and I staggered back, straight into hands that closed around me and scooped me up. I gave a protesting squawk and made a weak attempt to bite whoever would subject me to such undignified treatment, then smelled cigarettes and old books and the musk of secret magic. I collapsed against Callum as he settled me in the crook of one arm.

"I'm so sorry," he said, and I could tell he was using the dimples without even looking.

"Your cat … your cat attacked my dog," the woman said, already doing that human things where they talk themselves out of what their senses tell them.

"I really apologise. He's not allowed out, but he got past me. I've been looking for him all day. Is your dog hurt?" As Callum spoke the dog emerged from behind the woman and shoved its nose into his outstretched hand, wagging its tail happily. I could see a few little dots of blood on its snout, but it stared at Callum adoringly as he scratched its ears.

"I suppose not," the woman said.

"Okay. Sorry again, though." Callum turned and carried me toward the Rover where it sat grumbling wheezily to itself at the kerb. "Jesus Christ, Gobs," he whispered. "You *stink.*"

"Bite me," I said again.

CALLUM STARTED to put me on the passenger seat, then shook his head and set me on the pavement instead.

"*Hey,*" I protested, my legs all but giving way.

"Just hang on." He pulled his coat off and made it into a bed on the seat. "Jesus, you're really in a bad way."

"You should see the other ..." I considered it. "Lizard."

He lifted me onto the coat. "Just stay on there, okay?"

"Sure. It'll only improve your coat," I said, trying to get comfortable. Everything hurt.

"Well, at least my coat can go in the wash, unlike the car."

"Your coat should go in the bin. I intend to stain it dreadfully."

He closed my door and hurried around to the driver's side, folding his long legs in under the wheel. "It's already stained dreadfully. Adds character."

"Is character shorthand for 'makes you look like a dodgy flasher'?" I asked, then yelped as we pulled away from the kerb. "Ow! Take it easy."

He glanced at me, his forehead etched with anxious lines. "Do you need the vet?"

"Gods, no. Don't mention that filthy word." I shifted around. "What's digging into me?"

"My lighter, probably."

"Ugh." I tried to keep my head up so I could look at him, but it was far too heavy. I rested my chin on the crumpled folds of the jacket. "What're you doing here, anyway? Where's Art?"

"He came back an hour ago. You never turned up, and he was worried it'd look suspicious if he hung around. So I've just been driving back and forth on the outskirts, hoping you'd turn up."

"We should have synchronised watches," I mumbled, and he gave me a worried look.

"Are you sure we shouldn't just swing by the vet?"

"*No!* No. I'm just ..." Just what? Tired. Hurt. Hungry. Hungry? "Hungry."

"Well, if you didn't eat the whole time you were in there, it's probably the longest you've gone between meals since birth." He fished the tub of cat treats out of the doorless glovebox and upended it in front of me. "We'll get something better as soon as we're well clear of Dimly."

I was already chowing down on the biscuits, so didn't bother replying. He shook his head and kept us trundling steadily through the quiet streets, putting more and more distance between us and Dimly. Between us and tunnels and lizards and Cerberus dogs and murders of bloody crows and an armoury of magical weaponry that could tear the town – or the world – apart.

SOMEWHERE BETWEEN EATING as many biscuits as I could jam in my mouth at once, and drinking water from an old takeaway coffee cup Callum had wedged between the seats, my head got terribly heavy and the damp day seemed horribly bright, so I closed my eyes *just* for a moment. I was vaguely aware that we stopped at some point, and Callum left me in the car then came back with a bag that smelled of rotisserie chicken. He poked me a couple of times when I didn't get up to investigate, but when I hissed at him he gave up and started the car again, and then there was nothing but the touch of his hand on my back from time to time, as if he were reassuring himself I was still there.

A little later I became aware that the car had started lurching about to the tune of crunching gravel, and I half woke up as Callum climbed out to open the first of the gates.

"Why're we here?" I managed. "Why aren't we going home?"

He grimaced. "Art got another message from the kidnappers. Kara sounds like she's in a pretty bad way. We need to find those unicorns before they do anything more to her."

I licked my chops, trying to remember something desperately important. Something about kidnappers not usually calling their kidnappees by their first names. The words felt complicated, though.

We ground to a halt, and I heard Art's voice outside when Callum swung out of the car. I blinked blearily as Callum opened my door, handed Art the bag with the chicken in it, and scooped me up in my nest of his coat. I didn't even protest the indignity of it as he carted me inside and set me on the table, and when he plucked me out of the jacket I just stared at him like a stunned hamster.

He took two steps, holding me at arm's length, and deposited me in a sink of warm, frothy water.

"Hey!" I bellowed, exploding out of his grip and plunging nose-first into the suds. "Old Ones take you, you suppurating *turnip!*"

"You smell like you've been rolling in the sewers," Callum said, grabbing my sides to stop me climbing out.

"I have!" I wailed, trying to wriggle out of his grip.

Every time I tried to kick him my nose went under the surface. "Let me *go!*"

"You can't clean this off yourself. You'll be sick," Callum said, dolloping water onto my head.

"Stop that!" I twisted away from him, slipped, and gulped a mouthful of foam that set me coughing and spluttering. "What is this *poison?*"

"It's all organic," Art said from the safety of the doorway. I tried to glare at him balefully, but it was hard with gunk in my eyes and foam on my whiskers. "It's safe for cats," he added. "I checked."

"I won't be safe for humans when I get out of here," I muttered, and Callum scooped suds onto my head. "*Hey!*"

"Close your eyes, then," he said, and I bared my teeth at him. "No. Agreement, remember?"

"I call this a serious breach of your side of the deal," I complained, but didn't bite him. "Traitor. Garden weed. Soybean. Blemish on the name of PIs."

"Yeah, yeah. Shut up before you get soap in your mouth."

So I shut my mouth and stood there in undignified silence while he scrubbed mud and slime and nastier things from my fur, leaving me a small, soggy, drowned creature at the end.

I tolerated him towelling me off and examining my torn paws and scraped sides, which he smeared with stinking cream and told me not to lick it off. Finally I sat, still dripping slightly, on the worktop and glared at both men.

"Well? Happy now? Had your fun, have you?"

"Well, I can breathe around you now," Callum said. "So, yeah. It's an improvement."

"Really? I smell like a poodle's behind."

"I don't think so." He placed a bowl on the table and broke some chicken into it. "Come have some proper food."

I looked at the floor, which seemed an unfeasibly long way away, then at Callum. To my surprise, he didn't sigh, just lifted me carefully up and deposited me on the table with the care he usually reserved for books with broken spines.

"Thanks," I said, and investigated the chicken.

"Sure." He found a breadboard and looked at Art, who was still hovering by the door. "Want some chicken?"

"I suppose," Art said, with a glance behind him like he was afraid his own chickens might be watching. He took a chair at the table, pulling it away a little and eyeing me carefully. I bared my teeth at him, perfectly aware I had a scrap of chicken skin dangling from one fang, and he flinched.

"So you couldn't even wait for me," I said.

"I thought it'd look a bit suspicious if I was hanging around. I didn't want to draw attention to you."

"Oh, I got plenty of attention." I licked my chops. "You know what they're using unicorn horn for?"

Art gave me a puzzled look. "Well, trade, I should think."

"Trade? No baby goats, it's *trade*. But what *sort* of trade, is the point." I looked at Callum. "Was he always clueless, or is he just putting it on?"

"Eat your chicken and be nice," Callum said, hacking at a fat red tomato. "Art says Kara was in a bad way."

Art nodded, plucking restlessly at his trousers. "She was. Her hand was all wrapped in a towel, and she said they were being awful to her, and that I *had* to find the unicorns, or who knew what they'd do."

Callum put a loaf of bread on the table, and I shook myself off, scattering it with water droplets. "Jesus, Gobs."

"What?"

He just shook his head and went to get the chicken and tomatoes. "What do you think they're using the horn for, then?"

"Weapons." I kept my gaze on Art as I said it. "Spears, arrowheads, knives, anything you can think of. All smelted with unicorn horn."

There was silence, and Art stared at me, then at Callum. "I didn't … I mean, are you *sure?*"

"Very sure. They've got a huge stockpile. I saw this woman who seemed to be in charge talking to a guard-type about orders. They need more horn to fill the orders. He had a lizard."

"Who was the woman?" Callum asked, apparently not interested in the lizard.

"I don't know. Not the mayor – it sounded like the mayor doesn't even know about it. And I never heard her name. Wore trainers," I added, but this didn't seem to clear anything up. That's the problem with humans – they're always changing what they wear, and then you can't keep track of them.

"I'm not sure if that's better or worse than drugs," Callum said, putting the kettle on.

"The amount of weaponry there? Worse," I said.

"You didn't know," Callum said to Art.

Art shook his head, rubbing his knees with both hands. "I don't really have anything to do with Dimly these days."

"Just send them the horn," I said.

"Um, yeah. Just that."

We both looked at him, and after a moment Callum said, "What was the arrangement?"

"The arrangement?"

"Yes. How did you get the horn to them? How much did they take? How did you keep the Watch off the scent?"

"Oh, that." He fiddled with the bread knife, then cut himself a slice. "Well, like you said, I didn't give it *all* to them. I kept a bit back to destroy every full moon, in case the Watch checked."

"Who'd you deal with?"

"I ... I don't know his name. Big guy." He waved the knife around vaguely, scattering crumbs everywhere.

"What was the pay-off?"

"Um. Just, you know, it was like insurance money. They'd leave us alone if we gave them the horn."

Callum and I looked at each other.

"You always were an awful liar," Callum said, and poured water into the teapot.

"What? No!"

"Well, it was pretty hard to believe you were the brains of the outfit," I said.

Art looked at me like he didn't know whether to be offended or not.

"How long was Kara dealing with them?" Callum asked. "And when did you find out?"

Art groaned, and buried his face in his hands. "I'm sorry. I'm *sorry!* I was scared you'd drop it if you knew she was dealing."

"Well, I do feel a bit different about risking my tail for a drug dealer," I agreed.

Callum flicked my ear lightly. "We'd still have helped, Art. But you have to tell us what's actually going on. We can't help if we don't know the whole story."

Art made an unhappy noise and started picking his slice of bread apart. "It's not her fault. She was forced into it."

"Sure she was," I said, and Callum poked me. "What? I was being sympathetic!"

"I still can't tell with you sometimes," he said, and brought the mugs to the table. "Go on, Art."

"I didn't even know," he said. "Not until the unicorns went missing, and we couldn't find them. Then she came to me all scared, because they … they were threatening her. She was late on a shipment, and they said if she didn't find them, they'd feed me to the crows."

"But they took her," Callum said.

"I know. She asked me to find you really early on, said she'd heard you were a detective and we'd need your help. And I wouldn't, because I knew you wouldn't want to help as soon as you knew the truth. Then one day I came home from hunting for the damn things *all day,* and she was gone. She'd convinced them to take her instead of me. She *trusts* me. She really thinks I can find them before … oh, God." He rubbed his hands over his face. "Her finger.

They cut off her *finger.* And they said that was just the start. What am I going to *do?*" He stared at Callum, his eyes desperate and pained, and no one spoke.

I looked at the chicken in my bowl, thinking of the high, piled shelves of the warehouse, heavy with death and magic, and Trainers saying, *That's so Kara, you mean.* Not the unicorn chick, or the prisoner. Kara. And with such easy familiarity. Things still weren't adding up, and I didn't like that Kara had been the one to ask for Callum. I didn't like that at all.

"We need to go home," I said.

"We're not dropping this case," Callum said. "We need to find these bloody unicorns before anything more happens to Kara."

"But we're not doing any more tonight, are we?" I pointed out. "We need to rethink this. Consider the new evidence."

"It doesn't change anything. They've still got Kara. The only way we're getting her back is finding the unicorns. We'll deal with the rest later."

"Thank you," Art said. "Thank you *so* much. And I know I should've told you before, but I was just so scared you'd walk away once you knew the truth."

"We can still go home for the night," I said. "I'm knackered, and a sleep in my own bed would be nice."

"I don't think we should," Callum said. "The time we waste getting home and back again can be spent better. And the car's getting worse."

I growled. "There better be some prime fillets of salmon in that bag."

"You're doing better, then."

I didn't answer. As the warmth of the bath wore off, my legs were aching and my paws throbbed with a persistent, angry rhythm. But over it all was the conviction that we were missing something, and that staying here was like napping on the threshold of the enemy. Sooner or later someone was going to come at us with a broom and some well-placed kicks.

18

A ROCKY START TO THE DAY

As it happened, I was in no condition to have any say in whether we went home or not. All misgivings aside, I took a short break from my after-chicken custard and rested my stinging eyes, telling the two humans that if either of them tried to move my bowl someone would be getting bitten. That was sometime in the afternoon. Much later, when someone turned out the light, I sat up, shuffled stiffly from one side onto the other, and fell asleep again.

When I woke up properly the kitchen was still and dark, the big old range grumbling low and quiet, like a snoozing dragon of the non-Komodo variety. I pushed myself up to sitting, everything aching, and attempted a rough toilette. My fur was lying in strange directions and tasted of hippie soap, although I had to grudgingly admit that it was better than sewer scum. But my bladder was objecting strongly to all the water I'd drunk in the car, so I didn't linger over it long.

I jumped to the flagged floor, hissing at the impact on

my tender paws, and hobbled into the pantry. The window was still ajar, and I scrambled up to it ungracefully, then let myself out into the chill, damp quiet of a late summer pre-dawn.

The clouds were thick and heavy, their underbellies a gloaming orange from the lights of the city, and it felt like it had only just stopped raining. The grass was cold and soothing on my paws, and I limped to the veggie patch to take care of business. By the time I was finished the cool air had cleared my head a little, and I tottered to the gate, scaling it clumsily and perching on top to blink out at the night

It wasn't just the human lights flushing the clouds, I noticed now. Dawn was already coming in, even if it was a flat, uninspired one. I considered going back to the warmth of the kitchen to sleep a while longer, but now I was up all those sneaking, niggling thoughts were back in my mind. I was less concerned about the unicorns than I was about the weapons stash, the whole Art and Kara thing, and just what was pulling Callum back to places he'd been happy to leave behind. The sooner we were out of this whole mess, the better. Not that Callum was going anywhere until we found those stroppy ponies and rescued his damsel in distress. Ugh.

My whiskers flared in the low light as I cast around for scents, but no one seemed to be about, not even the fox. Other than the far-off roar of a motorbike, I could have been the only creature left in the world, the rest gone as surely as the unicorns. It was an uneasy thought.

I jumped softly to the grass and padded toward the barn, passing the chicken hut with its whiff of feathers and droppings and safe, sleepy mutterings. The barn door was shut, held to with a heavy bar of wood, but I found a gap near the hinges that I could probably drag myself under. I stood there and stared at it for a long moment, wondering if I could really be bothered with any more tight spots, especially considering all I'd got out of the donkey last time was babble, and goats were next to useless. Then again, I had no other leads. And who knew – maybe the pig would have got over her donkey-induced existential crisis and be willing to chat. I sighed and flopped to the ground, squeezing myself through with my ears back and my belly flat to the earth, the wooden slats scraping my spine. Inside was dark and homey-smelling, all hair and hay and dirt, and I could feel the warmth of the animals in their stalls.

I slipped past Kent as quietly as I could, not wanting to have my perception of reality questioned, and checked on the sow.

"Hey," I said to her from the top of her pen wall. "You sleeping?"

She flicked an ear at me.

"See, I'm not sure if you're sleeping or just not talking to anyone again."

Her flank twitched.

"I wanted to ask a couple of questions about the night the unicorns disappeared."

She sat up, looked at me, and flopped pointedly onto her other side.

I sighed. "Cheers." I jumped back to the straw-strewn floor and padded on, hearing sleepy belches coming from the end stall in the row. It was fully enclosed, no way for me to climb over or wriggle in, so I lay down, put my nose to a gap at the bottom, and said, "Hey."

"Intruder!" someone shrieked on the other side.

"Is it the fox?" someone else shouted. "Noooo, not the fox!"

"The fox!" the first one screamed. "Help, *help!*"

"I'm not a fox," I said.

"It's still there!"

"Help! Help! Help us!"

I sighed. "I'm a cat. I'm just trying—"

"It's a cat! *A cat!*"

"Fleas! There'll be fleas!"

"*Excuse* me," I said. "I do *not* have fleas. I only wanted to ask—"

"It's harassing us! It's scaring us with its claws! It's—" There was a thud beyond the wall, and a sudden silence, then the other goat started screaming.

"*It killed Clarence! The cat killed Clarence! Aaaaaahhhhhh! Aaaaaaahhhhh!*"

"I'm not anywhere *near* Clarence!" I shouted, and there was a second thud from inside the stall. "Hello?" No answer. "Um, goats?"

"Fainted," a deep voice said, and I looked around to see Kent looking over the door of his stall. "Their version of reality is terribly stressful."

"So it seems," I said, getting up and ambling back down the barn. "How's it hanging, Kent?"

He flicked his long ears at me. "I was considering the existence of nettles."

"I see."

"Yes. Is their sting a warning, or a prelude to pleasure? And, in identifying it as one, does that negate the other?"

I squinted at him. "I don't think about nettles that much, dude."

"No," he said thoughtfully. "But it is useful to do so, yes?"

I made a non-committal noise. Nettle ramblings aside, Kent had been right about the moon when the unicorns vanished, even if I'd thought he was talking kibble at the time. "You remember when the unicorns disappeared?"

"I remember my perception of that time, yes."

I swallowed a sigh. "Did you *see* anyone? Did you see the unicorns leaving, or anyone coming into the yard?"

Kent considered this, rolling his lips across his teeth. Then he said, "No. We are inside at night. Sometimes the unicorns were, too. Those are their stalls." He nodded at the row of stalls facing us. "But they're very difficult. Someone always ended up bitten."

"So they weren't inside that night?"

"No. Kara brought us in, but not them. Unless it was going to be really cold, they normally left them out. No one ever imagined someone would be foolish enough to steal such hostile animals."

I sat down and scratched my ear thoughtfully. "And did you hear shouting or anything?"

"Not until Art came home, checked in here, and realised everyone was gone. Then he and Kara shouted at each other for far longer than should be necessary for a civilised conversation."

"Do you remember when Kara vanished?"

He regarded me. "You talk as if she and the unicorns just *poof,* stopped existing. It's very imprecise."

I wondered if the goats had recovered yet. "Alright. Not vanished. When she ... was taken."

"Left," the donkey said.

I blinked at him. "Left?"

"Left. As in departed."

"She wasn't taken?"

He thought about it. "Well, someone came in a car and drove her away, but she wasn't forced to go."

I supposed that *could* work with Art's story that she'd gone to protect him, but somehow it didn't feel like it. "Did you see who took ... who she left with?"

Kent flicked his ears. "All humans look the same to me."

"Fair point. When did this happen?"

"Time is a rather human construct, but I would say about a week after the unicorns were taken."

I scratched the old scars on my shoulder with a back paw, shedding soap-scented hair. "Is there anything else you can tell me?"

"Well, there's a very interesting theory regarding the consciousness of small rocks I've been working on—"

"No, no," I said hurriedly. "I mean about when the unicorns or Kara left. Or were taken, or whatever."

He plucked a bit of hay from the floor and chewed it while he considered my question. "That young troll was around when the unicorns were taken. I could smell her."

And we were back to Poppy. Poppy, hanging around the field asking if we'd found them, and complaining Art and Kara hadn't been nice enough to them. Although that was an odd concern to have about one's dinner, but who knew. Humans get all into that happy lives for the meat they're just going to eat too. I got up. "Kent, you're a star."

"I'm a flaming ball of gas?"

"Something like that." I trotted to the door and wriggled my way underneath again, surfacing into the cooler air of the dawn and smelling rain on the edges of the sky. With any luck Poppy had either stashed the unicorns somewhere to eat at leisure, or had eaten them already and buried the bones somewhere handy. She seemed a good sort for a troll, and she wasn't exactly bright enough to stand up to a proper questioning, especially not now we had the donkey putting her at the crime scene. In fact, if we told Gerry that it was definitely her, he was new age-y enough to want her to own up to her crimes, and would probably ground her for a month or something, which'd do just fine for us. We'd get the truth out of her, then collect the bones, give them to Art to take to Dimly, and all would be done and dusted by lunchtime. Including any future unicorn horn trade. There'd still be the small problem of the weapons stash, but all I had to do was hand that to Claudia. We could walk away from Dimly and never come back. Job done.

I purred to myself, thinking of my heatable bed. Gods, it'd be good to be home.

"Cat?" Kent called after me.

"Yes?"

"Are you sure you don't want me to explain my theory of the consciousness of small rocks to you?"

"Maybe some other time."

He sighed. "Alright. Mind the car."

"The car?" But even as I spoke I became aware of it, the rumble of a powerful engine behind the house. I paused where I was, one paw in the air, ears flicking as I strained to tell whether if it was coming down the drive or not. It slowed, and a door clunked open, then there was the clink of a gate being opened. I broke into a sprint.

I shot into the garden and through the pantry window, stiff limbs forgotten, and charged up the stairs. Callum's door was ajar, and I raced through, leaping straight onto his belly while he snored steadily. He lurched upright with a yelp.

"Gobs, Jesus—"

"*Car.*"

The sleep cleared from his face instantly and he threw the covers back, almost taking me to the floor with them, snatched his clothes off the rickety chair and started pulling them on, shouting for Art. The other man appeared at the door a moment later in red flannel pyjama bottoms and a yellow T-shirt, his hair and beard both looking like something had been nesting in them.

"What?" he asked, scratching his chest, and my ears caught the quiet rumble of the car easing to a stop outside.

"*Hurry,*" I hissed.

"We've got to go," Callum said, kicking into his boots and pushing Art out into the hall. Downstairs, the latch clicked open on the kitchen door, the sound carrying clearly up to the landing.

"Gods, you don't even *lock* it?" I demanded.

"I'm sure I did," Art said, looking more confused than ever. "Well, I *think* I did."

"Get your coat on," Callum said, and I was disappointed to see he'd obviously washed his jacket. He hauled it on and added, "Can we get out your window?"

"I wouldn't do that," a man said from the stairs, and Callum shoved me unceremoniously back into the bedroom with one foot.

"Who're you?" Art demanded. "What're you doing here?"

"Come to collect you," the man said. "Let's move."

"Collect him for what?" Callum asked.

"Not just him. You plural. Come on."

Callum put his hands in the pockets of his coat and rocked on his heels. "What if we refuse?"

"Wouldn't go too well for Kara if you did that," the stranger said, and Art clutched his hands to his chest.

"Is she okay? I want to know if she's okay!"

There was a heavy sigh from the bottom of the stairs, and the man said, "Liam, have you got your phone?"

"Sure." There were heavy footsteps in the kitchen, then the sound of a phone ringing on speaker.

The ringing stopped, and a male voice said, "Yes?"

"He wants to know Kara's alright."

Still *Kara,* not *the girl.* And she went willingly. I edged forward, hissing Callum's name, and he held a hand out to me without even looking. *Stop.* I dropped to my belly, and a moment later a woman's voice came onto the phone.

"Art?" she said, the word wobbly. "Art, are you there?"

"Kara!" he shouted, and lunged for the stairs. Callum grabbed his arm, holding him back as he strained toward the phone. "Kara, are you alright?"

"Art, I'm so sorry!" she wailed. "They say it's taking too

long. They say you have to come, or they'll, they'll—" she was cut off with a muffled shriek, and the phone went dead.

"Kara!" Art screamed. "Call her back, call her back, please!"

"Come with us, and it'll all be fine," the first man said.

Art tried for the stairs again, pawing at Callum's restraining hand. "We have to go. We *have to!*"

"Callum, no!" I hissed, and he just did that hand thing again. "It's a *trap!*"

"Is the cat up there?" the man asked from below. "We need him as well."

"No," Callum said. "Besides, you know cats. He'd shift out of here before you could even grab him."

"Not from here. This whole place is shift-locked."

"Well, he's not here anyway."

"That so? Let's see." The stairs creaked as someone started climbing, and I bolted for the window, slipping out onto the windowsill and wobbling there for a moment. Then I slid my front paws down the wall, skittering as far as I could before gravity caught me and I leaped clear, landing in soft, overgrown grass and scooting under a squat little bay bush just as the window opened behind me. A big man with tightly cropped dark hair leaned out, checking the lawn below, and someone called behind him, "Leave it, Daryl. Shift locks or not, you won't find a cat that doesn't want to be found."

Truth, I thought, and watched the big man shrug and slam the window shut. There was a moment's pause, then someone shouted, and I caught the muffled sound of a struggle inside. I bolted to the front of the house and hunkered down in the cover of an overgrown rose bush, hearing more thuds from inside, and wondered if I should break the donkey out and see if he was up for biting anyone. Before I could decide, though, Daryl and Liam emerged from the front door, dragging Callum between them. His head hung loose, and there was blood trickling from the corner of his mouth. Art followed behind, a third man helping him along with one hand on the scruff of his neck.

"Can't I at least put my shoes on?" Art was asking, but no one listened to him. The two big men wedged a mostly unconscious Callum into the back seat of the glossy black SUV between them, and the equally huge third man (who I thought might be Boots. He was limping as if a coconut crab had taken a good chunk from his foot) pushed Art into the front passenger seat then got in himself. Art was still asking about his shoes when the door slammed heavily shut and the engine purred into life. They skirted the leaking Rover and headed for the gate without looking back, and I stayed where I was as the dull dawn blossomed grimly into a dull day, revealing the empty field and the silent yard, and I found myself more alone than I'd ever imagined I could be.

19

HERE COMES THE CAVALRY

As the sound of the car faded, I slipped out from under the rose bush and jumped to the gatepost, sitting there with my tail ticking softly behind me while the day brightened grudgingly. If I'd been able to shift, to step into the Inbetween and back out again somewhere new, I could have gone to Ms Jones, our fearsome local sorcerer, or even to Gertrude, the reaper for Leeds. Maybe even have found Claudia, although that was going a little closer to the Watch than I'd like.

But I couldn't. The Watch understands how to make punishments stick. The beasts that cruise the Inbetween are eternal. Vast patient leviathans and fast, toothed predators, once they have your scent they never stop looking for you. Some nights, when the moon hangs a certain way and the fabric of the world gets thin, I can feel them pressing around me, insatiable and unchanging. The odds of my making it through a shift were close enough to non-existent that it seemed like one of the less helpful things to do for Callum.

Which meant I was going to have to head for Dimly on foot. I wasn't at all sure what I was going to do when I got there, but that was where Callum had been taken, so that was where I was going. Art could rot in Dimly for all I cared, spend the rest of his sorry days counting snorting moon beetles in the warehouse or sorting hen's teeth by size and fineness, but I was getting Callum out. I didn't have the details of quite how just yet, but I'd figure it out on the way. I'm a great believer in improvisation. Callum calls it poor planning, and mutters on about it resulting in poor performance or what have you, but he's the one who just got dragged off by goons, so, you know.

I considered enlisting Kent's help again, but not only was he likely to question the philosophical implications of what we were doing, there was no way I was getting the barn door unlatched. By road was both a long way around and rough on the paws, so I jumped to the loose gravel of the drive and headed for the paddock. Canal path it was, then. Soft dirt tracks would be gentle on the paws, and it'd be quicker besides. Plus there was always the chance of hitching a lift on a passing canal boat if I was sneaky about it. I might even run into some water rats drifting a raft down, although that was less likely now it was light. However it went, I'd get there.

I had to.

The grass of the paddock, grown long without the unicorns to crop it, was damp with dew that soaked my paws and beaded my whiskers, and I started to run.

INITIALLY I MADE good time along the tow path of the canal, slipping into the weeds and long grass to dodge a handful of early morning joggers and cyclists who barely glanced at me, and baring my teeth at a couple of terrier-types being dragged along by a small woman in a big red coat. I'm not sure if hippie soap smells threatening to small dogs or if they were just smart enough to read my expression, but after a few half-hearted yaps they contented themselves with tangling around their human's legs instead. I kept going, trying to ignore the protests in my joints and the ache of my paws, looking for canal boats and wondering how far along here Callum had meant when he'd said you could walk to Dimly.

I kept to the tow path where we'd left it to find the sludge puppy, skirting the rundown canal boat we'd seen before. Even if they'd been inclined to help, it didn't look very mobile. And it was the only one I'd seen so far. It was too late for water rat rafts, too early for boaters, and I was limping already, slowing to a half-hearted jog that I pushed back up to a run every time I thought of Callum having pipe cleaners stuck in his ears or Komodo dragons let loose on his toes. I stumbled on small dips in the path, and gave up on dodging runners. One of them stopped and made smooching noises at me, asking if I was alright, but I just hissed at him and found a little speed from somewhere. That was all I needed, some good sanatorium or whatchamacallit grabbing me and carting me off to a rescue.

I splashed through a muddy puddle, too tired to even bother going around, and for the first time it occurred to me that I might not make it. That it was just too far, and everything just hurt too much, and I was just too exhausted. I stumbled on a little further, running on pure will, before I finally stopped, my head hanging and my belly dripping, and said, "Hairballs."

Which hardly seemed to do justice to the situation, so I followed it up with as many human curses as I could manage, then sat down wearily in the middle of the empty path, my paws throbbing as I tried to decide what to do next.

I'd just hobbled to the edge of the canal and shouted for the sludge puppy without much hope of success when there was the *ding ding! Ding ding ding!* of a bicycle bell behind me. I scooted for the cover of the nettles, spitting in the general direction of the cyclist, although at least they'd used their bell. The last one had just about run me into the water, and he'd been grinning as he went past. I lifted one front paw then the other, shaking them off gently, and the bike came to a stop next to me, brakes squealing shrilly.

"Hello, kitty," the rider said, her voice rocks rolling in a stream. "Want ride?" She frowned, all three eyes scrunched in effort. "Do ... *you* ... want ride?"

"Poppy!" I exclaimed. "You jewel among thorns! Sight for sore eyes! Be still my beating heart!"

She stared at me. "What?"

"You rock."

Her frown deepened, and she wobbled from side to side on the heavy bike frame, first one bare foot on the ground then the other. "Am troll, no rock."

"Right. Yes. Sorry. It's just an expression," I said, extricating myself from the weeds.

"'Spression?"

"Yeah, it's a human thing. You know, like good as gold, or run like the wind."

She considered this. "Wind blow, not run. And Gerry say objects no have moral value. Only munt— mun— value of penny."

I sat down in front of her, trying to keep the weight off my worst front paw. "Gerry has a good point. It's just something you say, and it means you're wonderful, amazing, stupendous. A lifesaver, right now."

"Me?" She looked at her feet. "You make fun."

Gods. The last thing I needed right now was an offended troll, especially as she was likely out of unicorn meat by now and probably had the munchies. Plus she was my best – and so far only – chance to make it to Dimly before Callum got made into a mummy or fed to magical coconut crabs. So she could have the unicorns as far as I was concerned.

"I'm absolutely not," I said. "I really need some help, Poppy, and you came along at the exact right time." I lifted my injured paw to her, the one I'd cut quite badly on something yesterday, and gave her my best big eyes, which are at least as effective as Callum's dimples. "I'm not in a good way. Callum and Art have been taken to Dimly by some really nasty people, and I *have* to get there. I have to!" Quite suddenly my whiskers were trembling. I can really turn on the emotion when I want to.

Poppy just about threw her bike into the weeds, dropping to her knees in front of me and cradling my paw in her massive hands. I almost pulled back. I'd seen smaller trolls than her break a dog's neck with two fingers. But she was gentle as she examined me.

"Poor kitty! Is dirty. I clean."

"Oh, no, that's okay," I said, trying to back away. "We really need to go."

But she had my foreleg pinched delicately between her thumb and forefinger, and she said, "Is okay. We wait for others anyways."

"Others?"

"I rides quick," she said, and grinned at me, pulling a pint bottle of hydrogen peroxide from the pocket of her overalls.

"Oh, hang on—"

"Shh, kitty," she said, and splashed a generous helping over my paw. I gave a strangled squawk as my poor abused paw started foaming like a gnome on pixie juice, and she plucked me up, cradling me in one arm as she ministered to my other paws and tail, and generally drowned me in the stuff, the excess splashing to the tow path and frothing in the dirt. "See? It no hurt. And now no infect."

"It doesn't *not* hurt," I spluttered, as the worst of the stinging started to subside. "You just carry that stuff on you?"

"Is part of kit," she said proudly. "I much interested in animal husbands." By the time I'd worked out that she didn't mean she was going to be some sort of wildlife chaplain she'd righted the bike and deposited me in the basket. "And look – others here!"

I hooked my front paws over the edge of the basket and peered down the path, expected to see Gerry and

William pedalling wildly after us on their own oversized bikes, but instead it was Kent, cantering clumsily down the path with the goats proinking along behind him and the sow trotting after with two chickens perched on her back.

"Kent?"

"Ah, I see young Poppy has found you. She has quite the turn of speed."

"What're you doing here?"

"I finds," Poppy said. "I opens barn, and Kent say kitty in trouble! So I helps. We all helps." She grinned broadly and rather alarmingly.

"Troll!" a brown and white goat shrieked, and promptly fainted. He fell over with all four legs sticking straight out in the air, and only the fact that he bumped into the pig stopped him tumbling into the canal.

"Clarence!" the second goat shouted. "Clarence! Clarence, wake up!"

Kent examined them, then looked at me. "We thought you might need some assistance."

"Right. Thanks."

"It was the ethical thing to do."

"*Cat!* It's the murder cat!" the second goat yelled, and fainted next to Clarence. The sow looked at him, then at us, and sighed.

"I probably should have left them behind," Kent admitted.

The chickens clucked happily, so at least someone was having a good outing.

Poppy looked at me and squared her impressive shoulders. "We go Dimly."

"Quite," Kent said. "Come along, Lady Grey."

The sow gave a long-suffering sigh, and Poppy swung one heavy leg over the bike and pushed off. We veered perilously close to the edge of the canal before she righted us and we wobbled off. I was still considering the wisdom of accepting lifts from trolls as we started to pick up speed, the ribbons on the handlebars streaming gracefully. Poppy was pedalling furiously, and I caught a glimpse of Kent and Lady Grey charging after us, the gap between us widening. I kept my paws hooked over the front of the basket and narrowed my eyes against the wind of our movement, tensed for the crash that seemed inevitable, given trolls' general lack of coordination and poor eyesight.

But Poppy pedalled on, her pale skin flushing a deeper grey with effort.

"*Whee!*" she yelled as we freewheeled down a slope by a lock, and two joggers in matching Lycra and headphones dived for cover as we thundered past. "Sorry!" Poppy called, dinging the bell rather belatedly. I hung out of the basket to look back at the joggers. They were staring after us, one of them with her hand pressed to her heart, and I snickered. If they thought a troll in orange dungarees riding past with a cat in a basket was the sort of vision brought on by a bad kale smoothie, wait until the rest of the ark came through.

KENT HADN'T LIED. Poppy really did have quite the turn of speed. Everyone knows trolls are strong, and the general consensus is that they're not the ripest bananas in the bunch, or what have you, but I'd never considered they could be fast. Poppy never slowed down, her shoulders a grim line of determination and her legs working steadily. We thundered down the tow path, bell dinging and ribbons flying, scattering dog walkers and joggers and more conventional cyclists in our wake. My eyes watered with the speed, and the mile markers flashed past.

Poppy grinned luminously all the way, letting out little whoops of joy on every downhill, and we only stopped once, when she spotted a half-grown duck swimming in aimless circles in the canal, one wing trailing uselessly behind it. She lifted me out of the basket, set the bike down, jumped into the canal, caught the duck, and clambered back out again as Kent and Lady Grey heaved into sight well behind us, still running hard but with rather less enthusiasm than before.

Poppy righted the bike and put the duck carefully in the basket, then gave me a stern look. "You is good kitty?"

"Well, mostly," I said, then as she frowned at me I added, "I'm not going to eat a *duck*. Come on."

"You is sure?"

The duck gave an uneasy quack, and I sighed. "I is – *am* sure."

She examined me for a moment longer, then broke into a huge smile and said, "Good kitty!" She scooped me up and tucked me in next to the duck, who belted me around the head a few times with its good wing, and I tried not to hiss at it too much. Then we were off again, and by the time we swung off the tow path and Poppy stared pedalling up a narrow, rough lane that ran alongside a dingy-looking stream, Kent and entourage were nowhere in sight and the duck had snuggled down next to me as if I'd raised it from birth. Which was hardly the most dramatic way for me to make my entrance to Dimly, but I wasn't about to complain. We'd been quick. I didn't think it could have taken us much more than an hour. I probably wouldn't have even made it to the first lock by now, even if my legs had still been working.

Poppy fell quiet as we headed up the new path, no longer *whee*-ing or pointing out dormice habitats and naming birds. She slowed down, too, shooting anxious glances into the undergrowth that grew heavy to the edge of the path. Big trees with twisted trunks reached hungry branches overhead, and the whiff of glamour crept up around us. The duck grumbled and cuddled a little closer to me, and I caught the dank scent of something dead in the bushes. The surface of the stream was greasy and still, pocked with bubbles and litter, and coils of barbed wire hung from a rotting fence across the water.

"Dear-oh," Poppy whispered. "Dear-oh-dear."

"Poppy, you don't have to go any further," I said, matching my voice to hers.

"But need you Dimly go," she said, then shook her head. "I *mean,* need go Dimly. You." She made a little frustrated noise, and it fell flat among the trees.

"I can walk the rest of the way. You've absolutely saved me, bringing me this far."

She looked at me doubtfully, and I could see little tremors running across her shoulders. "Sure?"

"Sure." I jumped out of the basket as she came to a

stop, and the duck gave an offended quack. "You get on home before the sun gets any higher, too."

"Is bad here," Poppy said, in that same anxious whisper, and I shivered. I didn't like to think what would make a troll scared.

"I know," I said.

"Bad trolls. Bad humans. Bad birds." She put one big hand protectively over the duck. "Kitty be careful."

"I will."

"Bad trolls hurts us, when Gerry says we leave." She rubbed her arm, a quick, reflexive gesture. "We fine was, different but fine, then sudden they says, you works for *her*, or else. Then bad trolls hurts us."

"I'm sorry, Poppy," I said, and meant it. Kinds will always turn on themselves – just look at humans – but it doesn't stop it hurting. And it's always the strange and the different and the weak that hurt the most. "You go look after that duck." Unless it was going to be breakfast. That was always possible, too.

She bobbed her head, grin surfacing briefly. "I fix duck."

"Nice one." I watched her turn away and start down the path, still pushing the bike and doing a rather exaggerated tiptoe, her shoulders drawn up to her ears.

She looked back before she had gone too far and said, "Peoples has choice – nice or nasty. Even troll has choice. People think trolls all stupid and nasty, but is choice. We choose good. Dimly choose nasty. Be careful, kitty."

I opened my mouth but couldn't find anything to say. And she didn't wait for a reply, anyway. She climbed back onto the bike and started pedalling, and a moment later she vanished around the curve in the path, leaving the place desolate and ugly and feeling very nasty indeed. There was no sign of Kent and the rest of the farm, and I didn't blame them. The goats had probably taken one whiff of the place and fainted on the spot. I stood there, feeling very small and very tired, smelling dead things and cruel magic and something gooey and unpleasant in the stream, wondering what exactly I thought I was going to be able to do.

Then I set my shoulders, lifted my nose, and started up the path. I wasn't going to do any of it standing here.

20

IT SEEMED LIKE A GOOD IDEA AT THE TIME

I TROTTED UP THE PATH, RESISTING THE URGE TO BOLT every time a twig snapped in the undergrowth or something *gloop*ed in the stream. It was entirely possible that the whole place was swarming with scorpion-tailed rabbits and cat-eating spiders and giant tusked bandicoots, but until one of them actually jumped out at me I was just going to keep calm and carry on. As long as I didn't fall in the water from sheer fright, of course.

Everything dripped with the sort of glamour that meant a human likely wouldn't have even noticed the path, and if they did they'd have turned back after a few steps with the sort of relief that comes from being sure you're just avoided walking into a serial killer's lair. The trail became more and more overgrown as I walked, and I kept checking back to see if Kent had turned up, but it seemed I was right in thinking he and his fainting goats had decided there were better things to do. Which just showed how dire the situation was, if I was hoping for the company of a donkey ruminating on the consciousness of small rocks.

I passed a few culverts, but they smelt stale and acrid, with no whiff of rat about them. I tried calling into the first one, and something started slapping and gurgling in the darkness, flopping its way closer and stinking of rot and sewers. I moved on fast and didn't do any more than check for scents on the others. I'd just have to hope I stumbled across the rats once I got into Dimly itself. They were my best way of finding Callum.

I knew the river ran through Dimly – most pockets were built on the water, boat transport being rather more secretive and reliable than road travel, and less subject to things like licenses and road tax. Although presumably the massive weapons stash would operate on slightly different logistics to a few packets of consciousness-expanding drugs and some singing cacti from Madagascar. But the river would still be used for plenty of things. I wasn't quite sure *where* in Dimly the river went, but I figured if I kept to the path I'd find out soon enough. I was still stiff and tired, but Poppy's rescue mission meant that at least I was still moving. And my sore paws and lack of breakfast meant I was kind of looking forward to introducing someone to my claws at the earliest opportunity.

For a long time the riverside path didn't get any prettier or better maintained, and I had an idea that to any non-Folk it'd look a lot like I was tripping though an impenetrable jungle of thorns and nettles. Cats see what's there, though, and eventually the path started to widen, bollards blossoming like white-painted mushrooms along the banks. A few had half-sunk wrecks moored up to them, but as the path widened further nicer vessels took their place, low-slung canal boats with deep green hulls and little varnished powerboats with covers stretched tight over them, and slim white rowing dinghies pulled up onto the banks.

The undergrowth gave way to landscaped gardens and rolling lawns patched with flowerbeds full of tall plants that whispered and sang to each other, and one leaned over the fence to snap at my tail as I passed. Houses lurked further from the banks, safe from flooding. Some were ancient, squat cottages that looked dank and unkempt, but as the gardens grew larger the houses grew taller and more sprawling, drawing even more distant from the water and watching over their grounds with supercilious windows. Some were elegant, all sweeping lines and gingerbread trim, and others hurt the eye with dimensions that didn't make sense, all strangely shaped windows and doors stuck in odd places. There were gazebos and boat sheds and tennis courts, old alters and guillotines and standing stones, and the whole place stood as silent and empty and wary as the town had the day before.

I slowed, searching for drains and culverts, risking shouts into some of them and listening for answering echoes. There was nothing – or nothing ratty, anyway. There was some alarmed and rapidly retreating splashing in one, and a growl that sent me on my way pretty quickly in another, but nothing else. Well, no matter. I'd do this myself. I'd start with the warehouse. Nothing that big existed solely below ground, not this close to waterways.

And given the preference for ghost ships over ghost cars, it'd back onto the stream somewhere. So that was where I'd start.

I WAS TROTTING PURPOSEFULLY past a scrap of a park, with a gated play area and benches nestled under the leaning trees at the edge of the water, when someone hissed, "*Cat!*"

I froze, looking for the speaker. It hadn't sounded exactly hostile, like *get the cat,* but it wasn't entirely friendly, either. It was almost an accusation.

"Over here!"

I spotted them. The two bookshop ladies were sitting on a bench by a ragged flowerbed, each with a sandwich in one hand and a mug of tea in the other, and they wore identical expressions of horror. We stared at each other for a moment longer while I considered whether to bolt or see if they'd help me.

Then the sister with the pink hair – Cherie – put her sandwich down on the greaseproof paper she had spread on her lap and hissed, "Come here! Hurry!"

I still hesitated. They might be harmless, but I didn't see how they could help. And something didn't feel right about them. *Nothing* in Dimly felt right.

Marie stood up and waved urgently with her mug, splashing tea over her hand. "*Quick!*"

"Marie, sit *down!* They'll see you!" Cherie tugged her sister back into her seat, both of them looking around anxiously, and I decided I had to try. After all, they'd protected us from the crows yesterday. If nothing else, maybe they could tell me where the warehouse was – or where prisoners were usually kept.

I ran across the short-cropped grass, stopping just out of grabbing distance and eyeing them both warily.

"Under the bench, quick," Marie said, and spread out the long skirt of her purple and green tartan dress. She had a matching headband on.

I hesitated, and Cherie flapped her hands at me. "Come *on!* They'll see you!"

I took a final glance around, then slipped under the bench, sheltering next to Marie's biker boots and peering up at both of them. "Who?"

"The crows, who do you think?" Marie asked, putting her sandwich down and adding a dollop of something eye-wateringly strong from one of her hip flasks to her mug.

"Marie, stop that. It's not the time," Cherie said.

"I'm very stressed!"

So was I. My heart was going too fast. It wasn't as if I'd forgotten the crows. I'd just sort of … had other things on my mind. But now the skies felt vast and unfriendly, and the trees hid platoons of danger.

"I don't see them," Cherie said, taking a bite of what smelled a lot like an egg mayonnaise sandwich. My stomach growled longingly.

"It doesn't mean they don't see us," Marie said, with a large slurp of spiked tea.

"Oh, those nasty birds. Stay quiet, kitty. Look normal, Marie."

We sat there in silence, the ladies swinging their legs

(Marie nearly clipping me with her chunky boot heels) and making little agreeable noises about their lunch. Finally Cherie said quietly, "Where's Callum, kitty? We did say you shouldn't come back here."

The question tugged a dull stitch into my side. "He's … I think he's here somewhere. I'm looking for him."

"You lost him?" Marie asked, sneaking another dollop from her flask while Cherie tutted disapprovingly.

"No. These big guys showed up and took him. They were from here, I'm sure of it." A flicker of movement closer to the stream caught my eye, and I flinched. Crow? But there was nothing there when I looked more carefully.

"Oh dear," Cherie said. "Oh, that's terribly bad news."

"Not good at all," her sister agreed. "What will you do, kitty?"

"Find him. Get him out."

"On your own?" they chorused. The double act was starting to get on my nerves, and I kept thinking I saw something on the edge of my vision, but every time I peeked out from my tartan shelter there was nothing there. I didn't think it could be crows, though – it was more grey than black. A squirrel, perhaps? A rat, if I was very lucky, but I didn't want these two to know about the little anarchists. In fact, I didn't want them knowing anything more at all. Something about them, the lingering scent of words and secrets, was making my skin itch.

"I suppose it'll have to be on my own," I said, and eased out from under the bench. "I best keep going."

"Oh, but kitty, you'll need help," Cherie said. "Don't you have help?"

"Friends, colleagues?" Marie suggested.

"Family, neighbours?"

"The Watch?" The last word hung in the still green air as they watched me with their bright, sharp eyes, and I took a step back.

"I'm not Watch," I said. "And does it look like there's anyone else here?"

"Oh dear," Cherie said again. "Poor kitty on his lonesome."

I felt the air shimmer rather than saw it, felt a thickening on the edges and sensed that flicker of movement again. I bolted for the river, ears back and weariness forgotten, and for a moment I thought I'd been quick enough, thought I was going to race along the towpath with nothing to show but some ruffled fur and a newly acquired dislike for bookshops. The women called after me, all pretence at stealth abandoned.

"Come back, kitty! Come back!"

"You can't be alone!"

"We'll help you!"

I ignored the shouts and concentrated on running harder, smelling the ozone whiff of magic mixed with something deep and slow and dark, like currents in deep water. My skin prickled, my fur rising to attention, and words flowed across the ground, overtaking me and swirling around my paws. *Stop halt wait pause cease desist enough.* They flooded toward me, turning the ground to swirling shadows and rising ahead of me like a breaking wave. I swerved, pelting across the grass into the depths of the park, and the words turned as smoothly as river water. They overtook me effortlessly, swamping the ground, the sky, the light, everything, and I was swept off my feet, enveloped in the insistence of them. They bundled themselves around me like a cocoon, sinking through my fur to press against my skin, still sending their orders shouting through to my bones. I struggled wildly. Cats aren't particularly open to being ordered around, and disembodied words are even worse than humans telling us to get off the table. You can't even bite words.

There was no scraping the words off, no scratching or gnawing them. It was like being swaddled in cold water that parted under your paws and reattached itself instantly. They even swam across my vision, and when the two women leaned down to look at me they were patterned with *stop halt wait*. I glared back anyway, thinking that arriving in a troll's bicycle basket with a wounded duck and a farmyard in train was proving to not be the most embarrassing part of the day after all.

I twisted, hard, and as I arched against the bonds of the words I met a set of small, sharp eyes watching me from under a petunia. Or, I don't know, a pansy. Some sort of flower, anyway. I froze, then wriggled my whiskers desperately. The rat just stared at me, then vanished into the shadows. I bellowed against the words gagging me, but it didn't come back, and Marie reached down to push the words off my face with small hands, breathing whisky and eggs over me. "Sorry, kitty," she said, and Cherie scowled at her.

"We have no choice. We took enough of a risk letting Callum go, and see where that got us. You *know* we can't let the cat go."

"We could have pretended not to see him."

"I bet they already know we saw him," Cherie said, checking the treetops. "They always know."

"You're a pair of treacherous toilet brushes," I told them.

Cherie frowned. "You should have left his mouth covered, Marie."

"He might not have been able to breathe."

"He's a *cat.* Hardly a tragedy."

"I take it back," I said. "You're not toilet brushes. You're overcooked Brussels sprouts with ... with mushy peas. In a dog bowl."

Cherie flapped her hands at me. "Words can hurt, kitty, but not yours. I don't care about them enough."

"Come a bit closer, then." I bared my teeth at her, and she laughed.

"You won't be doing that for long. There's a bounty on cats in Dimly."

"You're doing this for the *money?*" I demanded.

Marie flapped her hands at her sister. "*No.* Don't listen to her. We got in a lot of trouble for helping Callum. She was angry. She made us throw our favourite books in the river."

"Who was?" I asked. "The mayor?" They ignored me.

"We should never have helped Callum," Cherie said, and went to pick up their bag from the bench. "We're lucky she didn't burn the whole shop to the ground."

Marie gave a pained moan. "The *books* ..." She fumbled one of her hip flasks free, gave it a shake, and switched to the other, taking a swig as Cherie came back.

"*Marie.* Stop that. We have to take the cat to her. You

can't be falling down drunk."

"Is this right, though? Taking him to her? It'll be her people who took Callum. We always liked Callum."

"You know where he is?" I asked.

"She'll have him," Marie said. "Oh, I am sorry. Why did it have to be Callum?"

"Don't be soft," Cherie said. "We must protect the books, Marie. Now focus!"

"He cares about books," I said, talking to Marie. "He *loves* books. He won't let them hurt yours, if you help him."

Cherie snorted, and before I could say anything else she pulled the words back over my snout. "That's enough of your fanciful rubbish, cat. You're all the same. Sneaky, slippery, deceitful things. I think keeping you all out of Dimly is a good thing."

I narrowed my eyes at her, trying to convey exactly how unfair calling *me* deceitful was when she had me trussed up like a shoulder joint two days after feeding me tuna at her table.

"Come along, Marie," Cherie said, picking me up and putting me in the bag with the half-eaten sandwiches and empty cups. "Let's go and see her."

"It still doesn't feel right. Helping Callum get away *felt* right."

"Callum had his chance. If he got caught, it's his own fault for hanging around with animals. Besides, the cat isn't Callum."

"I can't imagine Callum doing anything bad," Marie said. "He likes books too much. Maybe she only wants to talk to him."

Cherie picked up the bag, and I swung uncomfortably in the soft bottom, a sandwich wedged under my ear. "That may be the case," she said, in a tone that suggested it was as likely as the unicorns appearing in the middle of the park doing a tap dance. "And think, Marie – she may reward us!"

"We don't need a reward. We don't *deserve* a reward. This cat is Callum's friend."

"Books, Marie. She may get us a new shipment."

There was silence for a moment, then Marie said, "Of *rare* books, perhaps?"

"Perhaps. Old, beautiful books. Secret books. *Unread* books."

Another silence, then Marie said, "Well, we did try to help Callum. And he is just a cat."

"Precisely. Now take one handle. He's very heavy for such a scrawny thing."

I screeched my outrage against the gag of living words as the women started walking, the bag swinging between them and giving me tantalising glimpses of grey sky and freedom. I wriggled and twisted, but trying to tear the words was like trying to wrestle seaweed. Well, I imagine. I've never actually had any desire to wrestle seaweed. The bag bounced and swayed, and the women ignored me, and eventually I gave up. The words wouldn't budge, and I was starting to feel distinctly motion sick. So I just lay there with my nose full of egg mayonnaise, trying to figure out what to do next.

At least I was going to find out where Callum was. Silver linings and all that.

I closed my eyes and waited.

21

THINGS DO NOT GO ENTIRELY ACCORDING TO PLAN

"MIGHT THERE BE HEMINGWAY?"

"Perhaps Woolf!"

"A little LeGuin?"

"Maybe some ... *special* books by *special* authors!"

I was fairly certain I didn't want to know what special books by special authors looked like to these two. They swung me between them as they hurried up the slope of the park, and the sound of their footsteps changed as they stepped onto tarmac.

"She'll be happy with us."

"I hope so. We made a mistake helping Callum. Sentiment is a terrible thing, Marie."

Marie made a small noise that suggested she wasn't as sure it had been a mistake. I wriggled around, trying to get my nose clear of the sandwich, but the bag was moving too much and the words were still burning cold against my skin. I wasn't going anywhere. A head appeared, staring down at me.

"He's making my words all hairy," Cherie said,

frowning at me.

I narrowed my eyes at her, as there wasn't much else I could do.

"Can he breathe?" Marie asked, joining her sister. Her glasses were sitting at an uneven angle, and from the smell of things she'd been fortifying herself with her flask quite heavily. I snorted air in the most sorrowful way I could manage.

"Does it matter?" Cherie asked.

Her sister straightened up. "Of course it *matters.* We should put him in something else, anyway. He's stretching our words."

My preference would be to make them eat their words, but beggars can't be choosers. I wriggled more enthusiastically.

Marie reached in to push the binding words off my snout while her sister tutted. "There you are. You can breathe a little better now."

"I'm going to be sick. I'll vomit all over your words if you don't move them."

"Ew," they chorused, and Cherie added, "It's true what they say about cats. Filthy animals."

"I'm not the one swinging people around in *bags,*" I shouted at her, and she flicked her fingers at me. The words clamped my mouth shut again and as much as I strained, they weren't going anywhere. I glared at the empty sky as the sisters started moving again.

"We should put him in a book," Cherie observed. "One where the cat dies at the end."

Before long we stopped again, and this time I caught glimpses of the front of a building. A lock turned, then we were inside the warm, musty confines of the bookshop. I was set on the floor, less gently on one side than the other, and footsteps retreated. I rolled myself against the side of the bag and it fell over easily, affording me a view across the empty floor. I wriggled wildly, working my way to the mouth of the bag and onto the faded rugs covering the old wood floors, but not even rubbing the words against the cloth would make them loosen. I flopped about like a landed fish, coming up with such inventive curses that it was a shame I couldn't say them out loud – although, given the magic in this place, flinging words might not have been wise.

The sisters reappeared, Cherie carrying a wicker laundry basket with a lid, and before I could do more than try the big eyes on them Marie had scooped me up and dropped me inside. The lid was dropped in place, and the words melted off me, leaving nothing behind but a faint itchiness and a longing for a pile of ageing hardbacks. There were matched sighs of relief from outside the basket.

"Ugh. My words feel so dirty," one of them said.

"I suppose," the other replied. "Warm, though."

"*Ew*. That's nasty, Marie. Let's go."

"I hope you're allergic," I called, shoving my nose against the lid of the basket. It was firmly tied down. "You'll never get the hair out, you know. Never!"

No one replied, and I was hoisted into the air again, the basket swinging gently as the sisters carried me back out into the cool air of the morning, for all the world like they were off to do the laundry rather than carrying me straight into the claws of the enemy.

BY PRESSING my nose right up against the wicker, I could get a patchy view of the world outside. The sisters marched down the street, heading deeper into Dimly and nodding pleasantly at the odd person we passed. There weren't many, and I didn't bother trying to shout. No one else around here was going to be any more helpful than Tweedlebook and Tweedleink here. So I just kept my eyes open so I knew where I was when I got my chance to escape. Or if.

We veered down a biggish street that ran toward the river, the buildings set back from the road and holding storefronts advertising magical locksmiths and traps of any sizes for the protection of your property. The poster in one window shouted, *20% off Instant Goblin Pits, this week only! Will hold any size prisoner!* It was faded and yellow at the edges. The sisters followed the road to where it dead-ended in front of a squat grey building, all sharp angles and hard edges and small, ugly windows. It looked like a bomb shelter or a prison – something made to both keep things out and keep them in all at once. There was a straggling line of saplings planted in front of it, and some bald flowerbeds that had obviously been meant to prettify things, but as the most life in any of them were some particularly virulent looking toadstools lining the path, it just made the place look as if it was leaking poison into the ground around it. And it could've been. It had that feel.

I was carted up three steps to the glass and metal double doors, and one of the sisters pushed the doorbell. I couldn't hear it ring, but after a moment an intercom rasped into life.

"Yeah?"

"Misses Silverfish," Cherie announced, leaning close to the speaker. "With a *captive!*"

A pause, then, "What sort of captive?" The tone sounded like the speaker was wondering what form he needed.

"A cat."

A pause, then the door buzzed and clicked open. "Bring it in."

"Him!" I yelled. "I'm a him, not an it! At least use *they!*" No one answered, not surprisingly. But, honestly. It's one thing to take prisoners. It's quite another to be rude about it.

The ladies carried me in, pushing the door shut behind us. It locked again with a solid *thunk,* and they trotted across polished concrete floors that matched the shiny concrete walls perfectly, coming to a stop in front of a glossy concrete desk. There must've been a special on at the concrete suppliers.

A young man with a soft blossoming of acne on his cheeks eyed the two women a little nervously and said, "Names, please."

"Misses Silverfish," Cherie repeated.

"First names," he said, clicking a few keys on a computer hidden behind the desk.

"Marie. Cherie." They spoke together, and the young man swallowed nervously, then clicked a few more keys, squinting in concentration.

"Captive?"

"A cat."

"A *black* cat."

"Very bad luck, you know," Cherie confided in the man, who looked even more worried.

I gave the wicker an irritated scratch. "That is *such* a human myth. And not even all human cultures think that. Plenty of them think we're *good* luck. So you're just being wilfully ignorant, and I shall vomit on anyone who says different." Although, I was having some doubts about my own personal luck, if we were being honest about it.

"He seems to have stomach problems," Marie said. "He keeps talking about vomiting on things."

I growled.

"Huh," the man said, and came around the desk to tap the lid of the basket. "Cat? Got anything to say for yourself?"

"I've been unfairly detained."

"Hogwash," Cherie said.

"Cats aren't allowed in Dimly," the man said. "You're breaking the law."

"You can't just keep cats out," I said. "We go where we want."

"Not in Dimly."

I gave up on arguing the point and just commented on the parentage of everyone in town, and how they were likely closely interlinked.

"Mouthy," the man observed. "Got a name?"

"Yep. But I'll eat my own earwax before I tell you."

"Suit yourself." He straightened up and addressed the sisters. "Good work. It'll be noted in your Good Citizen records, and I'm sure you'll be compensated."

I squinted through the gaps in the basket and watched Cherie pull herself up to her full, diminutive height. "We'd like to present the captive ourselves. There was an … unfortunate incident involving this cat and a human earlier in the week, and we want to prove our loyalty."

The man looked at the basket with renewed interest. "There was an incident here yesterday, too. It sounded like there might be a cat involved."

"It'll be this one," Cherie said. "It's *very* troublesome."

"Hey," the man said, nudging the basket with his foot. "Did you break in here yesterday?"

"Maybe," I said. "Maybe there's a whole army of felines about the place, sneaking through your streets and vomiting in your beds."

"There's not," Cherie said. "He— I mean, it told us it was alone."

"It sounds very reliable," the man said. "Look, I've noted down that you were the ones to bring it in. It's a busy morning for her. One of the outside teams brought two captives in this morning. She doesn't have time to see you right now."

Two captives. "Hey!" I yelled, drowning out Cherie's grumbles of disappointment and Marie suggesting they should just leave it. "Hey, reception man! It was me! I set the cocoon insect thingies loose on the Komodos and broke the freaky pumpkins free! It was me! *Plus,* I'm only the advance guard. I've got all the details on a veritable *invasion* of cats coming your way right now!"

"You said you were alone," Marie said. She had her fingers twisted together in front of her.

"I lied," I said. "Nasty, sneaky, cat, right?"

She looked unhappy, and the guard said to me, "I should really just throw you in the river. You know, since you confessed to the warehouse raid." But he didn't look too keen.

"Oh, sure," I said. "She'd love that. You know, when the place is overrun with cats and rats and the Watch is throwing people into the Inbetween, and she asks, wasn't there *any* sign …? Wouldn't want to be in your socks then."

"Shoes," Marie said, and her sister swatted her arm.

I hooked my claws into the wicker and pressed my eye to a gap. The guard was human, and even younger than I'd thought at first, not even a shadow of stubble on his chin. There was a gold name tag on his chest, and when I squinted I could just read it. *Parker.* He had the look of someone trying desperately to appear in control of the situation when the most important thing they've done before is make tea for the actual guards. And there was a blue tinge to the beds of his fingernails.

I lowered my voice. "You know, imp dust's a good cheap pick-me-up, but it does make one forgetful, don't you think, Parker? Makes it hard to be sure what you heard, even if it makes the time go quicker. Things get away on you. But she'd understand, right? All those hours at the desk, all those *forms*. Anyone'd need a bit of help to get through, right?"

Parker shoved his hands in his pocket, staring at me – or at the basket – with his face twisted into a frown. There were worried lines dug into his forehead, and I almost felt bad. But not that bad. He *had* just threatened to throw me in the river, and I doubted he'd meant in a life raft. Plus, Callum was here somewhere. I could almost feel him. So I just waited, and hoped it worked. None of my previous deaths had involved drowning, and I wasn't keen to find out how it worked.

"We should go," Marie whispered, and Cherie grabbed her arm. I could see the indent of her fingers from here.

"You know," Parker said, still keeping his hands out of sight, "it's best not to take a risk on this. Not with two captives already, and some cat hanging around yesterday." He nodded firmly, a *decision made* type of nod. "I'll take the cat to her. I can always take it to the river later."

Well, it was a reprieve if nothing else.

"What about us?" Cherie asked, grabbing hold of the basket before he could reach for it. "We want to come too! We *deserve* to come!"

He sighed and reached over the desk to push something. The door beeped an alarm. "Fine. Come on."

PARKER LED the way down a brightly lit hall, the walls the same glossy, polished concrete grey. There was nothing to alleviate it but the occasional painting, all done in shades of grey, and the yellow of the hanging lights. He hit an elevator button at the end of the hall, and machinery rumbled and chugged briefly before the doors clunked open. We piled inside, Cherie beaming triumphantly and Marie sneaking another drink, looking a little like she might fancy doing some vomiting herself.

The doors closed and we headed down with a lurch. I peered out, but there was no display and I couldn't see what button he'd pushed. We were moving for long enough that I guessed we were four or five floors down, though, and I had time to wonder if that made two huge warehouses stacked on top of one another, all packed with contraband, or if there were regular town council type offices sitting on top of the warehouse. I leaned toward the former. Nothing about this place suggested there'd be a meeting about dog parks happening two offices over.

We came to a stop and the doors slid open, letting us into a corridor of rather duller walls and a floor of unpolished concrete scuffed with the passage of feet and trolleys. The corridor stopped at a metal gate, and beyond it the ceiling soared upward, and the familiar huge shelving units crammed with goods filled the space beyond. Magic prickled my fur, and Parker pushed a button that set a buzzer echoing in the vast space beyond the gate. We waited.

I smelled him before I heard the scuffing footsteps – a troll of the non-Gerry type, musky and stinking, his heavy forehead plates all but obscuring his tiny eyes. He grunted at us.

"I've someone to see her," Parker said. "They've caught a cat, and I think it might be the one from the break-in."

The troll stared at my basket, and I could almost hear gears churning in his head. Finally he said, "She busy."

"I know, but this cat might be connected to the captives as well as the break-in."

More slow troll thought, then, "Give me. Put with rest."

"No," Cherie said. "No, he's *our* captive. We want to do it."

"I'm not sure," Marie mumbled, looking at her shoes, and Cherie scowled at her.

The troll looked from one to the other of them, then said, "No."

Cherie pushed Parker aside and started remonstrating with the troll, shaking her finger at him through the gate while he stared at her blankly. Marie tugged at her sister's arm, telling her to stop, and I pushed my nose against the top of the basket.

"Hey," I hissed at Parker, who was rather half-heartedly saying something about procedures. He looked down at me, and I could see sweat on his forehead. Fear was baking off him. He didn't like being this near the troll, or to the furtive things on these dark and secret floors. He wanted to be closer to the sun, where he could shuffle his forms and pretend the worst thing he was involved in was maybe a little light feline murder. Which was plenty, really, but that's how it goes. If it's not your own kind, you can reason a lot away. Hell, even if it *is* your kind. "Just leave us and go," I said. "Promise I won't tell."

He blinked at me. "I can't just leave you down here unsupervised."

"There's a troll," I started, then added, "Oh, too late."

The troll in question was swinging his enormous arms about, roaring in fury, as Cherie sent words whispering toward him, all of them screaming *give me give me mine keys mine give* as they went.

"Stop that!" Parker said, grabbing Cherie's arm, and Marie flung one *no* at him that splatted into his face like an octopus and sent him stumbling back, yelping and pawing at it.

"Cherie, what're you *doing?*" she wailed, turning back to her sister.

"Just explaining the situation," her sister said, still pelting the troll with words. I was starting to feel sorry for him. Words aren't a troll's strong point at the best of times.

He gave a final, frustrated roar, and stomped to the gate. He lifted it clear off its hinges, *do it let us in open the gate open open take us to her* festooning his ears, and glared at the sisters. "Come," he snarled.

They picked me up and hurried through, Cherie grinning and retrieving her words as she went. The troll waved the gate at Parker. "Come," he repeated.

"Um, well, I can't just leave the desk," Parker started, and the troll bared his teeth.

"Your fault. You come."

Parker stared at the teeth, which were large and filed to points. "Right. Coming." He scrambled up, jumping over *stop* as it scuttled after Marie, and the troll lifted the door back into place with a squeal of old metal.

He glared at all of us, then pointed at Cherie and said, "No more words."

"Of course," she said, smiling.

He huffed and stumped off, leading us into the echoing depths of the warehouse while magic twitched and whispered all around us, promising escape and death and glory.

22

SHAKE THE ROOM

THE TROLL LED US – THE BOOKSHOP SISTERS CARRYING ME between them, and the young guard trailing along behind, staring at the shelves as if waiting for something to launch itself at him – through the stacks, following a central corridor that carried us deeper into the building. Our footsteps skittered around behind us, taking on their own life although the shelves were too full to allow them to truly echo. I could smell ancient magics piled around us, roots and stems and preserved plants that grow in forgotten places, ancient stones and cloth woven by abandoned gods.

There were fiercer magics too, curses trapped in glass and amber, spears honed by basilisk tongues and shields fashioned from stolen dragon scales, and the rotting scent of darts dipped in the blood of the kraken. None of them as terrifying as the arsenal of unicorn horn weapons, of course, but the whole place dripped magic. It writhed and fought and scraped, both repelled and attracted, barely contained by hard-edged charms that divided the shelves from each other. It was a powder keg. One scrap of a mislaid charm and the balance would collapse entirely. The magics would rush to war on each other, and the whole place would just dissolve. Half the country with it probably, and the magical fallout would put the wars of the old gods to shame. I tucked my tail a little closer and tried not to breathe too deeply.

Eventually we approached the back wall, formed of old solid stone that made it seem we were in something that was more natural cavern than building. An arch a little bigger than a normal double door was set in it, heavy red curtains with gold trim sealing it shut. The troll pushed through them, and we followed into the domed chamber beyond. The air was heavy with heat and damp, condensation beading on the basket immediately, and it smelled of mudflats at low tide.

Figures loomed out of the mist, and the troll grunted at a hefty colleague. Two of the men from the house – not Boots, but the other two, Liam and Daryl – stood beside the troll, sweat running down their faces and their black T-shirts sticking to their chests. They had the same outsized proportions as the trolls, even if they weren't as big.

"Who's this?" a voice called, rather peevishly. "What's going on? I don't even know why these two are here yet!"

Either the murk of humidity had cleared a bit, or I was getting used to it, because I spotted someone sitting in a natural pool, a long blue dress floating around them and a slightly wilted crown of daisies perched on their bald head. The water was steaming softly.

"Cat," our troll escort said, waving at the sisters, who carted me forward triumphantly.

"We have a captive, your honour!" Cherie shouted.

Your honour? I squinted through the murk. This had to be the mayor, then.

"I'm not *deaf*."

"Sorry. I said, we have a captive."

"I heard you the first time, you were just too loud." The mayor dipped a fat pink sponge into the water and squeezed it over her head. "What do you want me to do with them?"

"Um. Well, we thought you might want to put it with the other captives?" Cherie said. Marie was swaying in the heat, looking distinctly unwell.

"*Him*," I shouted. "Him, not *it!*"

"It's mouthy," Cherie said. "But it came to Dimly with Callum."

"Callum? Oh, that's one of you, isn't it?" The mayor turned her bulky body to look at the other side of the pool, and I flung myself at the side of the basket, trying to see through the misty room. Marie dropped her handle with a whimper, and the weight of the fall ripped the other out of Cherie's grip. I yelped as the basket landed on its side and started rolling, flopping me about like a hamster in a runaway wheel.

"*Marie!*" Cherie shrieked, and I heard the dull thud of her shoes on the wet stone as she bolted after me. I found my feet and started to run, moving with the momentum of the basket, driving it faster and faster with no way of knowing what direction I was going in or what I was going to run into. Over the creak of the wicker I could hear more shouts and more running feet, and someone ahead of me gave a squawk of alarm. Well, they'd have to get out of my way.

"*Incoming!*" I yelled, just for the hell of it, and in that moment the basket hit a bump. I was airborne for a breath, my claws popping out as I flailed for a grip on the basket, then I was falling with it.

I hit the water with a hard, angry splash, and Callum yelled "*Gobs!*" from somewhere to the side. Water surged up around me, filling my nose, my ears, my eyes, stinking of expensive soap layered over something musty and unpleasant. The basket pushed down around me, trapping me beneath the surface, and I scrabbled at it frantically, not sure if I was trying to swim up or down or sideways, everything a confused mess of bubbles and water and a roaring in my ears that wanted me to breathe, *breathe* dammit! My nose broke the surface and I heaved a gasp that was more liquid than air, then the basket shoved me down and rolled me over again, and I had time to think that two baths in less than twenty-four hours was just insulting, and also proved my theory that it was dangerous to your health.

I bumped my nose on the wicker hard enough to make me splutter and suck in more water, and everything got a little dim and strange. I drifted in the confines of the basket, wondering what had been so urgent a moment ago. I was floating. Floating wasn't so bad. I could do floating. The weird green was even kind of nice on the eyes. I opened my mouth and watched a bubble drift away, and thought, *Well. That's up, then,* but I couldn't remember why that might be important. Not when it was so warm and floaty here.

The basket jerked, hard, then I was roaring upward with my belly flat to the wicker, water pouring off me like a whale breaching. Air rushed around me and I gasped it in with a whoop, then promptly coughed it all out again, along with about half the pool. Someone ripped the lid away, which happened to be what I was lying on, and I fell straight back into the water with a yowl of alarm. The dim green didn't feel so welcoming once I had a lungful of air again.

Hands grabbed me and hauled me back into the air, and I hung in their grip, still coughing and gasping and dribbling water everywhere. The abandoned basket bobbed below me.

"*Gobs!*" Callum shouted again, and I peered in his direction.

"Hey," I managed, when I finally spotted him. He and Art were on their knees, hands tied behind them, and two more of the black-clad guards loomed over them. There was blood on the side of Callum's face, and his jacket pooled on the floor around him.

"Are you okay?" he demanded.

"Wet," I said.

"Great rescue," Art said, and Callum gave him a look that suggested we wouldn't be taking any cases for old friends in the near future.

"Poor kitty," the owner of the hands said, and the next minute I was cradled against an extremely large, damp bosom. "How careless! You could have *drowned* him, throwing him in here like that! Do you know how many drowned cats I've seen? Puppies? Even *children?*" There was silence around the pool, and I blinked up at the mayor. She was holding me in two webbed hands and was shaking a third at Cherie. The fourth was set on her waist. I shook water out of my ears and stared down into the pool, which was quite a long way beneath me. Two pairs of legs were folded comfortably under the water, peeking out from under her floating skirt, and a muscular, finned tail curled and flicked behind her. It seemed an excessive amount of limbs. "No one was meant to get hurt," she shouted. "*No one!*"

Cherie clutched her hands to her chest, and Marie grabbed her arm, pulling her back toward the door. The troll stepped behind them, and they bumped off his huge chest with matching shrieks of alarm.

"I didn't say you could leave!" the mayor shouted. "Did I say you could leave?"

"No, your honour," Marie said. Cherie was opening and shutting her mouth, but nothing was coming out. "Sorry, your honour. We thought you might not want us in your sight, considering we disappointed you."

"Sit *down,*" the mayor snapped, and the troll put a heavy hand on the sisters' shoulders, pressing them firmly down to the ground. The room fell silent. The mayor lifted me up and held me at eye level. She had a large collection of very sharp teeth that angled inward, and translucent third eyelids slid across her bulging eyes as she examined me. "Are you hurt?"

"My dignity's mildly bruised," I said. "But nothing else. Thanks for the save."

"You're quite welcome," she said. "I don't like creatures

to get hurt."

I through of the crows and the d'wyrms, the vanished cats and destroyed rats, and said carefully, "That's nice."

She frowned at me. "You don't believe me."

"Well, no offence, but the Dimly civic code appears to be *tear outsiders limb from limb.*"

"It is not! It's ..." she thought about it. "Actually, I'm not sure I know. I've read all the Dimly history books, but I don't think it was in there."

"Maybe it's an unofficial code," I suggested.

"I'd never approve that."

I looked at her teeth, and said, "Well, that'd be why it's unofficial."

"But I wouldn't *allow* it, either."

"If you knew about it."

"I'm *the mayor.* I know everything that happens."

"Yeah, but there's such a thing as the power behind the throne," I pointed out.

We looked at each other for a moment longer, then she said, "Should I have a throne?"

"I don't know. We go in more for heated beds."

She blinked a couple of times, and licked her eyes clean with a long tongue, which seemed quite a feat given all the teeth it had to navigate. Then she set me on the side of the pool and said, "What're you doing here? I thought cats didn't come to Dimly."

"Cats aren't *allowed* in Dimly," I said. "Or rats. They get ... dispatched."

She frowned. "I never authorised that. That can't be right."

"It is."

She looked at the trolls. "Is this true?"

They shifted uneasily. It was like watching small hills who needed the loo.

"Answer me!"

"Can't," the door troll said, scratching the back of his head.

"I'm *the mayor!*"

"Can't. Boss say no."

"*I'm* the boss!"

"No," both trolls said.

The mayor glared at them, and pointed at the human guards. Or human-ish – they all looked terribly similar, as if they'd come off a production line, all broad chests and no necks and short hair. "You lot! Who's in charge here?"

There was a lot of shuffling, then Daryl, who was marginally shorter than the others and had a big scar curling over his cheek, said, "Well, *here,* it's you, of course, Madam Mayor."

She started to give me a *told you so* look, then stopped and looked back at Daryl. "Here as in Dimly, not this room."

He stared at her, expressionless. "You're the mayor," he said.

She frowned at him, then pointed at Art and Callum. "Why are they here? Where were you taking them?"

"It's a security issue, ma'am. We were going to put them in the cells for now."

"They don't look dangerous."

They didn't. Art looked on the verge of tears and Callum had his *I'm completely harmless* look on. He smiled at the mayor, adding the dimples for good measure, and said, "This has all been a misunderstanding, your honour. These men took us from my friend's house for no reason."

"We were under orders to bring them in. Corporate espionage, ma'am."

Callum laughed. "Do we look like corporate spies?"

The mayor examined him. "You really don't."

"Ma'am, we had an incursion into the warehouse yesterday. It was a black cat – almost certainly that one." Daryl was looking uncomfortable, and I had a feeling he was used to taking orders and passing them on, not arguing with multi-limbed city officials or thinking on his feet.

"That's outrageous," I said. "I suppose you think we all look alike, don't you?"

He gave me a look that suggested he was not a cat person.

The mayor looked at me, then back at the guard. "That seems very tenuous. Untie those two, at least. They're not exactly going to go running off with all of you here, are they?"

Daryl sighed. "I can't do that, ma'am."

"I'm the mayor, and I'm telling you to untie them *now*."

"We have our orders. They *were* to be taken to the cells. As you have asked us to bring them here instead, they will remain restrained."

"*My* orders supersede any others."

"I'm afraid not, ma'am. The security forces don't answer to you."

The mayor leaned her four forearms on the edge of the pool and examined him. He clasped his hands behind his back, squaring his shoulders and lifting his chin. She grinned, showing off those curving teeth. "Just who do you answer to, if not me?"

No one answered. Puddles were forming around my feet, and the air was so thick with damp that I didn't feel as if I'd be much drier even if I hadn't fallen in the pool. The mayor hefted herself out of the water, squeezing out the sodden skirt of her dress and arranging it over her tail and legs. She was as tall as the men, and her twitching, muscular tail made her a lot longer. She took two steps toward Callum and Art and repeated, "Let them go. Now."

"That's not possible, ma'am," Daryl said, his voice steady.

They stared at each other, and I said, "I suppose you're worried we might tell tales about your little arsenal of unicorn dust weapons. That's fair. I'd be worried if I was breaking that many treaties and conventions, too."

"*What?*" the mayor rounded on me, her teeth alarmingly close. "What weapons? What're you talking about?"

Daryl nodded at one of his clone-like buddies – it might've been Liam, but it really was hard to tell them apart. "Grab that bloody cat, would you?"

"You will not," the mayor hissed, as maybe-Liam started forward. "Tell me about the weapons."

"They're all locked up in the warehouse," I said. "Crates and crates of them. Could outfit an army with that lot." I sidestepped the guard as he made a grab for me. "Back off, Sasquatch."

"I never authorised *anything* like that!" The mayor turned back to Daryl. "Is this true?"

"I can't comment, ma'am," he said.

"You bloody will," she said, clambering out of the pool.

Sasquatch/Liam tried for me again, and I skipped after the mayor.

"It's not to do with you, ma'am," Daryl said.

"I am *the mayor!*"

A small sound caught my ear, a clatter of a pebble under a biker boot, and I looked around. Cherie was glaring at her sister, but Marie was looking at me. When I met her eyes, she flicked her gaze at the trolls. They were moving in hunting mode, that weirdly swift and silent gait that seemed as unsuited to trolls as a hippo is to gymnastics, hands helping them along and footsteps soft as a breath as they skirted the cavern to get behind the mayor. Parker was standing by the entrance looking like he wanted to run but was too scared to move.

"Hey," I said, turning to face the trolls. "Back off, dudes." My tail tried to do an impressive pouf, but I was too wet.

The mayor looked around, her eyes narrowing as she spotted the trolls. "What're you doing?" she demanded. "Stop that!"

They kept coming, still moving with slow, inexorable focus.

"Get back in your pool," Daryl said, and the mayor turned on him, her teeth bared.

"How *dare* you?"

He smiled at her, a tight, humourless grimace. "I'm sorry, ma'am, but you should not have seen these prisoners or heard about the weapons. I have my orders. Get back in the pool."

She glared at him, and he raised one hand. It wasn't a threatening movement. It was just a display. A small black gadget nestled in his palm, and I could smell the electricity from here.

"A *taser?*" I demanded. "Dude, you *suck.*"

"It won't kill her," he said. "Not even if she is in her pool. It's merely a persuasion of sorts. Would you rather I used one of *our* weapons?"

The mayor backed slowly into the pool, her eyes never leaving him. "You made weapons of unicorn horn," she said. "Who authorised this? And how *could* you?"

Daryl smiled slightly. "It's not me personally, ma'am. I'm just following orders." He nodded at Sasquatch. "Hurry up and put that cat back in the basket. She'll be here soon."

She. It had never been the mayor. The mayor wasn't the *she* the sisters had been talking about, and she had never been the one to suffocate the town and raise an arsenal. No one who worried about drowned kittens was going to do that. I sidestepped the guard as he grabbed for me again, not really paying attention.

"Who's in charge then?" I asked. "May as well tell us before she gets here." Sasquatch made another grab for me, and I slapped his hand casually. He yelped and clutched it to his chest.

"It *scratched* me!" he wailed, his enormous shoulders lifted to his ears.

"*He!*" I bellowed. "*He,* not *it!*" I threw myself at his legs, all claws and teeth, and the man staggered back, his hands raised in horror.

"It's just a damn animal," Daryl shouted. "Grab it!"

"Oh boy," Callum said, to no one in particular, and jumped straight from kneeling to his feet.

23

WELL, AT LEAST WE'RE ALL TOGETHER AGAIN

IT COULD HAVE BEEN AN IMPRESSIVE JUMP, BUT CALLUM tripped on his coat and staggered forward, head down as he turned the fall into a clumsy charge, barely keeping his feet. He barrelled into Daryl, who swore and shoved him to the ground. Sasquatch aimed a kick at me and the mayor surged out of the water, grabbing him up. She swung him over her head as he shrieked, then charged back into the pool, twirling like a dancer lifting a partner, and flung him into the oncoming trolls. They fell like bowling pins, and I ran for Callum, scampering straight to his shoulder as Daryl pulled him to his feet. I leaped at the man's face and he yelped, letting Callum go and fending me off with his forearm. I got one good claw to his nose and bounced away again.

"Callum, *move!*" I shouted at him.

"Art!" he yelled. "Art, come on!"

Art was still kneeling on the floor, staring around in alarm, and he gave a squeak as two of the giant guards grabbed Callum. The mayor lunged out of the water to rejoin the fray, and Daryl brandished his taser at her.

"*Stay there,*" he ordered her, and I raced straight up his back and bit his ear, making him squall. The trolls had regrouped and were splashing across the pool toward us, and the mayor spun back to face them, punching the first one in the eye and sending him crashing to the ground, where he lay rocking and groaning to himself. The second one grabbed her, and I threw myself off Daryl as he yelled, "Will someone get that bloody *cat?*"

I spat at him, running to join the mayor as she threw off the second troll, bouncing him bodily off the rim of the pool and sending him slamming into the first troll, who was just sitting up with one hand still over his eye. They crashed to the floor in a thunder of colliding forehead plates and stony troll muscle, and the mayor and I turned to face Daryl together. Two of the other guards were sitting on Callum, holding him down as he bucked and swore, and Sasquatch was still lying on the far side of the pool making small sad noises to himself.

Daryl looked at the trolls, who were struggling to disentangle themselves, then spotted Parker, and yelled, "Get over here and make yourself useful!" Parker looked like he was about to faint, and Daryl made a disgusted noise. He pointed at one of the trolls, who had managed to get to his feet but looked a bit dazed. "On three," he told him.

"Tree? Is no tree."

"Jesus *Christ.* Just *grab her.*"

"Ah. Okay." The troll hulked forward, circling to one

side of the mayor as Daryl went to the other. The taser looked ugly and vicious in his hand.

"Move, cat," the mayor said. "Don't get hit." She dropped into a crouch, two hands out to each of her opponents, tail and legs braced. I hesitated, then shot toward Callum, leaping at one of the guards with my teeth bared. The guard yelped and jerked back, bumping into his buddy, and Callum wriggled away from them, flopping about the place helplessly as he tried to get to his feet. The mayor gave a ululating battle cry and charged the troll. He grabbed her as she slammed into him and they plunged into the pool together, hitting the bottom with a thud I felt in my paws, and as Daryl ran toward them with the taser brandished, a clear voice rang across the murky chaos of the cavern.

"What the *hell* is going on here?" it demanded, and everything stopped.

"MA'AM," Daryl said. He wasn't moving, but he still had the taser in his hand and his eyes on the mayor.

The mayor sat up, the water reaching her non-existent waist, but didn't let go of the spluttering troll. The second troll sat up with a groan beside the pool, one hand pressed over his eye.

"Ow," he announced, then seemed to notice the silence of the room.

Callum rolled to his knees, the blood on his face standing out starkly against his skin. Marie and Cherie retreated from the door, not quite looking at the new arrivals. I squinted at them. The low light and steam made it hard to make things out, but it looked like Boots, with another couple of black-clad guards and a woman standing in front of them. Trainers. She was still wearing skinny jeans, her hands hooked into the back pockets and her thick, messy hair pulled back from her face.

"Is anyone going to answer me?" she asked.

"A slight problem with a cat, ma'am," Daryl said. "Bloody nuisance of a thing."

"Not a thing," I snapped, then added (not without pride), "And that has been said before."

"A cat," Trainers said. "Two trolls, four – no, *five* guards, since you left your post, kid – and you're having trouble with a *cat.*"

Parker looked like he was going to faint.

"You obviously don't have much experience with cats," I said. "We're disproportionately troublesome."

She ambled further into the room, her hands still in her pockets, and smiled at me. There was something disquietingly familiar about that grin. "We'll have to deal with you in a disproportionate manner then, won't we?"

"How? With unicorn horn weapons? Take all my lives, just like that? You know how much of a contravention of *all* treaties using horn is? Wouldn't like to be in your socks when the Watch get wind of it."

"Gobs," Callum said, a warning in his voice, but I ignored him.

Trainers' smile tightened. "I see we've got a snoop."

The mayor put one hand over the troll's face as he tried to get up, dunking him under the surface while he thrashed in alarm. "I've got some questions for you, Ez.

What's this about unicorn horn weapons? What are you doing with these men? And … and these guards *threatened* me! I'm *the mayor!*"

Ez?

"Of course you are," Ez said, the way humans sometimes tell me *of course* I'm the best little cat in the world. The mayor's expression didn't change, but her tail swirled the water like a crocodile's. Apparently she liked that tone about as much as I do.

"Why have we got *any* sort of weapons, let alone those?" the mayor asked. "When I was elected, it was on a promise to clean the town up. To eliminate any illicit trade, not make it worse!"

"I think I used the term *control* rather than *eliminate,*" Ez said.

"This is *unacceptable.* Those weapons must be destroyed at once. And why are you taking prisoners without my knowledge?"

Ez sighed and looked at the floor. "I'm sorry. But this is just how it is. There must always be a figurehead, and there must always be one in charge. And they're very rarely the same person."

"I won't stand for it," the mayor declared, climbing to her feet. "I won't let you hurt people. I *won't!*"

"Where's my sister?" Art shouted suddenly. "I want to see my sister!"

"Art, shut up," Callum said.

"No, I won't! I want to see Kara!"

Callum looked at Ez and said, "Let Art go. You've got me now. What do you need him for?"

"What?" I demanded. "Why do they need you? Who is

this fly-blown cabbage, anyway?" And then I remembered. *Ez*. Esme, although no one called her that to her face. Callum's sister. "Hang on, shouldn't you be dead or something?"

Ez snorted. "You do keep bad company, little brother."

"Not since I left here," he said, his voice flat.

I glared at Ez. "Bloody Watch. The one time you actually want them to do a decent job."

Ez gave me a cool look, the familiarity of her slim, slouching stance making perfect sense now. "Business is business, cat. It pays to make yourself useful to the right people."

I scooted across the floor to stand in front of Callum, baring my teeth at his sister. "So, what? This was all a set-up, just to get Callum back here? You and Kara cooked it all up?"

"Kara *wouldn't,*" Art snapped. "Where is she? Kara! *Kara!*"

Ez rubbed her face with one hand. "God, Art, *shut up*. She's fine."

"You cut her finger off!"

Boots burst out laughing. "Sure we did."

"I *saw* it!"

"Art, it's okay," Callum said, and the mayor shouted over him, "You cut someone's *finger* off? What is *wrong* with you people?" The troll had another go at sitting up and she shoved him back under the water.

"Great. Now you've set her off," Ez said, and bent down to grab Callum's arm. "Get up."

"Someone tell me what's going on," the mayor demanded. "I won't have this!"

"Everything is under control," Ez said, helping Callum to his feet.

"Let him go," I told her, and she gave me that amused look again.

"Or what? What're you going to do, all on your lonesome?"

"Gobs," Callum started, and she burst out laughing.

"*Gobs?* Aw, that's so cute—"

I went for her ankles with every drop of pure fury in my heart. Anyone who knows cats realises just how much that is. Look, we're perfect killing machines and everyone keeps telling us we're cute little poppets. And we generally can't *do* much about it, because treaties and the Watch and all the rest, so we just have to take it. So, yeah. We have a *lot* of rage.

Ez yelped, letting go of Callum and staggering back as she tried to knock me off, but I was already swarming up her jeans, laying my claws as deep as I could. All I could think of was Callum and his lost friends, his lost childhood, his lost *years* even when he did get away from his poisonous family, drowning in human drugs as surely as he'd drowned in Dimly ones. Callum and his hard-won silence, his fragile centre of peace. And she'd take that away from him. She'd pull him back in here to rot, just because she could. Just because she couldn't stand to see him free. I'd tear her heart out if I could find it.

"*Gobs, jump!*" Callum yelled, and the words sank in far enough that I threw myself free just as he charged Ez, catching her in the belly with his shoulder and taking them both crashing to floor.

Art scrambled up and took off for the mouth of the

chamber at a sprint, dodging Boots and his guards with surprising agility, shouting his sister's name. The mayor galloped toward us and grabbed Daryl, flinging him bodily into the pool to collide with the troll and sending the taser flying with him. I half-expected the whole place to get zapped, given how damp everything was, but there was just a sharp snap, then the scent of melted electrics joined the damp stink of the place as Daryl clung to the troll with a dazed look on his face.

I threw myself at Ez's arms, clawing hard as she struggled to shove Callum off. She swore and caught me a belt across one ear that made me hiss and jump back.

"Run!" Callum snapped at me, then yelped as Ez's knee caught him somewhere sensitive.

She rolled him back onto the floor, jumped to her feet, and bellowed, "Can we *please* get this lot under control?"

Parker took a hesitant step to stop Art, then flinched back when Art screamed in his face like he'd been the one kneed in sensitive places. Art charged through the curtains and vanished, and Boots took off after him with two of the guards following. The sisters started throwing words about the place frantically, but Marie was squinting through one eye and her words got tangled around one of the trolls. I couldn't quite tell if it was deliberate or not. Cherie's words went straight for the mayor, though, tugging at her dress and tangling around her feet, whispering *stop halt don't move freeze trapped trapped trapped frozen stuck*. Ez grabbed the back of Callum's coat and hauled him to his knees, and when I hissed at her she just smiled.

"What're you really going to do, kitty? I've had worse than a few scratches in my life."

"You want me to get the cat?" Daryl asked. He was dripping wet and looked mildly concussed, but he'd disentangled himself from the troll and discarded the taser in favour of a large knife that glittered with the rainbow tint of unicorn horn. I took a step back, baring my teeth at him.

"Not with that," she said. "We'll just let the lizards have him."

"Can try it," I said. "But I've already outrun them once. Got a couple mummified, too."

Ez sighed and hefted Callum to his feet, checking his hands were secure. "That was some very expensive sabotage, you know. But at least I know there's only one of you running about. That's handy."

I glared at her, trying to think of something smart to say, and Callum flung his head back hard. He caught his sister in the nose with a solid crunch and she yelped, letting him go and staggering back as she clutched her injured face. He scrambled to his feet, managing not to trip himself on his coat this time.

"Nice," I said, and broke into a sprint as Daryl swiped at me with the knife. Callum kicked him in the knee and took off after me.

We slalomed across the floor, jumping words and swerving away from guards, and the mayor thundered after us, trying to rip herself free of the clinging words as she went. The trolls lunged after her, grabbing her dress to hold her back and ripping gauzy handfuls of it away, which only meant she ran faster with her scaly legs bare.

Parker hesitated as we passed, then stepped forward and snatched up the pursuing train of *stop halt hold* in both hands and tore it effortlessly.

"Hey!" Cherie shrieked. "Our *words!*"

"You broke them!" Marie said, staring at the young guard with wide eyes.

"Come on!" Callum shouted at him, dropping his shoulder and charging through the heavy curtains into the warehouse – and straight into a woman on her way in. She crashed to the floor with a yelp, a crossbow clutched in her hands. She jerked the trigger as she fell but the shot went wild, the bolt scattering softly singing dust behind it.

"*Kara!*" Art screamed behind her. A guard with a Komodo dragon was standing over him, the lizard straining toward Art's face with its teeth bared. Boots was right behind Kara, and he gave the sort of sigh you'd expect from a long-suffering civil servant of some sort.

"Honestly," he said to no one in particular, levelling his own crossbow at Callum. "Just settle down, alright?"

Callum hesitated, then Parker plunged through the curtains and sent both of them sprawling to the ground.

"*Move!*" I yelled. "She's not on our side!"

Kara swung the crossbow to bear on Callum as he struggled to get to his knees, and he said, "I see that."

Boots grabbed the back of Parker's shirt and hauled him up, the young man squeaking in fright.

"Finger grew back well," I told Kara, and she glanced at me, a smile quirking the corners of her mouth.

"Gobs, *go*," Callum said, and I opened my mouth to tell him exactly what I thought of that just as the mayor plunged through the curtains with both trolls on her back. She dropped to all eight hands and feet, bellowing wordlessly as she sprang forward, her tail whipping in fury and sweeping Boots' feet out from under him. He yelped, letting go of Parker as he fell into the pile-up, and the young guard grabbed Callum, dragging him clear. Kara screamed, rolling to the side as the mayor landed right where she'd been sitting, and the mayor's tail brought the heavy curtains billowing down over all of them.

Callum scrambled back, away from the tangle of curtains and limbs and shouting, and Parker helped him to his feet. "Art!" Callum yelled, and Art made some incoherent plea as he strained away from the Komodo.

"Leave him – we've got to get out," I shouted at Callum, struggling to be heard over some highly creative swearing from the curtains. The other guards were running in from the pool chamber, Ez striding after them, the bookshop sisters' words chasing around the curtains and grabbing hold of people indiscriminately. "We'll come back for him! You're the one the dodgy sister tag-team wants anyway!"

"Open the weapons store!" Kara shrieked over the roaring trolls and the curses of the mayor as she struggled out from under the curtains. "Call more guards and seal Dimly! No one leaves. *No one!*"

"Callum, God*dam*mit!" Ez shouted. "Just stop! *Stop!*"

A crossbow bolt whistled past my ears, and I used one of my favourite human swearwords. Parker yelped and dived to the stacks on one side as Callum sprinted to the other, and I pelted after him, fleeing into the magic-laden air of the warehouse.

24

A GOOD OLD-FASHIONED BRAWL

I CHARGED AFTER CALLUM AS HE VANISHED DOWN ONE OF the aisles in the centre of the vast warehouse. I leaped to the first shelf and raced along it, dodging through the twitching limbs of bone and hide chairs. Callum sprinted for the wall at the far end of the aisle, where there looked to be a gap between the shelving and the wall, and I yelled, "Left! The lifts are to the left!"

Running feet charged into the aisle behind us, and I could hear Kara still screaming for more weapons and Ez shouting for everyone to stay where they were. A crossbow bolt tore past Callum and headed for the far wall, and he dived into the shelving across the aisle from mine. There was the clatter of small, probably priceless and almost definitely dangerous things breaking, and I leaped after him. I hit hard, skidding across the metal shelf and ploughing nose-first into a collection of stuffed mice in bell jars, all of them with too many teeth, extra limbs, and some interesting weaponry.

The jars rocked alarmingly, and I kept going before

anything broke out and tried to eat me. Callum rolled out of the shelf underneath me and ran straight across the aisle, a bright yellow feather boa clinging to his shoulders and wriggling hopefully toward his neck. I bunched my hind legs under me and launched myself across the gap, and slammed straight into a large troll who was moving far too quickly to be reasonable. I smashed into his back with a squawk, slid to the floor with my nose hurting and my ears ringing, and staggered into a run as he tried to stomp on me. Callum had already rolled through to the next aisle along, shouting my name, and I scooted into the cobwebby space under the bottom shelf to follow him, the troll's fingers passing close enough to my tail that I think I lost a few hairs. Not that there were many left to lose after the crows and lizards, mind.

The bottom shelves on the next aisle were stacked with massive, stained wooden crates, all sealed shut with nails and chains, so we sprinted straight down the aisle as Callum searched for a gap to crawl through. The troll thundered along the aisle we'd just left, keeping pace with us, and more crossbow bolts whistled past us, but they went wide. I glanced back and spotted two guards running after us, and one of them held a hand up to show he wasn't going to shoot and shouted, "Stop! Just stop, okay?"

Callum picked up the pace and I jumped to the first shelf, scooting between some large sealed jugs to peer into the next aisle. I came almost face to face with a crossbow, and threw myself back behind the nearest jug, which promptly exploded in a rush of warm, honey-scented oil.

"Hey!" I yelped, jumping sideways before I could get

oil on my paws and shaking the drops off my back. I peered at the damp spots anxiously, making sure I wasn't sprouting tiny hairy gargoyles or something. "Magic stuff up here! You don't know what you're unleashing!"

"Unicorn horn bolts, cat," Kara said, stooping to grin at me. I didn't like that grin. I knew that sort of grin. The last time I'd been near one, the owner had been grinding lit cigarettes into my kitten-sized shoulder. And this time I didn't think Callum could come charging to my rescue armed with nothing but cat-friendly outrage. "They'll kill anything."

"Sure, if it's alive," I retorted. "You've got no idea what it might do to inanimate objects."

She hesitated, grin fading, and I shoulder-barged the next jug along, hefting it off the shelf and straight at her face. She jumped back with a curse and I followed the jug, flying across the aisle and diving for the shelter of the next row of shelving. I skidded through a thicket of Russian nesting dolls, sending them rolling in every direction. They immediately started unpacking themselves, all waving their arms and scolding me in thin voices, and I kept going.

"Callum!" I yelled as I jumped the next aisle, and caught a glimpse of someone sprinting along the wall at the far end of the shelving.

"Here!" he shouted, then was gone again, a troll lumbering after him. I dodged a large collection of ashtrays in the shape of fanged ladybirds, one of which rolled over and sprinted after me, whistling with excitement, and jumped to the floor as the shelves gave way to open space that led all the way to the gate Parker had brought us to about three days ago, as far as I could tell. I zigzagged across the floor, the ladybird ashtray still running after me and a pack of Russian dolls waving splinters and nails following on behind. Although I was less worried by them than by the two crossbow bolts that clattered to the ground as I dodged and dived with no idea where the next shot was coming from.

But I was almost there. Two final hard turns, one more near-miss, and I dived behind a small waste-paper basket (I guess even magical goons need somewhere to put their sandwich wrappers) as Callum emerged from the shelves, running hard with the troll still lumbering after him. The troll had gone an interesting neon yellow, and had feathers sprouting on his tail and head, so I guess Callum had put the feather boa to good use. The troll was unfortunately still very mobile though, and looked even angrier than trolls usually do.

"Come on, come on!" I shouted, and Callum came skidding to a stop next to me, grabbed the gate and pulled.

It didn't move. Callum ducked behind a big amphora in a stand as a crossbow bolt whistled past his head, and said, "It's locked."

I blinked at him. "The troll just lifted it off the hinges."

He looked at the huge gate. The troll had stopped mid-reach for Callum when one of the bolts nicked his nose, and was now advancing on two guards who looked like they wished they were anywhere else but here.

"Who shoot?" the troll thundered. "*Who shoot?*" His nose had gone a bright pink that clashed violently with the yellow.

Callum took the opportunity to grab the gate again and try lifting it. It squeaked a little on the hinges, but didn't move. "No good."

"Awesome," I said, and the lift *ding*ed. Callum ducked back down next to me and we both peered around as the lift doors slid open. There was a *buzz,* a click, and the gate popped ajar, but before we could decide if that was a good thing or not half a dozen giant lizards came thundering out of the corridor, followed by the same amount of the big, broad, indistinguishable guards, all armed with crossbows and looking suitably determined.

"Hairballs," I said.

"Run," Callum suggested, but when he stood up he was faced by a pink and yellow, irate troll and a close-up view of three crossbows. The fourth was pointed at me.

"Hairballs," I said again.

"What a bloody mess," Ez said, wiping blood from under her injured nose, then waved at the yellow troll and two of the guards. "Bring everyone up here." They hurried off, and she looked back at us with her hands on her hips. "Absolute mess," she said again.

"Like that's surprising," Kara said. She was methodically crushing the Russian dolls under her boots, her crossbow hanging from one hand and her curly hair tangling down her back. There was a fat red lump on her cheek where something had hit her or bitten her. I hoped it got infected.

The new arrivals marched through the gates and surrounded us, the Komodos staring at me and licking their lipless mouths. A couple of guards grabbed Callum and dragged him out from behind the amphora to the middle of the floor, leaving him there on his knees with his hands still trussed behind his back and his jaw set in a hard line. A few stray feathers and some cobwebs decorated his hair. The remaining guards kept their crossbows trained on us, and Kara kicked the last of the dolls away.

"Let's just get rid of them," she said. "What're we waiting for here?"

Ez gave her a cool look. "When did you get a crossbow, anyway? I didn't say you could have one."

"I've got every right to defend myself," Kara snapped.

Ez shook her head and gave Callum a *kids, what can you do?* look. He just looked back at her, his expression unchanging. There was silence for a moment, broken only by dragging footsteps as the mayor and Art were ushered back by the guards. The mayor looked furious and the regular-coloured troll had a black eye. The bookshop sisters hurried along behind, clinging to each other, and there was no sign of Parker.

"So, it was all a trap?" I said to Ez. "You just wanted Art to get Callum back here?"

She glanced at me, but addressed Callum. "I never wanted you back here—"

"That was me," Kara said, bouncing on her toes. "I was like, bonus, right? He'll find the unicorns *and* we can show him what happens to people who leave Dimly. But you're a useless investigator. You can't even find a whole herd of stupid bloody animals."

I growled, and she aimed a kick at me. I jumped her foot and hissed at her. Callum didn't say anything, just looked at the ceiling as if he were bored.

"I don't *understand,*" Art said. "Kara, what's going on?"

She sighed rather extravagantly and swung the crossbow onto her shoulder, standing with one hip cocked out. She was wearing skinny jeans too, but with boots and a leather jacket. "No one ever accused you of being the brains of the family, Art. But it's alright. Just shut up, do as you're told, and you'll be back to your farm-yard animals before you know it."

"The trade never stopped after the raids, did it?" I asked. "Kara took it on."

"We had a break," Ez said, before Kara could answer. "I was away when the Watch came for our families. When I came back … well, I laid low for a while, then set up again. The town needed some structure."

"That was meant to be *me,*" the mayor protested. "I was going to make this place safe. Instead you've turned it into some *weapons factory.*"

"Oh, shut up, flippers," Kara said, waving the crossbow at her. "Honestly, you're so boring. *Ooh, my poor river. Ooh, the poor animals. Ooh, the poor town*. Ugh."

"I'll give you flippers," the mayor snarled, and both trolls wrestled her back as she tried to grab for Kara, who just laughed.

"It doesn't make sense," I said. "The Watch left the unicorns, which is strange enough. But they left you alive, and didn't even check back? That doesn't seem right. They don't tend to like loose ends."

Ez gave me a crooked smile that was far too like Callum's. "Even the Watch keep up appearances at times. Especially if you prove useful."

"Who're the weapons for, then?" I asked. "They're not

exactly cat-accessible." And wasn't that a gruesome thought, the Watch allowing those things here?

"Oh, sodding hell," Kara said. "Why are we even listening to this animal squawk?"

I hissed at her, but didn't do anything else. There were four crossbows pointed steadily at me, and the lizards stared at me with flaring nostrils. Even if she didn't get me, someone would.

"None of this should be happening," the mayor said. "This is just *awful*."

"Oh, stop your whinging," Kara snapped. "You were in a *puddle*. Sitting there mourning your bloody reeds or whatever. Just be thankful we pulled you out of it."

A little movement caught my eye and I glanced at it, thinking it was one of the sister's words. They seemed very subdued, though. Cherie had a handful of wilted vowels she was stroking mournfully. And I couldn't see any words on the floor. I looked back at Ez, who was smiling at the mayor.

"Nothing changes," she said. "You'll go on just as normal, and so will we. This is just a business deal that got … complicated."

"Go on as *normal?* I can't go on as normal! I'm not even a proper mayor!" She pointed at us. "And what about them? You think I can just ignore the fact that you've got *prisoners* here?"

"Jesus, let's just get rid of her, too," Kara said. "She stinks, anyway."

"Kara," Art said, his voice pleading. "You didn't really know about this, did you? I mean, it's okay, I understand you dealing horn. I know you wanted more than the herd—"

"Honestly, Art, just shut up before I shoot you," she said.

I caught that movement again, and glanced at Callum. He shifted where he knelt, flaring his fingers. Had that been all I'd seen?

"Dude, your sister is even worse than Callum's," I told Art.

"She's just confused," Art said. "Kara, look, I know things have been so hard since, well, you know—"

"I really am going to shoot you," she said, levelling the crossbow at his head.

"Kara, stop it," Ez said sharply, and the younger woman laughed, then shifted the bow to point it at me.

"Fine. I think I'll get rid of the cat, though. Even the pit's too good for cats."

"You won't touch him," Callum said, his voice flat. It was the first thing he'd said since we'd been caught at the gates.

"Don't shoot the cat, Kara," Ez said, rubbing her forehead.

She smiled. "Fine. There are other ways." She gestured at the guards, and they slipped the leashes off the Komodos. Art gave a strangled squawk.

"No, *stop,*" Ez said, and one of the guards stepped forward, grabbing for the lizards' collars, but Kara levelled the crossbow at him.

"*Don't*. It's just a bloody *cat.*"

"Kara, stop it," Ez snapped, and the younger woman took a step away from her.

"Back off, Ez."

"*No.* This is *not* how we do things."

I stared from the advancing lizards to the guards, who still had their weapons trained on me but didn't seem sure what to do. I looked at Kara and said, "You're a horrible, rotting cabbage forgotten in the veggie bin for six years."

She burst out laughing, and I went from sitting to airborne in one leap that wrenched the muscles in my back and strained my poor exhausted legs. Kara raised one hand to fend me off, still laughing as she stepped back, and the Komodos burst into a sprint, thundering toward us. Then someone snatched me out of the air, and Boots yelled, "What the *hell?*"

Ez said something stronger.

Small furred movement surged across the floor, a wave of tiny bodies and nipping, snapping teeth. The rats were sprinting through the Komodos, diverting them, and the lizards forgot about me and started chasing the tasty little morsels instead. More rats were running up the legs of the guards, setting them staggering back in surprise (and Daryl screaming in horror), forgetting to keep their weapons on us. The mayor grabbed the nearest troll and head-butted him so hard that the crashing of heavy skulls rang across the warehouse like bells.

She dropped him to the ground and bellowed, *"I'll show you who's mayor!"*

Callum deposited me on his shoulder, red marks eaten into his wrists from the cable ties the rats had gnawed through, and ducked as Kara tried to train the crossbow on him. Ez grabbed her, jerking the weapon away.

"Stop that!" she shouted. "It's not a bloody toy!"

"He deserves this!" Kara shouted back. "He *left!* I brought him back for *you!*"

"I didn't ask you to!" There were rough edges in Ez's voice. "It was better he was gone."

"He deserted us!"

"We should go," I whispered to Callum. "They seem busy." He shushed me and took a cautious step back.

Ez glanced at him, then back at Kara. "His friend died. Your *brother*. From drugs *your* family supplied and *I* dealt. I'd have left if I could."

Kara stared at her, then punched her full in the face and snatched the crossbow back as Ez staggered back with a yelp. "Is *everyone* in this place completely bloody soft?" she bellowed, and swung the weapon back to bear on Callum.

"Now can we run?" I asked Callum.

"You stay right there," she snarled, then it turned into a yelp of alarm as rats swarmed up her legs. "Jesus *Christ!* What've we got these bloody lizards for?" She swiped at the rats wildly with one hand, and Ez tackled her from the side, sending them both spilling to the floor. Kara's finger jerked on the trigger and Boots screamed as the bolt tore through his ankle. He collapsed, wailing about coconut crabs and unfairness.

"I think so," Callum said, and grabbed Art to haul him up from where he knelt, gulping, on the floor.

Cherie dropped her injured vowels and flung a stream of words at Callum. He let go of Art and jumped away, tripped over a Komodo, and went windmilling backward. I leaped clear, landing hard, and looked up at a large set of very sharp teeth at very close range. The lizard hissed. I hissed back, but it sounded a bit puny and unimpressive, and the creature lunged.

I raised my paws rather hopelessly to meet it, and four small furry bodies hit me from the side, throwing me to the ground as the lizard's teeth snapped shut on thin air. More rats piled up the Komodo's tail and it whirled around with an outraged roar, slamming its muscular tail into Kara and Ez and sending them tumbling away from each other. It reared up over Kara on its hind legs, hissing mightily, and the yellow troll rugby-tackled it before it could bite her face off, more's the pity.

I looked up to meet a small, sneering grin. "Patsy, you're the jewel in the crown of all rats," I told her.

"Utter bollocks," she said, and jumped one of the bookshop sister's words as it crept across the floor, spelling *immobilise* at us. "Move your tail, Mogs. There's a gap in the wall calling your name."

"I can't leave Callum," I said, then scrambled up as another Komodo rushed past, teeth bared as it ran down two desperately scampering young rats. "*Hey!*"

I ran after the lizard, yowling wildly until it turned its attention from the rats to me. I turned hard, paws sliding in the hard ground, and bolted with the horrible scratch of its claws behind me. I charged two guards who were trying to wrestle the mayor to the ground with the Komodo plunging after me, and shot between their feet. The lizard followed, taking the guards and the mayor to the ground in a shouting heap.

I yowled in triumph and spun back to see where Callum was, then stopped dead.

Kara had the crossbow trained on his head, and his feet were mired in a swamp of words.

"Kara, *don't,*" Ez shouted, but Kara just grinned.

I bolted for Callum, but I wasn't going to make it. There was no way anyone could make it, and there was a Komodo coming at me from the side, teeth bared, but I just kept going, my stomach sick and empty and lost.

And the elevator gave a single, civilised *ding,* then the doors exploded off it like someone had taken a battering ram to them.

25

ENTER THE UNICORNS

ALL EYES TURNED TO THE GATE, EVEN KARA'S, AND PARKER burst from the cover of the shelves. He tackled Callum, and the words exploded around them like inky confetti, showering shattered vowels and broken consonants everywhere. Marie and Cherie gave identical shrieks of horror, and Kara spun back and fired. The bolt bounced off the concrete as Callum and Parker rolled away, and the Komodo hit me from the side, scooping me up in its jaws while I screeched in fury.

The thing's teeth were far sharper than necessary, but we'd both been running too fast. The lizard tripped as it grabbed me and I bounced free, my sides stinging. I rolled twice, found my feet, and bolted as the metal gate to the corridor burst off its hinges and flew across the floor, taking two Komodos with it. Gerry marched in, wearing a rather fetching dusky pink skirt and a mint-green blouse that matched his dangly earrings, closely followed by William testing the limits of the seams on his flannel shirt.

There was more movement behind them, but that was

all I glimpsed before I hit Kara with the Komodo trailing me by about half a pace, and all three of us went to the floor. Patsy and Ernie ran past, Patsy cursing me out as she nipped Kara's ears, setting her screaming, and the lizard clawed its way toward the rat eagerly, never mind that the woman was in the way. I jumped on Kara's hand, biting her fingers as hard as I could until she let go of the crossbow and concentrated on trying to fend the lizard off.

Ez snatched up the crossbow and shouted, "Take them down! They're probably from Appleforth!"

Callum scrambled up, kicking away the last of the words. "They're not! They're local!"

"Shut up and get out of here," Ez snarled at him, training the bow on Gerry. Callum lunged forward, and she swung the weapon toward him instead. "Don't push it, little brother."

"Shoot him!" Kara shrieked, sitting up with her jacket in tatters and scratches on her face as the Komodo raced off after the rats. "Shoot them *all!*"

"This is *quite* enough!" Gerry shouted. "Where are your manners?" The yellow troll took a swing at him, and Gerry ducked it and hit the other troll so hard he flew back into the shelves. An aquarium tipped over on the top shelf and rained murky water on him, which set tentacles sprouting wildly all over his shoulders while he wailed in horror.

"There's only two of them," Ez called to the guards, keeping the crossbow on Callum. "Let's get this under control before any more turn up. Hurry!"

They started forward obediently enough, then hesitated as William took a step forward, cracking his knuckles. Gerry straightened his skirt and checked his earrings.

"You've got *weapons,*" Kara screamed at the guards, staggering to her feet. "Unicorn horn will stop trolls just fine. *Use them!*"

"Oh dear," Gerry said. "That's a bit of a sensitive subject around here."

Hooves thundered in the corridor. Poppy appeared at a run, her face scrunched in fury, Kent cantering along next to her and the big sow clattering to the other side. Behind them came the unicorns, all eleven of them, their hooves shining like moonlight on still water and their manes flowing soft and silkily silver. Their coats shone with the rich, indefinable lustre of pearls, and their tails ran with magic. And sure, their horns were little stumpy things, but muscles rolled under their hides, and their hooves were sharp and fast as they dropped their heads and charged through the gate, snorting with fury.

EZ DROPPED the crossbow and sprinted for the stacks without a word, Kara racing after her. They vanished down the aisles, and the guards scattered, still clutching their weapons. Callum grabbed Art, hauling him to his feet and pulling him into the dubious shelter of the amphora as the herd thundered past, teeth bared and eyes rolling. The mayor sat on the floor and watched them pass, clapping happily. The sisters ran for shelter, and Parker scuttled after Callum and Art, staring at Gerry in fright.

Gerry currently had the second troll in a headlock as he explained what a bad name he was giving troll-kind, and the yellow, feathered and tentacled troll was still sitting on the floor whimpering. He was developing suckers on his chest. William picked up the gate and ran after the guards, whirling it over his head with a cheery "*Vroom!*" The goats staggered in after the unicorns, took one look at a confused Komodo, and fainted. Kent and Lady Grey ambled in to stand guard over them, and the lizard took a step back. Turns out even a Komodo isn't too keen on a kick from a donkey.

I turned to check on Callum and found myself facing another Komodo, this one looking more irate than confused. I gave a squawk, but before I could even run Poppy scooped it up under one arm. It writhed helplessly, flailing about with its claws, but Poppy didn't loosen her grip.

"Shh, lizard," she said. "Good lizard."

The good lizard tried to bite her face, and she tapped its snout lightly, then grabbed another by the tail as it went past.

"Um, Poppy, I'd be careful with those," I said, flinching as she bundled the second lizard up. There were huge rents torn in her orange overalls already, and she gave both Komodos a squeeze that made their legs stick out in alarm.

"I is good with *all* animals," she said proudly.

"Um, good," I said, and started to suggest she put them somewhere safe when a shout interrupted me.

"Mogs, *duck!*" Patsy yelled. The rats had scattered when the unicorns appeared, and the shout came from the stacks. I flattened myself to the floor, not having any idea where the attack was coming from, and a fireball exploded on the floor between Poppy and myself. We both yelped, and she hugged the lizards closer to her then ran for the gate. I took a step after her, then hesitated as more fireballs hit around us, and a scream went up deeper in the warehouse. A unicorn raced past, trying to outrun the spreading burn on its hindquarters.

"No!" Poppy screamed, and dropped the lizards to run after it. The mayor leaped to her feet and grabbed the creature as it ran past, bringing it to the ground while it swore with the sort of vocabulary I could only aspire to. The mayor ripped the last shreds of her sopping dress off and smothered the flames as Poppy dropped to her knees next to them, sobbing big angry tears.

Another fireball hit the ground just in front of me, then someone grabbed me and carted me at a sprint toward the shelves the missiles were raining from.

"Alright?" Callum panted.

"Is that your bloody sister?" I asked Art, who was following us. "I don't like her. Not that I'm sure about yours, either," I added to Callum as he threw me into the shelter of a tall shelf and scrambled in after me, dodging a fireball. Two unicorns raced past, chasing a guard and describing in delighted detail what they intended to do with him. I spotted another guard battling a rug that was trying to assimilate him into its weave while four rats laughed hysterically.

"My sister's quite nice," Parker said to no one in particular as he clambered after us. "Well, she's never fire-bombed anyone, anyway. Not that I know of."

"Come on." Callum grabbed the edge of the shelves, peeked out, then climbed up to the next shelf.

"Where're we going?" I asked, clawing my way after him. It wasn't easy, with my aching limbs.

"To deal with Kara," he said. "Parker, come on. Do that breaking the words thing if the Silverfishes turn up again."

"How do you do that?" I asked the young guard, as Callum checked the next shelf up, then ducked as a fire-ball sizzled past him.

Parker shrugged. "I don't know. Words just don't work for me."

"How do you mean, don't work?"

"They look all funny. The letters make no sense."

I blinked at him. "How do you do forms and stuff, then?"

"My sister helped me memorise them. And I record everything on my phone so I can do them slowly later."

"Huh. Fair enough." I watched Callum stick his head out again. One of those souvenir snow dome thingies barely missed his nose as it spun past to explode on the floor. A small webbed creature stood up in the wreckage and shook its tiny fist at the stacks. "Can we not get up?"

"No, they're watching for us."

"Try the other side."

Callum did, and almost got another snow dome in the face. "Well, at least they've run out of fireballs."

"That's something." I snuffled around the shelf. "There has to be something we can use here."

"Um," Art said, and we all looked at him. He was staring into the aisle, where Gerry was looking in at us with an elevator door held over his head like a shield. He had one arm protectively around Poppy's shoulders, and she was still snuffling.

"Oh, no," I said. "The unicorn ...?"

"Will be fine," Gerry said. "Angry tears." A rain of new missiles bounced off the door and crashed to the floor around them. Large holes started to eat their way into the concrete.

"I'm sorry, Poppy," Callum said. "That was such a cruel thing to do to the unicorn."

"I breaks her face!" Poppy sobbed, and Art looked alarmed.

"Help!" the guard in the rug called, his voice muffled. "Someone help, please, I'm stuck!"

Callum glanced at him, then looked up. The rain of missiles had eased. "Can you help me get up there?" he asked.

"We can deal with this," Gerry said.

"No. It's kind of a family thing," Callum said, and I groaned.

"Will someone roll their eyes for me, please?" I asked. "This seems to call for eye-rolling."

"I understand," Gerry said, ignoring me. "But I may have a better idea."

LOOK, new age trolls seem to be quite a bit smarter than your average troll (Gerry says it's to do with night classes and breaking stereotypes), but this idea seemed neither smarter nor better than mine, which was *leave now and let the mayor deal with it.* Patsy sat next to me by the gate, her good eye bright.

"This is fascinating," she said.

"This is ridiculous," I replied. The other rats were watching from the safety of the shelving, while the Komodos had been corralled into the pool room to bask in the heat. The mayor had rallied the guards, who seemed more than happy to switch allegiance to someone who wasn't ordering them to fight trolls or unicorns. She'd armed them with dragon scale shields against the missiles that were still flying from the top of the shelves, although they were becoming less frequent. The unicorns were trotting around flexing their muscles and preening, and Kent and Lady Grey stood next to us. The goats regained consciousness every now and then before seeing a troll or a rat and fainting again.

"One has to admire the grandiosity," Kent observed. "The sense of scale and drama."

"Bollocks," I said, and we watched the trolls and the mayor pick up the huge ropes that had been attached to the shelving, as high up as Callum and Parker had been able to climb without being bombed. The mayor gave a shout, and they took up the slack on the ropes as the humans kept the shields over everyone, then began to pull.

"Stop that!" Kara yelled from the top, and threw some sort of fossilised egg at the shields. Halfway down it sprouted wings and zoomed off.

"This is actually a really bad idea," Ez agreed. "If all this stuff smashes—"

"Well, you're doing a good job of that already," Callum called. "Why don't you just come down?"

The shelves creaked and swayed, and the trolls and the mayor pulled in grim silence. A few bottles rolled off and smashed, releasing little whiffs of coloured smoke.

"Kara, he's right. Let's go down," Ez said.

"Kara, come on," Art pleaded. "I know you didn't mean to do any of this. You were coerced!"

"Can *anyone* here roll their eyes?" I asked my companions. They all just looked at me, except Lady Grey, who obliged with a very small eye roll, although I wasn't quite sure who it was directed at. "Thanks," I said, and she did it again.

The shelving shuddered and jerked, and four boxes slid off. They smashed to the ground, sprouted antennae and suckers, and suckered off into the depths of the warehouse. Kara teetered on the edge of the top shelf, waving wildly as she tried to catch her balance, and Ez pulled her back to safety.

"Alright!" she shouted. "Alright, we're coming down. Stop before we blow the whole bloody place up."

"Aw," Patsy said. "I really wanted to see that go over."

I stared at her, then looked back as the mayor put her rope down. "Throw down any weapons," she said.

"We don't have anything," Ez said, showing her hands.

Kara folded her arms, glaring down at everyone. "I *don't* agree to this," she shouted.

"Just shut up and come down," Ez snapped, lying on her belly and wriggling her legs over the edge, feeling for the next shelf. "Know when to accept defeat, Kara."

"Screw *that,*" Kara said, and shoved the other woman straight off the edge.

"*Ez!*" Callum yelled, as his sister tumbled backward with a scream that was as much shock as fright. He started forward, but Gerry was quicker. He pushed William out of the way and sprinted for the shelves, snatching Ez out of the air as she tumbled toward the ground. He caught her clumsily, knocking the air out of her as he grabbed her waist, but set her shaking and pale back on the floor without any broken bits. I wasn't entirely jubilant.

"Nice," Patsy said appreciatively.

"Aw, look at you!" Kara called. "Saved by a *troll!*"

"That enough!" Poppy shouted. "You mean to unicorns, and mean to dinky—"

"Donkey," Kent said.

"—and mean to everyone, and you just *mean!*"

"Yeah, I'm so worried about your opinion," Kara said, and Poppy took a large, perfectly shiny green apple from her pocket and threw it. Kara was still laughing when it hit her between the eyes with a *thwock* and a splatter of juice, and she fell back onto the shelves with a solid and rather final thump.

No one moved for a moment, then Art said weakly, "Kara?"

"Oh, shut up," the mayor said, and pointed at the guards. "Go get her down, will you? And everyone else get out before we get turned into toadstools by all the loose magic."

"She's my *sister,*" Art protested. "She's very easily led—"

"She's not," Ez said, holding her side. "She's a bloody liability. I never should have done business with her."

"Yes. We'll be talking about that," the mayor said. "And how amends shall be made. But no one will be hurt. You have my word as mayor, which is going to mean something around here now."

Callum looked from the mayor to Ez, and said, "Sounds good." He put his hands in his pockets and ambled toward us.

"Callum," Ez called after him, and he ignored her, looking at me instead.

"Shall we go?"

I watched a unicorn headbutting a shiny metal box and hurling abuse at it, and said, "About bloody time."

THE LIFTS HAD BEEN TORN APART by Gerry and the unicorns' rather dramatic arrival, so Parker led us to some dull, skinny stairs winding up behind a fire door. We traipsed our way up them, me balanced on Callum's shoulder and Art trailing behind us. Kent and Lady Grey were waiting for the goats to recover from their latest fainting fit, and Patsy had tipped me a wink and vanished into the walls.

The stairs went on for far too long, but eventually Parker pushed through into the glossy grey lobby, the yellow lights hanging bland and unchanged over their reflections on the floor. He unlocked the doors from behind the desk, and we staggered out into the day. I was surprised to find it was still day, to be honest. It felt like we'd been trapped under Dimly for a lot longer than the hour or two the light suggested. It probably didn't even qualify as lunchtime yet.

Callum dug in his pockets, found his cigarettes, and lit one with a satisfied sigh, then sat down on the steps with his long legs out in front of him. I sat next to him, watching for crows. Dimly didn't feel any different.

Art paced up and down the path. "What if they *hurt* her?" he asked us.

"Dude, she was running a drugs trade right under your nose, and totally set you up to get Callum in here," I said. "She tried to *kill* Callum. She kind of deserves a bit of a kicking."

Callum clicked his tongue lightly. "She won't get a kicking. Gobs is just being Gobs."

Art ran both hands back over his long hair, tugging at it. "I know, but … she's my *sister.*"

"I know." Callum offered his pack of cigarettes to Art, who waved it away. "Doesn't make her a good person, though. And doesn't mean you can save her. Or have to."

Art went back to pacing, and Parker said, "Does anyone want a cuppa?"

"Oh, God, *yes,*" Callum said, and the young guard went inside to put the kettle on.

I went back to watching the sky, and Callum ruffled my fur, inspecting the toothmarks from the lizard. "We should clean these," he said.

"A troll bathed me in peroxide this morning," I told him. "I dare even lizards to get through that."

"Still," he said, and then it was silent, punctuated only by the slap of Art's bare feet on the pavement.

We were drinking tea and eating biscuits when Kent and Lady Grey appeared, leading the goats. Well, the humans were eating biscuits. Parker had sacrificed his lunch to a better cause and given me the cheese from his sandwich when I complained that I was about to faint from hunger and digestive biscuits weren't good for cats. I was warming to him.

"Kent!" I exclaimed. "You really are one donkey in a million, you know. Getting Poppy this morning was just genius."

He looked at me out of liquid brown eyes and said, "One must act for the greater good. I must say, the whole experience was a little immediate for my taste, though. One had so little time to reflect on what one was actually seeing versus what one *thought*."

"How about you?" I asked the pig. "Has this convinced you of your own reality yet?"

She blinked at me, then picked up the packet of biscuits and walked away with it.

"I think she feels more real when she's not talking," Kent said. "Or that is my theory."

"Clarence," one of the goats said wearily. "Clarence, cat."

Clarence looked at me. "He's just not that scary anymore."

I bared my teeth at them both, but they just followed Lady Grey and tried to steal the biscuits off her.

"Where's everyone else?" Callum asked.

"And what about my sister?" Art demanded. "I need to see her! Even prisoners get visitors!"

Kent flicked his ears. "I am, in truth, merely a donkey. I have no knowledge to impart regarding your sister."

"I'm going back in there." Art started for the doors and Callum grabbed his arm.

"Sit down. You can't help her. She's not a kid, and this is all on her."

"But it's not her fault! First Rory, then all our family taken by the Watch – she can't help but be affected by that."

"We all make our choices," Callum said. "They're not always right, but we all make them."

"Some better than others," I observed. "And look – we did find those bloody unicorns."

Everyone except Lady Grey and the goats turned to look inside as Poppy led the unicorns across the polished floors of the foyer. She had a Komodo slung over each shoulder, and half a dozen more on leashes that she'd tied to her waist. The unicorns ambled next to her, and only one of them tried to headbutt his own reflection in the floor, which seemed pretty restrained.

"Awesome," Parker said, in a wondering sort of voice.

26

A DIMLY SORT OF PEACE

WE ALL MOVED ASIDE TO GIVE THE UNICORNS ROOM. ONE stomped at me and I hid behind Callum without even hissing. There was blood on its hooves and its teeth were yellow and far too big. One bumped into another and they both started shouting at each other, chests pressed together and eyes rolling as they spat insults.

"Bad 'corns!" Poppy snapped, slapping both of them on the hindquarters. "Behave or go back to mean people!"

"This sucks," one complained.

"No respect," another agreed.

"Where're our grooms? Our jewels? You're going to put us back in that bloody field again, aren't you?"

"Not even a crown in sight!"

"Or a silver chain!"

"No maidens. We need *maidens,* troll!"

I looked up at Callum. "Such romantic creatures. So beautiful. So noble."

He nudged me, the corner of his mouth twitching, and

Poppy put her hands on her hips. "I gives you back to mean peoples!"

The unicorns glared at her, but subsided.

"Did you have them all along, Poppy?" Callum asked.

She twisted her huge fingers together. "They no happy there. No groomed proper. He mean." She shot Art a disapproving look, and he waved his hands helplessly.

"Well," I said. "And here I thought you might have … you know."

She frowned at me. "I vegetarian troll. I loves all the animals. Bad cat."

"I'm very sorry. I was perpetuating stereotypes."

"I knows," she said with a sniff. "Now I takes home."

"Oh, great," Art said. "I just need to check on Kara, then I'll be right there."

Poppy gave him a look that made the unicorns mutter in approval. "Not your home. I no give back. You no nice, and unicorns no safe. No *hidden*. They has new home."

"What? No! I have to take them! The Watch—"

"You want try?" Poppy demanded, and the unicorns all lowered their heads and glared.

Art looked at Callum pleadingly, but he just shrugged.

"I hired you to help!" Art snapped.

"Hey, we found the unicorns and your sister," I said. "And where's our payment, anyway?"

"My sister is still down there! And this … this *troll* is stealing my property!"

"Dude, did you just call us property?" one of the unicorns demanded.

"Did he think he *owned* us?"

"Like a *hat?*"

"Shut up!" he yelled at them, and glared at Callum. "*Help me!*"

"We're done." Callum offered his cigarettes to Parker, who wrinkled his nose and shook his head.

"No!" Art was almost shouting. "No, you have to help! It's not fair—"

"Shut up," I snarled at him. "You lied to us right from the beginning. You almost got Callum killed. You and your sister can both rot for all I care."

"Goddamn *cats*—" He aimed a kick at me that I dodged easily, then suddenly seemed aware of where he was. He looked at the mostly four-legged creatures regarding him with disapproval. "I didn't mean that. I wouldn't really kick him."

"We know," Callum said wearily. "Just sit down and shut up, Art, will you?"

He did, burying his face in his hands, and no one spoke for a while except for the unicorns, arguing among themselves.

GERRY AND WILLIAM were the next to appear, ushering Marie and Cherie ahead of them.

"Off you go now," Gerry said, shooing them down the path. They went, Marie hesitating as if to say something to Callum, then her sister dragged her away. Both of them skirted Parker like he might bite them.

"That's it?" I said. "They just about suffocated me."

Gerry clasped his big hands together. "They thought they were doing the right thing."

"Yeah, I've heard *that* before."

Gerry nodded at Parker. "You head home. Have the rest of the day off."

"Really? I mean, shouldn't I check—"

"I'd stay away for a few days," Gerry continued. "It may take a little time to get everything sorted out."

"Am I *fired?*" Parker asked, his eyes wide.

"No, no, lad. Nothing like that." Gerry gave the young guard a reassuring clap on the shoulder that almost sent him face-first onto the path. "Paid leave. A little extra holiday."

"Right. Wow. Okay." Parker hesitated, then nodded. "Got it. Thanks." He hurried off down the steps like he was worried Gerry might change his mind.

The big troll straightened his skirt and said, "We'll be off too. And so should you be."

"No, I need to see Kara," Art said.

Gerry shook his head. "Not right now. Go home. Come on, Poppy." He stooped to pick up a Komodo dragon that was favouring one paw and headed down the path, Poppy following with the unicorns and rest of the slightly confused-looking lizards, and William bringing up the rear.

Art rubbed his mouth and glared at Kent. "I suppose *you're* going with them too."

Kent considered it, then said, "A little too busy for me. Too much attention. It doesn't leave enough time for philosophical reflection." He looked at Lady Grey and the goats. "We'll expect some carrots tonight, though. I feel we've earned it." He ambled off, and the other animals followed him, all looking a little tired and dishevelled. I knew how they felt.

Art looked at me and Callum. "Cal," he started.

"No," Callum said, and got up. He looked at me. "Need a lift?"

"So much," I said, and he picked me up, depositing me on his shoulder as he headed down the street in his easy, long pace, threading our slow way out of Dimly.

WE WALKED down the river and along the towpath all the way back to Art's, which took a lot longer than a troll bike ride. The car, astonishingly, started, and we went home. Mrs Smith saw us coming in and gave a great dramatic gasp of horror, clasping her hands to her flat chest. Then she insisted on showering us both with antiseptic and copious quantities of food, which I was sure did more to fix us up than the smelly cream she put on my bite marks. She also took Callum's jacket away and brought it back all repaired and clean, which was unfortunate.

We ate. Slept. Argued over some cheap DVDs Callum had got from the charity shop, then went back to eating and sleeping when the laptop wouldn't play them anyway. Callum wanted to call Art and I told him I'd vomit on the mobile if he did. I didn't go to Claudia, the Watch lieutenant, but I sent a message. Finding her myself would've meant poking around Watch houses. That sort of behaviour was likely to get me back in the Watch bad books (if I'd ever got off them), and a claw in the nose for my efforts. If they heard I'd been meddling in Dimly, it'd be even worse. So I told a certain hairless cat I trusted, and she took the message on.

I didn't hear anything back, and maybe that was best. We were out in one piece, the unicorns were with a rather more responsible caretaker, and the horn trade in Dimly had just ground to a very abrupt halt. I didn't think it'd restart, not with the mayor actually in charge.

But neither of us could stop thinking about Dimly. The rats running the gauntlet of their monster-infested drains, and the crows patrolling the streets above. And that damn warehouse of terrible magical things, humming beneath the earth like a boil waiting to erupt. It was hard *not* to think of it. I'd wake in the night with the taste of sewer scum in my mouth and the scent of Cerberus dog in my nose. And Callum probably thought about it even more than I did, being such a bleeding heart and all.

And we didn't know, did we? Didn't know if the mayor had truly taken the place in hand, or if Ez and Kara had more allies we hadn't come across. Maybe nothing had changed. Maybe we just wanted to believe it had, that we hadn't gone through all that for nothing.

Which is why we were parked on the outskirts of Dimly two weeks later. My tail was still a bit bald from the Komodo dragon and the crows, and Callum had a new scar on his cheekbone, but other than that we were doing okay. He'd even managed to get the car running almost smoothly again. As smoothly as it ever did, anyway.

The sun was full summer, and it was one of those days when the wind had quietly wandered off to more interesting places, so the heat hung still and bored around us. Windows were flung open and duvets aired on sills, and a man in hot pants walked past with a one-eared greyhound on a leash. I huffed at it from my perch on the car roof, and it huffed back in a polite sort of way. Callum leaned on the car next to me, skinny arms bare in a faded T-shirt, and smoked absently. No one bothered to look at us. If there was anywhere a man talking to a cat was going to go unnoticed, it was on the edges of a pocket.

"Anything look different?" he asked me.

"Hard to tell," I said, squinting at the fringe of glamour across the street. "I mean, it's still there."

"It was hardly going to get up and walk away."

"Ha."

We were quiet for a moment longer, then he said, "How do you think Poppy's getting on with the unicorns?"

"Well, let's see. She has absolutely no fear, a team of Komodo bloody dragons to guard them, and a parent troll with a better moral compass than a travelling monk—"

"Is that still a thing?"

"—and she has very firm convictions regarding how animals should be treated," I continued, ignoring him. "Which I mostly agree with."

"Only mostly?"

"I really didn't like those lizards."

He snorted, and a cat stepped out of nothing on the pavement across the street, just beyond the edge of the glamour. A Labrador almost walked into her, and it jumped back with a howl, diving behind its human's legs. I squinted at it. It looked like the same one I'd bopped on the nose. Poor silly creature.

The woman swore and pulled the dog tighter against her, not that it was showing any inclination to chase the cat. The cat looked the woman up and down with cool, mismatched eyes and strolled across the street. A moped had to swerve to avoid her, the young man on it shouting curses, but she ignored him and jumped onto the bonnet of our car. Her pale coat, with its patches of tabby and ginger, glowed in the warm light.

"Alright, Claudia?" I asked her, displaying my newest scars.

"Alright, Gobbelino. Callum," she said, curling her tail over her toes as she sat down.

"Claudia," Callum said, and finished his cigarette. He ground it out on the heel of his boot and went to drop it in an overflowing bin. "How's things?"

She looked at the sky in a considering way before she answered. "Interesting," she said finally. "Things are interesting."

I wasn't sure about that. *Interesting* tends to have unfortunate consequences.

Claudia glanced at me, her one green and one blue eye washed paler than ever in the sunlight. "Thanks for the tip-off."

"Yeah. Sorry I had to go through Pru, but, you know. The Watch." I shrugged, and she shook her head.

"You were right to. And to tell her to come to me and no one else. I got ahead of the unicorn thing, got the Watch leader to tell the original team that they'd been reassigned."

"No consequences for Art, then?" Callum asked.

"Not from us," Claudia said. Her whiskers twitched. "He's still homing old animals, and those unicorns haven't been safer since old Gordon Lightfoot had them all prancing around the Scottish Highlands with cork on their horns."

"What about the weapons?" I asked. "You know where they were going?"

"No." She regarded us both. "And all I've got to go on is *some black cat*. I have a few ideas, though. It took too many blind eyes on the Watch for this one to slip past. No cats in Dimly? I mean, I know it's a pocket, but come on."

"So what're you doing now?" Callum asked.

"Same as before. Watching. Waiting. Someone'll slip up at some point."

"You think it's connected to the zombie juice thing?" I asked.

She snorted. "Either that, or the Watch is even more rotten with corruption than we thought."

I shivered. Claudia wasn't just Watch. She ran some strange, secret team that answered only to the new Watch leader and tried to keep a check on the more megalomaniacal tendencies of the actual Watch. It sounded like the sort of thing that didn't leave a lot of time for custard and heatable beds.

"What about Dimly?" Callum asked.

"What about it?"

"Has anything changed?"

She gave us an amused look and said, "You haven't been back?"

Callum and I looked at each other. "Why would we?" I asked. "I almost got eaten several times, drowned, set on fire, squashed – it wasn't the best week of my life."

"Come on." She jumped to the ground and looked expectantly at the car.

"What?" Callum asked.

"Go on. I've not had a car ride in years."

WE DROVE into Dimly with Claudia sitting bolt upright on the seat next to me, her ears flicking at the clatterings and groans of the old car.

"I don't think the last one was this loud," she observed, and put her paws on the door handle, lifting her nose to the window for some fresh air. "Or quite so smoky."

I gave Callum a pointed look, and he put his cigarettes away.

We puttered our way through streets that looked more friendly with the sun flushing the walls and sparking off windows, flooding gardens with light and giving even the more hungry, crouched buildings a warm blush. There were people out walking, faeries in high fashion and fauns in punny T-shirts and less easily identifiable creatures showing off their twelve-packs with their shirts rolled up. Dogs trotted next to some of them, and sparrows bounced through the gutters, and heat rose from the streets.

We wound our way to the town centre, where the pavements were crowded with groups and couples eating ice cream and takeaway chips from the vans parked by the green, and kids with horns and wings and a variety of limbs ran shrieking across the grass. It was hard to find parking, but eventually Callum found a spot in a side street, and Claudia led us across the main square, heading for quieter streets. The bookshop was open, books stacked in trolleys outside, and I hissed at it.

We turned down the street that ended in the squatting warehouse, and it was still there, but the trees outside were in bloom, and flowers packed the bare dirt. Even the walls seemed brighter. I looked at Claudia.

"Come on," she said, and led the way to the door. There was a new sign above it.

"Dimly Municipal Swimming Pool," Callum read, and we both stared at Claudia. Callum pushed the door open, and let out a wave of shouting and shrieking that was very much in the joyful range. We went inside and found ourselves standing on the edge of a shallow pool full of young creatures waving an assortment of inflatable and foam toys and creating small tidal waves that slopped water onto the concrete sides. The next pool over was scattered with people charging purposefully up and down, puffing and blowing. Another was crowded with elderly Folk and humans doing star jumps in the water. And beyond them, through a wall of glass, the river coursed peaceful and green, trees leaning over it to examine their reflection.

"Where'd it go?" Callum asked. "I mean, the warehouses. The *weapons."*

"Sludge puppies are as powerful as they are tenacious," Claudia said. "Once the mayor understood what was happening, she took care of it."

"Hayley," I said. Of course the mayor had been a sludge puppy. You just don't expect to encounter one wandering around in frilly dresses.

"Who?" Callum asked.

"The sludge puppy's missing friend."

"That's the one," Claudia said.

"She did all this?" Callum asked.

"With a little help." She nodded across the pool. A troll in a ruffled one-piece swimsuit and matching swimming cap was standing on the side demonstrating backstroke to a gaggle of smaller trolls. They all had enormous life belts on.

"Trolls can't swim," I said. "They're too heavy."

"You try telling Gerry trolls can't do anything," she said, and there was a huff of laughter in her voice.

Callum ran both hands through his hair and shook his head. "What about Ez and Kara?"

Claudia tipped her head to one side. "Ez is still here. She and the mayor came to an arrangement. Ez is good at what she does. She just needed to see that there was a different *way* to do it. That a well-run town helps the many, not the few."

Callum scratched his chin. "That's quite a shift."

"Any more than yours, Callum North?"

He and Claudia stared at each other for a long moment, then I said, "And Scary Spice?"

Claudia shifted her gaze to me, that huff of laughter back in her voice. "The mayor prefers moral re-education to capital punishment. So she found Kara a teacher."

"Oh, gods," I said. "It's not the donkey, is it?"

Claudia wheezed helpless laughter. "He's making her give verbal presentations on the intrinsic value of good will, and in her spare time cleaning all the drains to accommodate the rats. Unpaid, of course."

Callum stuck his hands in the pockets of his ancient

jeans, staring around like an alien who's just had his first earth encounter at Glastonbury festival. "Well. That's … optimistic."

"The world needs more optimism," Claudia said. "Even if it is misguided. Things can always be corrected later."

"I hope it's optimism with sharp objects kept out of reach," I said. "Especially for Kent's sake."

Claudia snorted. "It is."

We were quiet for a while, the sunlight washing warm through the tinted, UV-filtering glass in the roof, the whole place ringing with the shouts of the dryad leading water aerobics and the shrieks of small creatures hitting each other with pool noodles, and Gerry shouting, "Kick! *Kick,* Emily!" as he dropped a small troll in the water. She vanished, flailing, under the surface, and he jumped in after her.

"Optimism looks risky," I observed, as Gerry swept Emily to safety.

"Of course it is," Claudia said. "But without it, what? Nothing changes. Everything stagnates. And we all just hate each other a little more. Ourselves, too, sometimes."

"More than sometimes," Callum said, still watching Gerry. "And, you know, why not? Everyone should get the chance to change, right?"

"I don't need to change," I said, and they both looked at me. "I don't! What would I change?"

"Oh, God. Don't get me started," Callum said, and I glared at him as Claudia gave her soft, huffing laugh.

"A few changes might give you longer lives," she said. "You know, just a thought."

I sniffed. "Those deaths were totally not my fault."

"Of course they weren't," Callum said, digging his wallet out. "Anyone fancy ice cream?"

"Wouldn't say no," Claudia said, and turned to lead the way out.

I looked up at Callum. "Don't want to visit your sister?"

"Not particularly," he said.

"Not too optimistic about her changing?"

He smiled, a lopsided little effort. "When I decided I had to get out, it was Ifan who helped me, and her who tried to stop me. Ifan who tried to help me get clean, and her who always had drugs. I'm not sure I'm ready to be optimistic yet."

I shrugged. "You don't have to be. Changing is her deal, not yours."

He stooped to scratch my ears. "You don't talk complete rubbish all the time, you know."

"I know," I said. "See? No need for me to change."

He snorted, and we followed Claudia out into the warm, heavy heat of a Yorkshire summer's day. Before us lay all the things that were possible, because everything can change, and behind us lay the past with its sharp, unforgiving teeth, but it felt like there weren't so many now.

It felt like some things had been laid to rest, because some things have to be. We can't carry them forever.

And family – whether by blood or not – can help us put them down when we don't know how to.

Plus, there was ice cream. And everything's better with ice cream.

THANK YOU

Lovely people, thank you so much for picking up this book. I know there are huge demands on all of our time these days, and I appreciate it hugely that you've chosen to spend some of yours discovering the truth about unicorns (sorry).

And if you enjoyed this book, I'd very much appreciate you taking the time to pop a review up at the retailer of your choice.

Reviews are a bit like magic to authors, but magic of the good kind. Less world domination via dodgy weaponry, more get-more-readers-and-so-write-more-books variety. More reviews mean more people see our books in online stores, meaning more people buy them, so giving us the means to write more stories and send them back out to you, lovely people.

Plus it pays for the cat biscuits, which is the primary reason for anything to happen in life …

And if you'd like to send me a copy of your review, theories about cat world domination, cat photos, or anything else, drop me a message at kim@kmwatt.com. I'd love to hear from you!

Until next time,

Read on!

Kim

(And head over the page for more adventures plus your free story collection!)

MAGICAL DIFFICULTIES, CUBED

Sorcerers, magicians, and necromancers, oh my

"We'll do it," Callum said.
"Of course we will," I said. "Why would we not stalk the scary magician who might be trying to raise his son from the dead? ***For free?****"*

Like it or not, when a sorcerer asks you to track a magician, you track a magician. It's that or spend life as a hamster.

But the scary magician is the least of our worries. Between raging squirrel mobs, My Little Ravenous sewer monsters, and bungalow-dwelling necromancers with a good line in attack dogs, it's all we can do to keep ourselves the right side of dead …

Join G&C London, Leeds premier magical investigators, in A Melee of Mages today!

Just mind those squirrels …

Scan above to grab your copy, or head to the link below:
https://readerlinks.com/l/2392832/g3pb

A POPPY'S WEIRD ANIMAL RESCUE SHORT STORY

But what's wrong with lemons? Download your free story now to find out!

Even the most enterprising of young trolls can't take in *every* animal. And all the best animal rescues have adoption days.

Poppy just *knows* it's going to be a success. The unicorns hooves are polished and their manes are brushed. The Komodo dragons have been over-fed to prevent any unauthorised nibbling. The basilisks are on their best behaviour, and the donkey's even promised not to philosophise at anyone.

But it is Dimly. Things were never going to go *quite* according to plan. And Poppy certainly wasn't expecting lemons ...

Download your free story today!

Scan above to claim your free story, or head to the link below: https://readerlinks.com/l/2392830/g3pb

ABOUT THE AUTHOR

Hello lovely person. I'm Kim, and in addition to the Gobbelino London tales I also write other funny, magical books that offer a little escape from the serious stuff in the world and hopefully leave you a wee bit happier than you were when you started. Because happiness, like friendship, matters.

I write about baking-obsessed reapers setting up baby ghoul petting cafes, and ladies of a certain age joining the Apocalypse on their Vespas. I write about friendship, and loyalty, and lifting each other up, and the importance of tea and cake.

But mostly I write about how wonderful people (of all species) can really be.

If you'd like to find out the latest on new books in *The Gobbelino London* series, as well as discover other books and series, giveaways, extra reading, and more, jump on over to www.kmwatt.com and check everything out there.

Read on!

amazon.com/Kim-M-Watt/e/B07JMHRBMC
bookbub.com/authors/kim-m-watt
facebook.com/KimMWatt
instagram.com/kimmwatt
twitter.com/kimmwatt

ACKNOWLEDGMENTS

Always the first thanks are to you, lovely reader. Thank you for continuing the adventure with me, for accepting that cats can be detectives and unicorns may have been misrepresented just because they're a bit fancy. You are entirely wonderful, and I would buy you an ice cream if I could.

Thank you to my wonderful editor and friend Lynda Dietz, of Easy Reader Editing, who somehow, after seven books, still seems to find my habit of forgetting character names and re-using them in every book funny rather than frustrating. I'm working on that, honest. All good grammar praise goes to her. All mistakes are mine. Find her at www.easyreaderediting.com for fantastic blogs on editing, grammar, and other writer-y stuff.

Thank you so many times over to my fantastic beta readers, who never do anything but make my stories better - and even managed to beta for me during a pandemic. You know who you are, and I also hope you know how amazing you are. Which is very.

Thank you to Monika from Ampersand Cover Design, who somehow just knew how to illustrate a cat detective confronting unicorns. That's a skill. Find her at www.ampersandbookcovers.com

And, every single time, thank you to my small but perfectly formed family, providers of love, support, inspiration, and laughter. And, in the case of the Little Furry Muse, bites. But I think they're loving ones. Sometimes, anyway.

ALSO BY KIM M. WATT

The Gobbelino London, PI series

"This series is a wonderful combination of humor and suspense that won't let you stop until you've finished the book. Fair warning, don't plan on doing anything else until you're done ..."

- Goodreads reviewer

The Beaufort Scales Series (cozy mysteries with dragons)

"The addition of covert dragons to a cozy mystery is perfect...and the dragons are as quirky and entertaining as the rest of the slightly eccentric residents of Toot Hansell."

– Goodreads reviewer

Short Story Collections

Oddly Enough: Tales of the Unordinary, Volume One

"The stories are quirky, charming, hilarious, and some are all of the above without a dud amongst the bunch ..."

- Goodreads reviewer

The Cat Did It

Of course the cat did it. Sneaky, snarky, and up to no good - that's the cats in this feline collection, which you can grab free by signing up to the newsletter on the earlier page. Just remember - if the cat winks, always wink back ...

The Tales of Beaufort Scales

Modern dragons are a little different these days. There's the barbecue fixation, for starters ... You'll get these tales free once you've signed up for the newsletter!